Two Right Feet

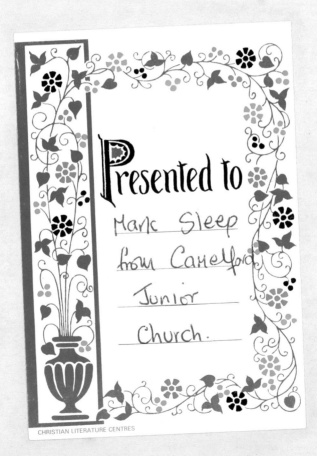

Presented to

Mark Sleep

from Camelford

Junior

Church.

CHRISTIAN LITERATURE CENTRES

Two Right Feet

CATHIE BARTLAM

Illustrated by Pat Murray

SCRIPTURE UNION

© Cathie Bartlam 1998

First published 1998

Scripture Union, 207–209 Queensway, Bletchley, Milton Keynes, MK2 2EB, England.

ISBN 1 85999 059 2

British Library Cataloguing-in-Publication Data.
A catalogue record of this book is available from the British Library.

Printed and bound in Great Britain by Cox & Wyman Ltd, Reading.

Chapter one

George Marcus Thumbleton had a secret. In fact he had two secrets. If anyone found out about his secrets, then he hated to think what would happen to him.

George Marcus Thumbleton did not like football. He did not like playing football, watching football or supporting United. No one knew this terrible secret. Everyone thought George was mad about football. Everyone that George knew was mad about football.

His sister Susie was the maddest of the lot. Her bedroom was covered in footballing wallpaper. Her duvet cover and curtains

5

were blue, just like United's colours. She had got all the team's kit. Her walls were covered with posters of all the players. And George knew that she had even got pants with United's badge printed all over them. He saw them on the washing line. Susie thought she knew everything because she was three years older than George. When she grew up, she was going to be a footballer.

When George, who was seven-and-three-quarters, grew up he wanted to... well I'm not sure I could tell you what he wanted to do. You see, that was George's other secret. The secret that was even worse than not liking football. The secret that no one in the whole wide world would understand. The secret that everyone would laugh at. George wanted to be a concert pianist! Shocking, isn't it? A concert pianist playing wonderful music for people. Not a footballer scoring goals in front of thousands of fans. You can see why George could never let anyone find out about his secrets. They were so weird.

So George spent his days trying to pretend he was as excited about football as the rest of his family.

It was Monday teatime. George had just walked home from school with his mum.

"We'll have a pot of tea," said Mum, "and look at the paper."

George got out the sports section. No one in his house read the rest of the paper. In fact George didn't know why the shop couldn't sell just the back pages of the paper.

"If United carry on like this," said Mum, pouring him a milky cup of tea and passing him a plate of biscuits, "we've a good chance of winning the league. There are only eight matches left in the season. We've lost our best winger..."

"With the broken leg." Even George knew that. "So he won't be playing for ages."

"At least not until next year, I reckon. We need four wins and two draws. We can afford to lose two games. Even then I'm not sure if we can be top of the table." Mum scribbled numbers in blunt pencil on the folded newspaper. She was always doing this. She liked working out what United needed to do to win some championship or other. George hadn't a clue what the figures all meant but it kept Mum happy.

"You can play out until tea," she said. "Your football boots are in the back porch.

Dad cleaned them last night."

Slowly George shoved his feet into the boots. Dad needn't have bothered cleaning them. They never got muddy or scuffed. That was because George never seemed to be able to kick the ball. It didn't matter how hard he tried. He saw the ball coming towards him, pointed his foot in its direction and nothing happened. Well, the same thing always happened. The ball went sailing past him.

Once George had shut his eyes as the ball came towards him. That was the only time he could remember thumping the ball so hard that it flew down the length of the pitch. The kick had really hurt his foot. His big toenail had gone black, then yellow and, weeks later, had fallen off. George kept it in his treasure box, a biscuit tin with pictures of Father Christmas all over it.

"You're late," said David, who was already covered in dirt. "We've been waiting for you."

"For ages," added Peter. "I'm fed up with being in goal. That's your place. We're

United, they're Rovers and we're winning four-nil." He pointed to a sweaty band of boys and girls who were charging all over the big grassy area in front of the houses.

George knew his place. He walked slowly over to his goal. He hung his jumper on the sign that said,

"No ball games allowed. By order."

As he watched the others running around, George talked to himself. "I don't want to be in goal. I'm always in goal. Every day I stand here while they all run up and down. It's so boring. I want to be playing the piano in Grandad's room. I want to make music dance out of my head and through my fingers."

George sat down and drew pictures in the dirt. He piled up the soil and made mountains for the ants to climb. Then he made a bridge by twisting some grass together. He had just got a woodlouse to hang upside down from the bridge, when a white and black leather object zoomed past his face and knocked him sideways.

"Goal! Goal!" shouted Jenny, as she did a handstand. George noticed that she had got United pants as well.

"You great lump," shouted Dave. "Goalies don't sit down in the Cup Final!"

"This one does," said Peter, as he hauled George upright. "Try to stop the next goal."

"Okay," said George, looking to see if his woodlouse had survived. He couldn't see it anywhere. George hoped it could fly. He was a bit worried because he hadn't seen any wings on the woodlouse.

By teatime George had let in two penalties, stopped one free-kick by throwing his jumper at the ball, got a yellow card from the ref, who was only Mark Pratchett from number thirty-seven, a boy in the year below George at school, and had got muck all over his new T-shirt from when a ball hit him in the chest.

"Well," said George's proud mum, "I can see that my little hero has been a real star today. Look at all that dirt, my little 'Two Right Feet'." She patted the filthy T-shirt with great pride. "To think we've got such a good player in our family, worth two of any of the others. Clean up and I'll get tea on the table."

As George washed himself in the bathroom, he pulled evil faces in the mirror. George hated his nickname. 'Two Right

Feet'! It made him sound like a Red Indian. George would have quite liked to be a Red Indian. They didn't play football, at least they didn't in films on the telly. But 'Two Right Feet', I ask you, because he was supposed to be as good as two players put together. The truth is, thought George, I'm hopeless and I hate it.

Chapter two

Mum had never seen George play football. If she had, she would have known that he was hopeless. Susie knew but pretended that George really liked being in goal all the time. Dad thought that George was United's number one fan.

After tea Dad said, "You'll soon be eight, George. We've come up with some great ideas for your birthday."

"Go on, tell me," said George, who was bursting with fish and chips and chocolate ice cream.

"Shall I tell him?" said Dad.

"You'll have to," said Mum. "You're

15

more excited than him."

"You could never keep a surprise quiet," said Grandad. It was Grandad's house they all lived in. They had lived there ever since Grandma died, long before George was born. "Tell the lad. Put him out of his misery."

So Dad told him. "On your birthday you and five friends..."

"And me and Mum," said Susie.

"And me," added Grandad.

"Are going to United's ground for a tour behind the scenes. Then we can have a posh tea there," continued Dad.

"And, between us all, we're buying you all the team's kit." Mum said this with a big smile on her face.

"All?" squeaked George, who didn't want the kit, or the trip to the ground. "All?"

"Yes," said Mum. "Nothing's too much trouble for our little 'Two Right Feet', is it, Dad?"

"Course not," replied Dad. "Can't you see the boy is taken by surprise? He's speechless!"

"I knew he'd be delighted," added Grandad, "but I didn't think he would lose his voice!"

"We'll get the kit after the next home match," said Susie. "Dad hasn't told you that part. He will get tickets for you and me and Mum. We'll sit together and Dad and Grandad will have their season tickets. Brill, eh?"

"Brill," echoed George. "Really brill."

George escaped into Grandad's room. It was the big one at the front of the house. Grandad had a bad leg and couldn't manage the stairs, so his bed was in there. The room was full of Grandad's special things, boxes of football cuttings and match programmes, photo albums of all the relatives, a helmet taken from a soldier in the war and, best of all, Grandma's piano.

George sat at the dusty piano and lifted the lid. Inside him music was trapped, waiting to get out, but it couldn't. He ran his fingers up and down the yellowy keys. Then he hit all the black notes. It sounded awful, as awful as George felt. What a birthday treat! He didn't want any of it. What George wanted, more than anything, was to learn how to play the piano.

The dog, a scruffy thing called Shearer that looked as if it had a goat for a mother, crawled into the gap by George's legs. George talked to him in a soft whisper.

"Listen, Shearer, what am I going to do? I don't want to go to the match. I hated it that last time, when Grandad's leg was really bad, and I used his season ticket. It was freezing. I couldn't see anything.

I hated the smell. That fat bloke behind me dropped cigarette ash all over my head. The noise was awful. I didn't even see the goals, let alone who scored them. My feet were like ice blocks. I hated it, Shearer, and I don't want to go again." George paused as the dog found some spilt chocolate buttons and ate them.

"I don't want the kit, or the party, or the tea at United's ground. And they all think I really want it. They're so happy for me but I'm not happy for me at all."

19

George played 'chopsticks', the only tune he could manage on the piano. He played it thirty-three times. He knew it was that many because he marked each time down on a piece of paper. Even after thirty-three times, George was no nearer solving his problem.

"If I tell them," he said, poking Shearer awake with his foot, "they'll think I'm mad – barmy. They won't understand. Everyone else would think it was marvellous. Dave and Peter would die for it all. I suppose I'll have to invite them, and Mark Pratchett, but I don't want to go. I want to learn the piano, but no one will let me."

Shearer looked at him. "Okay, Shearer, so I haven't told anyone what I want, but I can't."

Mum burst into the room. "Have you finished playing that ghastly tune? It's time for bed. Footballers have to get their rest, you know?"

"Yes, Mum."

As George got ready for bed he wondered

if concert pianists had to get their rest. George wasn't quite sure what a concert pianist was. When Aunt Ellie was over from America she had wanted to watch one on telly. George had sat up with her, while Mum, Dad and Grandad had gone down the local pub to watch United play an away match on cable TV.

This man, in a black suit and a shirt as white as a washing powder advert, had sat down at this huge thing that Aunt Ellie said was a 'grand piano'. Everyone had clapped and cheered. An orchestra had played some music. Then the man had started to play the piano. George had never heard anything like it. The music seemed to creep into his insides. It flowed through his legs and arms. It made something come alive inside him, something he didn't even know was there. He couldn't take his eyes off the man who was flinging himself all over the keyboard. That night George knew that he wanted to be like that man – a concert pianist, Aunt Ellie had said. The music had stayed with him. He'd never heard anything like it again but he knew that it lived deep inside him.

It was hopeless though. All he could play was 'chopsticks' on the same piano that Aunt Ellie had made alive with her music. He would never be able to do it. He didn't know how. He didn't know what he could do to learn. However much he pressed the piano's keys, he couldn't get anything nice to come out of them. But somewhere, inside the piano, inside him, there was a way of letting the music free. If only George could find the way.

He never would. Far better to be a footballer, wear the kit and go to the matches than dream of being something impossible.

"I'll try harder at football," said George to himself, after Dad has come up to say his 'goodnight' prayers with him. George thanked God for his birthday treat, and wondered if God knew he didn't really mean it. Dad was more excited about the treat than anyone. George wondered what Dad would say if he asked for piano lessons instead!

Chapter three

George decided to try hard to be good at football. Every day, after school, he went out to play with his friends on the big stretch of grass outside the houses. The green grass was very patchy now. The summer was coming and it was nearly the end of United's season.

Dad couldn't get tickets for any of the home games that were left.

"I'm really sorry, George," he said. And he meant it.

"It's okay, Dad. I don't mind," said George, and he meant it as well. Dad thought he was just being brave.

"I'll make sure I get you some tickets for next year," Dad promised. George hoped that he would forget. "We'll go and buy your kit the week before your birthday."

"Okay," said George. That gave him three weeks to think of a way of not having the kit as a present.

Meanwhile George played football.

"I'm not going in goal," he said to Peter. "I'm going to be a striker."

"Fat chance," said Peter. "You couldn't strike a drum with a drumstick." But he let George run around in the centre of the pitch.

The ball was coming towards him, skipping over the bumpy, lumpy grass, straight for his shiny boots.

"Wallop it!" screeched Jenny.

"Belt it in!" yelled Mark Pratchett, who was fed up with being ref and had decided to be captain.

This was it! George's moment of glory. Carefully he turned and faced the ball. He watched it skimming towards him, lifted his right leg in the air, kicked his foot as hard as he could... and fell over. The ball carried on until it hit a tree metres away.

"You're hopeless," said Peter. "Why didn't you turn sideways?"

"Yes," added Dave. "You can't belt it like that, full on. You have to turn with it. Don't you know anything?"

George knew that he had hurt his bum when he fell over. His face went bright red.

He couldn't stop it. It made his pale blond straw-like hair look even whiter.

"I'll be okay next time," said George.

"You'd better be," threatened Mark Pratchett. "We should have scored then."

But George wasn't better, not the next time, nor the time after that. He ran around, getting very hot and sweaty. However hard he tried he couldn't make his foot kick the ball at the right time. He made one spectacular save, though.

The ball soared through the air and George just happened to be in the right place. It started to fall out of the sky, down, down, straight towards him. George reached up his hands, squinted into the strong sunlight, and caught it. He actually caught the ball, and didn't drop it straight away.

"Save!" he yelled. His friends rolled around laughing.

"You're not in goal!" shouted Dave.

"Did you forget?" asked Jenny.

"Handball!" screeched Mark Pratchett,

who was being ref again. "You can only handle the ball if you are goalie. You are a striker. Remember?"

"Some striker," added Peter. "Swop with Sunil, in goal, before one of us kills you." Peter was joking, but George saw sense and went back to his place by the dumped coats.

And that's where George spent most of his time for the next couple of weeks. As the ball hardly ever came his way, he daydreamed.

George didn't mind being hopeless at football. It was a lot better for George to be in boring goal all the time than to have no one to play with. He would have minded if his friends told him to get lost and not to play. George would hate that. He would be lonely.

Sometimes, not very often, Peter, Dave and Mark played with him on their bikes, or if it was raining, they came round and got all the Lego out. They always made football grounds, or coaches to take the players to away matches. George was quite happy with that. He was good at fixing Lego bricks together. He could always find the right brick, even the hard ones, like a blue block with a hook on it.

Everyone was getting very excited. United needed to win the last two games to be top of the table. Everywhere people were talking about their chances: at school, at home and even in church.

The minister, who looked more like a rugby player than anything else, was called Samuel Peasby. He was as mad on football as everyone else. He had got a season ticket, like Dad and Grandad, and he went to all the away games. That's if he hadn't got a wedding to do on a Saturday. Not many people round St Michael-in-the-Fields dared get married when United were playing.

The church had got a weird name. There wasn't a field for miles, just rows of big, blackened, terraced houses, the park and the open stretches of grass, like the one by George's house. A long time ago all this area was fields. George couldn't imagine what it would have looked like then.

George really liked Samuel Peasby. Not because he supported United. Not because he laughed a lot. Not because he once preached a sermon wearing a football kit and balancing a ball on his shoulders. Not because he ran the Friday Club where everyone aged seven to ten charged around causing chaos. No, Samuel Peasby had got

something that George really wanted. Samuel Peasby had got music inside him and his music spilled out all over the church.

Samuel Peasby played the piano and the electronic keyboard. He could make it sound like anything he wanted to. At Harvest Festival last year, he made it sound like a cow moo-ing and a sheep baa-ing. He even made it sound like corn growing, though when George said that, Susie told him he was nuts. Sometimes Samuel Peasby played his big brass trombone and the notes sent shivers down George's neck, as if someone was tickling him gently with a feather. Once the minister had played bagpipes in the church. George thought he was the only person who had liked the sound of fighting cats in the sun-filled building.

George wanted to be like Samuel Peasby. He was the only person George knew who could make music come alive. Mrs Henderson at school couldn't. She bashed away at the piano as if she hated it as the children sang with wobbly voices. No, Mrs Henderson hadn't got music living inside her, but the minister had. And so had George. It had got to get out soon or he would burst!

Chapter four

It was raining, the thin sort that you don't notice much until you are wet through. It was the last match of the season and United had got to win to become champions. Everyone in George's house was very tense and snapping at the others.

George escaped to play football. He was soaked through and so was everyone else. As usual he was in goal. The rain had made everything slippy. George decorated his bare legs with mud, making patterns like fierce snakes and frightening spiders.

"George! Go for it!" Dave's yell stopped him halfway through making a mud python on his leg. "Save it! Go on, you can do it!"

And he could, Dave was right. George saw the ball coming, high and fast. No way could he try to kick it. It'd have to be a header. Like a rocket on a launch pad, George went into orbit, up, up, the ball glancing off his forehead and dying on the grass in front of him. George started to come back to earth and then crash-landed straight onto the "No ball games allowed. By Order." sign.

The wood splintered and cut into George's face, taking a thin slice of skin with it. It bled all over the place.

Peter knocked on George's door.

"Mrs Thumbleton, George has saved a goal!"

"Great, and...?" Mum wasn't usually informed of George's successes.

"And there's sort of blood and stuff on his head."

Mum went into action, sprinted across the wet grass in her United track suit and reached her blood-covered son.

"Well, 'Two Right Feet'," she said. "You're a real hero this time! Saved the goal. Got your team to win. We could do with you at this afternoon's match."

"Yes, Mum." If she called him that stupid nickname again, George would be sick.

Mum dabbed at the blood which took no notice and kept on running. "Trust this to happen today. We'd better clean you up."

Mark, Dave, Peter, Sunil and Jenny followed Mum into the house, splashing muddy splodges all over the carpet and onto the wall. Shearer ran round in circles, barking his head off. Grandad appeared in his pyjamas and Dad got a bucket and sponge.

"Just like the real thing," he said, washing George's face in the same way he washed down the car when it got really filthy.

"This might need stitches," said Mum, "at least those butterfly strip things. You'll have to take him to casualty.'"

"But the match!" Dad was worried.

"You'll have plenty of time," said Mum. "I can't drive, so it's no use me taking him."

In the end Dad drove Mum, Grandad, Susie and George to the local hospital. The nurse told them it was not a deep cut, but that it was bleeding a lot.

"I know that," said George, and got told off for being cheeky.

"It'll need cleaning up and some butterfly stitches," said the nurse.

"I told you so," said Mum.

"But I'm afraid there will be a good hour or so's wait. We're busy," she smiled. "Some people have been celebrating United's win before they have even played the match."

Dad went into a panic. Kick-off was only ninety minutes away and he'd be stuck here with George. Grandad came to the rescue.

"You and Mum go to the match, take Susie to Jenny's house and I'll stay here with George," said Grandad. "We'll get a taxi home. George will be all right with me, won't you?"

"Course. It doesn't hurt much, honest," said George.

"But we can't get your kit if you're stuck here," said Dad.

"We can go down in the week," said Susie, taking charge. "The shop is always open."

After they had had the same conversation about twenty times and George felt like screaming at them, Mum, Dad and Susie went. George and Grandad were left in peace.

"Why did you let Mum have your season ticket?" asked George.

"Oh, I don't mind her seeing the game," said Grandad. "I've seen United win the championship at least three times before. Your mum never has. I was going to let her have my seat, anyway, before you did your fantastic goal saving. You'll have to take it a bit easy on the football front, though, our George, for a while now."

"That's okay, Grandad." George thought before he spoke again. "Grandad. You know the piano, in your room?"

"The piano?"

"Yes. Why do you keep it? I mean it's big and no one plays it."

"Except you and that blooming tune 'chopsticks'." Grandad was thoughtful. "I keep it because of your grandma. You never knew her but she loved that piano. She used to give lessons on it. The money came in handy, especially after I injured my leg and couldn't work overtime."

"What was Grandma like?" asked George.

Grandad seemed to go off to some place far away from the noisy, busy hospital waiting room.

"Oh, she was lovely. She loved her music. You've seen the photos of her, you know, the ones at her dancing classes. She loved playing the piano for the children's ballet lessons. Week after week, year after year, she never got tired of playing the same tunes. And she used to play down at St Michael-in-the-Fields. It wasn't like now, you know. Freezing cold, that place was. Grandma would sit there playing the music while her breath floated like a little, cold

cloud up in front of the piano."

"Can you play it, Grandad?" asked George.

"Me? No lad, I can't. I never wanted to. You see, Grandma used to say that you've got to have the music in you, sort of living somewhere inside you, then you can play. Mind you, it takes a lot of hard work and practice too."

"Samuel Peasby's like that, isn't he, Grandad?" said George.

"Oh, him, he's got the gift all right."

"The gift?"

"The music."

"So, it's all right for men, for boys, to have the gift?"

Grandad looked straight at him. "What a funny question. Are you sure you didn't bump your head when you cut your face? Of course anyone can have the gift, boys or girls."

The doctor came and taped up his cut and the blood stopped dripping everywhere. It looked dead good. George felt proud of his long, thin wound. He felt good in another way as well. Grandad had said that it was all right for boys to like music. Did that mean it was all right for George? Was it okay for George to want to let the music come out of him? What would Grandad say if George told him he wanted to play the piano? What would Mum and Dad say?

George didn't dare risk it. Not yet. Maybe if United won, but even then George didn't know if he could tell his family what he really wanted to do.

Chapter five

United did not win. They drew. Mum and Dad were gutted.

"They can still do it," said Dad. "If Rovers don't win their midweek match, we'll still win the championship."

"I can't stand the tension," said Mum. "When the score was two–all at full time I felt like crying."

"You did cry," stated Dad. He turned to George. "I got you a programme to keep. How's your face? It looks sore."

"Not bad." George's cut just tickled, but the butterfly stitches made it look as if he was a really tough guy. "I liked coming home in the taxi with Grandad. It cost eight pounds forty pence. Grandad gave the driver a ten pound note and told him to keep the change."

"Grandad would," said Mum. "At least that should heal up without much of a scar."

"And if you do have a bit of a scar," added Dad, "then when you are older you can grow a sort of beard."

"Halfway up his cheek? Don't be so ridiculous," said Mum.

George couldn't ever imagine growing up. He didn't want to have a beard.

The family had a late tea. Mum was too worried about United to cook. Dad went to fetch a Chinese takeaway. George liked trying to eat with chopsticks. He got into a mess. Shearer, the dog, liked George eating with chopsticks as well. The animal ate up all the bits that dropped on the floor. Shearer really liked beansprouts.

There was a thundering knock on the door. Dave and Peter were standing there.

"Can we see George?" asked Peter, and walked straight into the house. "My mum has made him a cake."

"And I've got him a football mag," added Dave. "Wow! George, you look great!"

"Does it hurt?" asked Peter.

"Terrible," said George. He would get all the fuss he could while it lasted. "Agony. The cake looks great."

Grandad whisked the cake away, cut it up and they all sat round the table eating it.

The table was still covered in all the foil containers from the takeaway shop.

"How was the game, Mr Thumbleton?" asked Dave.

"My dad told me their last goal was offside," said Peter.

"That ref was as blind as a bat," said Mum. She was still upset about the result.

"It was like this," said Dad. He cleared a bit of the table. Some crispy fried duck fell off the edge, only to be caught by Shearer before it reached the floor.

"That dog plays better than most of our team," said Grandad.

Dad ignored him. He was turning the table into a football pitch. The foil dishes were players, the chopsticks marked the touchlines and the ball was a leftover pork fritter.

For the next hour the family, Peter and Dave discussed the match. They decided the ref was bribed, the linesmen needed their eyes testing and that United should have won two–nil. Susie was too upset by the

result even to join in. She had gone to her room to play her music and drool over her posters of the players.

George came to a decision. Now was not a good time to mention music lessons. It was not a good time to say he didn't want the football kit. They would never understand.

In George's family you supported your team whatever the results. If he said he didn't want the football things now, they would think he was a traitor. Not to support your team when they were down was about the worst thing you could do in the Thumbleton family. Not to support your team at all would be unbelievable.

George escaped to Grandad's room and went to the piano. He sat there, staring at the pictures of Grandma. She looked very fuzzy. The early evening sunlight darted into the room and showed up all the dust on the photos. George picked up a frame

and rubbed it with his sleeve. A smear of chocolate cake joined the dust.

"Hello, Grandma," he said. Grandma looked back at him. "If you were here, you could tell them what I think. I could have told you. Grandad said you had the music inside you. You would know what it is like to be me." George paused and started to walk round the room, still holding the photo.

"In fact," he said, "you could teach me how to play the piano." He opened the scratched piano stool and took out a piece of music. He looked at the lines drawn closely together. There were dots all over them, and little sticks, some with curly bits at the top. George knew that this was music. But how did you get these black scribbles to become something beautiful? George hadn't got a clue.

He sat down and played 'chopsticks'. For a moment he wondered if he could use the real chopsticks to play the tune. That would mean going back into the big kitchen and hearing yet more about the offside goal and the match.

There was another knock on the door.

"I've come to see how George is," said Peter's dad. "I've got him a pile of my old magazines to look at. He'll not be running round for a day or two."

Not more football mags! thought George. Susie would grab them anyway.

"So, how is he?"

"Oh, gutted, like the rest of us." Mum sounded concerned. "He couldn't believe United didn't win. How he'll last out until Wednesday's result I don't know."

I do, thought George. Quite easily. At least after Wednesday they would know if United would be top of the table. Then there would be a few weeks' peace before the start of the next season.

"Then there will be my birthday," he said, banging on the piano keys as loudly as he could. "I don't want it."

"Don't want what?" said Dad, coming into the room.

"Oh, nothing."

"You're not worried about your face, are you?" Dad gave him a hug. "You'll still be our 'Two Right Feet', don't worry."

"I'm not worried," said George, who was worried, but not about football.

"Peter's dad has brought you some mags to read. Come and say thank you. And George, I wish you'd stop playing that awful tune. It drives me mad."

Football drives me mad, thought George, but he kept quiet.

Dad carried on, "I don't know why Grandad keeps this old piano. It's out of tune and takes up too much space. I think I'll have a word with him. See if he wants to get rid of it. He might even get a few pounds for it." Dad chuckled. "Not that I'd give him a penny. It can go to the dump for all I care. I'll do that, George, I'll have a word with Grandad. Time he chucked out some of this stuff."

George was horrified. What could he say? Dad noticed his face had gone pale.

"Hey, you look a bit queasy. Too much food on top of that nasty cut. I reckon you need to go to bed." And Dad took him upstairs after he had said goodnight and thanked Peter's dad for the mags.

No piano! He would never find a way of learning how to play it, if they gave it away. George had got to keep the piano, but how?

Chapter six

The next morning George woke up and stretched. His face felt very stiff. If he grinned, he thought the cut would open up again and blood would pour everywhere. His cheek had gone a lovely purply-blue colour. George couldn't wait until everyone saw it.

He got dressed and found Dad and Grandad downstairs. No sign of Mum.

"She's too fed up to go to church," said Dad. "Susie has been awake half the night, so it is just you and Grandad. I'm not sure that you should go."

"I want to go," said George. Not only

would he hear all the music but everyone would look at his face. He couldn't miss that.

"I'm not sure you should, what with your face," Dad mumbled.

Mum came downstairs, still in her dressing gown. "Oh, you'll be all right, George. Don't make a fuss."

"It wasn't me making the fuss," said George, but Mum just headed for the kettle to make herself a mug of coffee. She was really moody in the mornings even on a good day, and today was not a good day. George decided to keep out of her way.

Dad looked at her. "I'll cook us a nice dinner," he said. "You go and relax."

So only George and his grandad walked to St Michael-in-the-Fields. It took ages. They kept meeting people they knew. They all said the same thing.

"What have you done to your face, George?" and "United should have won yesterday."

At church George stayed with Grandad. Samuel Peasby seemed a bit sad. He must have been upset about United as well. They sang some songs. Even the electronic keyboard sounded sad. Then the minister told a story about everyone working together, like in a football team. George could tell that all the people were thinking about United, rather than about being on God's team. Samuel Peasby jumped up and got out his trombone. After ten minutes of loud, happy songs of praise they all felt a lot better.

"I don't know what God thinks of this," whispered Grandad. "I expect he's as worried about United as I am."

George thought. God? Thinking about football? If God thought about football he must think about music because he liked music. If he didn't they wouldn't sing all those hymns and songs in church. Some of the songs were so old that they were written down in the Bible, thousands of years ago. George had seen them. Psalms. He liked the one about God being a shepherd. Perhaps when St Michael's really was in the fields, real shepherds came here and sang about God being the shepherd.

George was enjoying his thoughts so much he didn't realise that he should have gone off to his group. He stumbled to the front and through the little side door. Everyone could see his injured face. They all felt sorry for him. George felt good. Perhaps he'd get some more presents. Not football mags though!

Amy Entwhistle was taking his group. She

had long hair which always fell out of her pony tail. It had grey streaks in it some weeks and other weeks it looked black all over. George once tried to count the grey hairs, but it was too hard. Amy was a very good friend of God's. She liked telling the children how much God loved them. She hardly ever talked about football. George thought she didn't know much about it. That made him like her even more.

She had a nice smell, a bit like a clean baby, and wore baggy tops with pictures on them, and black leggings. George couldn't imagine her in a dressing gown, drinking coffee and worrying about United.

"I've brought some flowers today," said Amy.

George groaned. Girly stuff! That was all he needed. He'd rather have a few adventure stories from the Bible than flowers.

"I want you all to choose one, and hold it carefully," said Amy.

The girls rushed and grabbed the pretty

ones while the four boys who were George's age hung back.

"Come on, boys as well."

There was one flower that looked like something from outer space. It was dark purple, darker even than George's bruise. It had big spikes on it that curved inwards and it looked as if its head was too big for its stem. It was a lot bigger and uglier than the others. It looked like George felt. He picked it.

"Ah, George, you've gone for my only dahlia," said Amy. "Beautiful, isn't it?"

George wasn't sure. It was certainly different to the others. Steve ended up with some straggly honeysuckle, Mark Pratchett held a wilting dandelion as if he wanted to choke it and Billy was left with a pink rose. They all felt stupid.

"Are we going to draw them, Miss?" asked Mark.

"You can in a bit," said Amy. "I want to talk to you about them first." She paused. "What are they?"

"Flowers," said the group, not impressed.

"But are they all the same?" asked Amy.

"Course not." It was one of the girls, Lisa, who thought she knew everything, just like Susie. "Mine's a carnation."

"And mine's a Queen Elizabeth rose," said Billy. "We've got them all down the side of our garden."

"Yes," said Amy. "You are right. They are all flowers, but they are all different. You can't say that one is better than another."

"What about my dandelion?" asked Mark Pratchett.

"It is just as special as the rest. I know it is different, but it is special. And do you know what?" Amy stopped. George hadn't a clue what she was going to say. "The flowers are a bit like us. We are all people, all made by God and loved by God and yet all very different."

"So, Mark is a dandelion," joked Lisa.

"That's not quite what I mean," said Amy. "What I'm trying to say is that God thinks of us all as special. He made us to be different and that was his idea. In fact if we were all the same it would be very boring. Can you imagine everyone exactly the same?"

"Looking the same?" asked Billy.

"At least I don't look like you," said Lisa. "That's something to thank God for."

"And I don't play with dolls, like you!" said Billy.

Amy interrupted. "You've got the idea, but I don't want you to be unkind to each other. I want you to think about the ways you are different and be happy about them. It's okay that Billy doesn't like dolls..." Billy pulled a face. "And that you can all have different hobbies and interests. Being different to each other is special. God loves us all and wants us to enjoy our differences."

The group carried on talking. They made a collage of all the things they liked. George thought quickly and talked to himself.

It is all right to be different. I don't have to love football. God has made me so I like music, like Grandma and Aunt Ellie and Samuel Peasby. God knows all this. I'm special. It is okay to be me.

George felt a little bubble of happiness pop up inside his tummy. The bubble was growing. It was going to explode into a huge grin. He didn't dare to laugh in case he split his stitches open. It was going to be okay. George didn't know how, but Amy said God thought he was special and it was okay to be different. And Amy should know. She was God's friend. He would have to tell Grandad all about it.

Chapter seven

As soon as George finished in his group he rushed out to find Grandad. He was in the back hall, drinking weak tea and talking.

"Course, I said to them all, that ref wants locking up. If he'd have been looking we'd have been celebrating United's victory about now." Grandad turned and saw George. "Hello there. What on earth have you got?"

"It's a special dahlia." George tugged at Grandad's arm. "I've got to tell you about it. Can we walk home?"

"Better not keep the wounded hero waiting," said Grandad. "I tell you, this lad could have made a better job of it than our team, yesterday. It's not for nothing that his mum calls him 'Two Right...'"

"Grandad!" George felt he would die if Grandad told his friend the nickname.

At last Grandad left the hall and George could tell him what he wanted to.

"I'm like the dahlia, and Billy is the dandelion and Mark was a rose, a big pink one."

"Queen Elizabeth," said Grandad. He knew his roses.

'And, anyway they're all special, even though they are different and they are all flowers. So that's great, isn't it Grandad?'

Grandad hadn't the slightest idea what George was on about. "You've lost me somewhere," he said. "Try again."

"It's obvious. Obvious," George liked that word. They kept saying it yesterday when they were talking about the match. "It means it's all right to be me."

"It always has been, I think," said Grandad, no clearer in his understanding.

"But that's where you are wrong, Grandad. You see, I can be the me with the piano, not the me with two right feet. God doesn't mind about the football and the kit. It's okay to have the music in me."

"The piano. What's this about the piano?"

"Dad wants you to get rid of it..."

"I know."

"And if you do, then it'll never happen."

"George, what won't happen?" asked Grandad.

George stopped and looked straight at him. At times grown-ups were so stupid. He had just told Grandad all about it and still he was asking a dumb question. "I said, what won't happen?" repeated Grandad.

"I won't be able to learn the piano, if we don't have one. I can't get the music out of me unless someone teaches me and gives me lessons. And," George added bravely, "I don't want a United kit for my birthday."

Grandad had understood that bit.

"You don't want a kit?"

"No, Grandad."

"Well, why ever didn't you say so?"

"I couldn't," said George. "I mean you're all mad about football, but I'm not." His voice dropped to a whisper. "I don't like football, Grandad."

"Don't like football!" George wished Grandad would stop repeating everything he said. It was like talking to a parrot.

"That's what I said, Grandad. I'm like the dahlia." He looked at the drooping flower in his sweaty hand. "I'm different, but it is

okay. Amy Entwhistle said it is all right to be different. That's how God made us."

"Well, if Amy Entwhistle said it," said Grandad, "it must be right! You'll be the first Thumbleton in living memory not to like football."

"And is it all right, Grandad?"

"Of course it is. Just takes a bit of getting used to, that's all."

"But I wouldn't be the first Thumbleton to like music, would I, Grandad?" George looked anxiously at him.

"You know the answer to that, my lad. Your grandma would have been very proud of you. Very proud. If she were here, she could teach you."

"Perhaps I could have lessons, instead of a kit," said George.

"Aye, perhaps you could," said Grandad. "We'll have a good talk over dinner. I wonder if your dad has cooked it yet?"

As they walked home Grandad kept asking George questions. At last he seemed to understand what George was saying. No football but music.

It would take a bit of getting used to but Grandad was quite glad that someone in his family wanted to keep the old piano. He was not so sure what the others would say, though.

"I tell you what," said Grandad. "You go and put that dahlia in a vase, on top of our piano, and we'll leave the talking until after the meal."

"Our piano"! Grandad had said, "our piano". Not his, not Grandma's, but ours!

That must mean that he was going to keep it and George could play it.

Carefully George dusted the piano. He even took all the photos off the top first and he found some proper polish. The smell twirled round with the casserole that Dad was still cooking.

George polished the piano until he could see his face in it. He looked like a monster. The curved wood made him look a really funny shape and the butterfly stitches looked like something out of a cartoon film.

George put the dahlia on the piano next to all the photos and under the big framed picture of United when they won the cup. He felt as excited as United must have felt then. Excited but a bit scared.

What if Mum and Dad didn't think it was okay to want to play music? What if they were cross about him not wanting the football kit? What if Dad thought he was a wimp? And what would Mum say when she found out that his nickname was stupid? He was not as good as half a football player, let alone as good as two.

George played 'chopsticks' softly, until Dad shouted that dinner was ready. This was it. George went to face his family.

Chapter eight

Everyone ate Dad's casserole in silence. It was a bit chewy but no one dared say so. After they had munched their way through it, Dad produced an ice cream dessert from out of the freezer. At least that was easier to eat.

"How's your face?" asked Mum.

"Okay," said George. Actually, it hurt more today than when he did it. "It's a bit sore."

"You look like a monster," said Susie. She hadn't got dressed yet and was still wearing her United pyjamas. "Can I finish the ice cream off?"

"Let George have it," said Dad. George refused. He wanted to be in everyone's good books, even Susie's. He wanted them to be on his side when Grandad told them about the music.

"I think we'll all have coffee," said Mum. "I don't feel like rushing and doing anything much today. I'm still trying to get over the match yesterday."

"Bit of a shocker," agreed Dad. "I really thought they'd win, and now we've got to wait until Wednesday to see if they are the champions."

George gulped and nearly choked on his coffee, which was too hot. If they started talking football he would never be able to tell them about the music. He sent a look at Grandad which meant please, tell them. Grandad got the hint.

"I've got another 'bit of a shocker'," he said, leaning back on his chair and undoing his belt a couple of notches.

"What did you say, Grandad?" asked Susie.

George picked up Shearer and hugged him. This was never allowed when the family were eating but George didn't care. Hugging Shearer would give him a bit of courage. Shearer sniffed at the plates and tried to reach the runny blobs of ice cream. He couldn't, so he let George stroke him.

"I said," repeated Grandad. "I've got a bit of news for you all." He paused. "Are you all listening?"

"I bet it's something one of your friends told you at church," said Dad. "It's not that rumour going around, is it, you know, the one about them looking for a new manager for next season?"

"Well, I don't believe that," said Mum. "The manager is fine." If he had been there, the manager of United would have been pleased to hear this. All the newspapers were saying that he was not as good as he used to be.

George felt like screaming, "Shut up! Listen!" He kept quiet, though.

"It's nothing to do with football." Grandad paused. "Well, actually it is in a way. It's young George, here."

"George?" said Mum. "What's he done now?"

"He hasn't done anything, and he doesn't want to. That's the problem. He thinks you want him to, but he doesn't. He wants to do something else, but he hasn't told you. He thinks you won't like it."

Grandad stopped and looked pleased with himself.

"Are you losing your marbles?" asked

Dad. "What on earth are you on about?"

George thought Dad was being really thick. It was obvious what Grandad was saying. It made perfect sense to him. But not to Mum or Dad or Susie.

"The football," said Grandad. "The boy doesn't like football."

Grandad got the effect he wanted.

"Doesn't like football!" shouted Mum.

"Doesn't like football," whispered Dad.

"Doesn't like football?" asked Susie.

Grandad laughed. "Well, you seem to have understood me, anyway."

"You mean it's true?" asked Dad.

"Ask him yourself," replied Grandad. So Dad did. George had to tell them that he didn't like playing football, watching football, supporting a team, going to matches, even if they were supposed to be a special treat, and that he didn't want a football kit.

Stunned silence. Followed by more stunned silence. George twisted Shearer's long fur into a series of ropes. Mum poured herself another cup of coffee.

"It's not the bang on the head, is it, George?" she asked, hopefully. "I've heard about these things, they can make people go all funny."

Grandad laughed. "He's told you – he doesn't like football."

"I think we've got the message," said Dad. "Why didn't you tell us before, like years ago?"

"I thought you wouldn't like it, wouldn't like me," mumbled George into Shearer's neck.

Dad jumped up and came over to George. He squatted on the floor beside him and turned his head so that he could see into George's eyes. This was difficult as George had now buried his head in Shearer's long fur. Dad ruffled his hair. George sat up. Dog hairs were stuck to his sticky butterfly stitches.

"You daft boy," he said, kindly. "Of course we like you. We love you. You don't have to like football, or anything else for that matter. I only wish you'd told us ages ago."

"Good job we hadn't bought the kit," said Mum. "Really, George, you are the limit. Pretending all this time."

Grandad interrupted. "I don't think he was pretending. I think we all just thought that because we are mad on football, George would be as well. I don't think we ever gave him a chance to say what he really wants."

"And I suppose you know what that is," said Mum.

"Oh, yes, me and George had a big chat. He knows what it is, all right. Tell them, George," said Grandad.

George looked up and took a deep breath. "I want to have piano lessons and learn to play Grandma's piano. I want to so much, it is like something bursting inside." He looked so serious that Dad laughed.

"We can't have that," said Dad. "You bursting inside. We'd better do something about it."

"I'll ask around," said Mum. "See who does lessons." She thought for a minute. "So, I can't keep on calling you 'Two Right Feet'?"

"No, Mum, I'm hopeless," said George.

"I'll think of another name," said Mum. "How about Mozart?"

Grandad came to the rescue. "I don't think George wants to be called anything other than George. Let's just call him that!"

Chapter nine

Mum did what she said she would do. She found a piano teacher for George. The best teacher in the whole wide world: Samuel Peasby! The minister took just a few pupils for lessons after school. So every Thursday George went off to his lesson.

It was strange, but the music didn't come flowing out of George's fingers straight away. In fact he sounded no better than when all he could play was 'chopsticks'. George hadn't realised that he would have to practise so hard.

"Why can't I play like you?" said George, one Thursday.

"How old are you?" asked Mr Peasby.

"Eight." George had had his birthday. He got some music books and tapes, and a party at McDonalds as well as the lessons.

"And how old do you think I am?" asked Mr Peasby, with a crinkly smile.

He looked pretty ancient, but George decided not to tell him that. In fact Mr Peasby was thirty-one. "And I've been practising and playing since I was five years old, so that makes," he counted on his fingers, "twenty-six years' worth of playing. And how long have you been playing, George?"

"Three weeks and two days, if you don't count 'chopsticks'," said George.

Mr Peasby laughed. "We don't count that," he said. "Don't worry, it'll come. But only if you work hard and practise. It's like football." George groaned. "You don't think our lads in the team got to where they are today just by wanting to be footballers? No. They had to work hard, train, eat the right foods, give it their all." Samuel Peasby was getting excited now, like he sometimes did in church. "These things don't come overnight, George. A bit of talent and a lot of hard work."

"But I can hear the music inside me," said George, "I want it to come out, to become real music, but when I try, it sounds awful."

"It will," said Mr Peasby, "for ages. You are trying to run before you can walk. What you need to do at the moment is learn the scale of C and practise 'Three Blind Mice' until you have got it perfect. By Christmas we might have got to 'Away in a Manger'."

"Christmas!" said George. That was ages away!

"Only if you practise. Here don't look so glum." Samuel Peasby passed him the trombone. "See if you can get a note out of that."

George took a deep breath and blew. Nothing happened. He tried again and again. At last a sound like a strangled mouse came out of the trombone. George was red in the face. His thin scar showed up like a white line painted on a road. He laughed.

"I see what you mean," he said. "It must take ages to learn this."

"And what about this," said Samuel Peasby, producing the bagpipes. George got one breathy screech out of it, like a lorry suddenly putting on its air brakes.

George practised every night. The rest of the family tried to get out of earshot. That was difficult.

"At least," said Dad, one night when George was having difficulty with the scale of F, "we haven't got to listen to that dreadful 'chopsticks' all the time."

"Do you think he'll ever learn to play a tune?" asked Susie.

"I expect so," said Grandad. "Then there'll be no stopping him. He might be famous one day. On the telly!"

"He might," said Mum, not believing it. "And United might win the championship next year!"

United had only been runners-up. Rovers had won their midweek match. The family had all gone to the runners-up celebration though. Even George. Well, they wouldn't leave him at home on his own, so he had to go.

Actually it wasn't too bad: lots of people wearing their kit, waving as the players went past on their open-topped bus. Susie was overcome with emotion. Her favourite player had smiled at her. She took lots of blurred photos of the players on the bus and insisted that they were all looking at her. All George saw on her photos were blobs and vast chunks of moving bus. But it kept Susie happy.

Susie wasn't happy at all when she found out about George's secrets. She made him swear that he would never tell her friends that he didn't support United.

"I promise," said George, "that I will support them, but not like you lot."

Susie had to put up with that, but she was not very happy. It was much better to have a brother who was an ace footballer than one who kept playing 'Three Blind Mice' or 'My Bonnie Lies over the Ocean'. She had heard all about the flowers and the dahlia but was still not sure that it was really okay to be different and special. Not when being different and special wasn't what she wanted to be or do!

George was sure. He knew he was special. He knew that God loved him and made him with the music inside him. One day when he was really old, like Samuel Peasby, the music would come flooding out. Until then he needed to learn all he could.

Now that he didn't have to like football, George didn't actually mind it so much. He still played out with his friends after school on the big stretch of grass by the houses. They didn't expect him to be any good. He still stayed in goal. Someone had to. Twice in the last few weeks he had saved a goal, but his friends didn't mind when he missed. He was a bit of a hero, with his scar, which would take ages to fade.

The council had replaced the "No ball games. By Order." sign. Someone's dad, probably Peter's, carefully dug it up and put it right at the edge of the grass. That way there would be no more nasty accidents.

George and Shearer were happy. Shearer played football with George and dug up the grass when the ball was far away. Shearer lay on George's feet when he practised his piano. *His* piano now. Grandad had given it to him. It still lived in Grandad's room.

Only one thing got George cross. He couldn't do anything about it. It was the price that he had to pay for liking music. Here it came now.

"'Beethoven'! Tea's ready. Get a move on." It was Mum and her nicknames. "And, 'Beethoven', don't forget to wash your hands if you've been playing with that dog."

So, George, also known as 'Beethoven', smiled to himself, as he closed his piano's lid and joined the family for tea and a discussion on United's team for the new season.

More exciting books to enjoy in the *Read by Myself* series...

Mrs Turnip's Treasure
Anne Thorne
When Mrs Turnip asks Adam to look after her 'Treasure' he assumes it is some kind of booty from her great-uncle's pirate ship. But Adam's in for a big surprise!

ISBN 1 85999 052 5
Price £3.50

Message in a Bottle
Heather Butler
While helping with the milk round on Saturdays, Robert starts swapping notes with the mysterious Alf. These include puzzles, secret codes and jokes – which the reader can do too!

ISBN 1 85999 053 3
Price £3.50

Becky's Pony
Pennie Kidd

Becky falls in love with the little grey pony. She longs to be able to ride but thinks it will be impossible. Discover how Becky's courage helps her make a dream come true.

ISBN 1 85999 062 2

Price £3.50

Nobody's Dog
Eleanor Watkins

Luke cannot forget the lonely dog with its hungry brown eyes. It seems to be nobody's dog, so Luke and his friend decide to look after it. But it is not as easy as Luke thinks.

ISBN 0 86201 983 4

Price £3.25

Kangaroo Daniel and the Runaway Pony
Dilys Gower

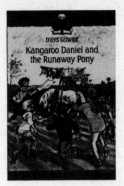

Kangaroo Daniel enjoys helping at the stables but his friend Ashley is not so keen. The horses all seem so big – except for the little pony Sparkie, who becomes his favourite. Discover what happens when Sparkie goes missing and the boys try to find him.

ISBN 0 86201 965 6

Price £2.99

Available from Scripture Union, PO Box 764, Oxford, OX4 5FJ Tel: 01865 716880 Fax: 01865 715152

BOKKIE

· TOECKEY JONES ·

BOKKIE

· TOECKEY JONES ·

The Bodley Head
London

1 3 5 7 9 10 8 6 4 2

Copyright © Toeckey Jones 1995

Toeckey Jones has asserted his right under the Copyright,
Designs and Patents Act, 1988 to be identified as the
author of this work

First published in the United Kingdom 1995
by The Bodley Head Children's Books
Random House, 20 Vauxhall Bridge Road, London SW1V 2SA

Random House Australia (Pty) Limited
20 Alfred Street, Milsons Point, Sydney,
New South Wales 2061, Australia

Random House New Zealand Limited
18 Poland Road, Glenfield,
Auckland 10, New Zealand

Random House South Africa (Pty) Limited
PO Box 337, Bergvlei 2012, South Africa

Random House UK Limited Reg. No. 954009

A CIP record for this book is available from the British Library

ISBN 0 370 31973 7

Printed in Great Britain by
Mackays of Chatham PLC, Chatham, Kent

In memory of my mother. And for Chris because she has always believed in this book. Also for Bokkie's friends.

Toeckey Jones would like to thank South East Arts for their award for Bokkie.

1

My first memory of her. She is sitting cross-legged on a carpet, sketching. We are introduced. She looks at me, and I am transfixed. There is a peculiar sensation in my midriff; I can't speak. I am mesmerized, until she looks away.

It all happens in the space of a second. Suddenly, my life is different. I am involved with her from that moment. And all because of a peculiar sensation in my solar plexus. Sentimental. Crazy. Illogical. True. But then love isn't logical. Love simply is. I know that now. However, I didn't know anything then. I had to live it all through. And so it is a long story.

It begins on a hot summer day in early 1968. I'm at a loose end; living in a sort of limbo; having completed my school sentence and waiting to enrol at the University of the Witwatersrand. It is a Saturday afternoon. My mother and Nick have gone out to tea with a theatre producer. I have the house to myself. Janet, our African maid, is entertaining a female friend in her room in the back yard. They are enjoying themselves. Their shrieks of laughter are audible in my bedroom. I assume they're laughing at the foibles of their white madams.

I flip through my records. But I don't feel like listening to music. I wander listlessly around the house. My mother's bedroom door is shut. I open it. My mother had the room redecorated when she married Nick, although she kept the old furniture. I resent Nick's clothes being in my father's wardrobe. My father has been dead for five years, yet I feel his presence in the room this afternoon. I shut the door.

There is a presence in my bedroom too: my old dog,

7

Jock, who died not so long ago. As I sit down at my desk and stare out of the window, I imagine I can hear him scratching in his basket. I don't want to stay in the house. The problem is, I don't know where I want to be. So I get in my mother's Mini and go for a drive.

Without making a conscious decision about it, I end up at Robert Thornton's house in Wendywood. Robert is one of my school friends. I haven't seen him since the Matric dance, when he took a fancy to my blind date and spent most of the evening dancing with her.

Robert isn't at home. Mrs Thornton tells me he is playing squash, and she doesn't know when he will be back. 'But come in, anyway,' she says, 'and have a cup of tea. And you can meet Pixie.'

I'm thinking I must have misheard her, as I follow her into the living-room. She couldn't have said Pixie, unless she said a pixie, in which case ... At first glance, the living-room seems to be empty, confirming my sudden doubts about Mrs Thornton's sanity. Then I notice the figure sitting on the floor under the window. All I can see are two jean-clad knees sticking out from either side of a huge sketch pad, and two elbows, and a thatch of caramel-coloured hair.

Beside me, Mrs Thornton says, in a tone intended to impress, 'Pixie, you know the actress, Deborah Mane? Well, I'd like you to meet her son, Samuel.'

I clench my teeth. Two of my pet hates are being introduced as Deborah Mane's son, and being called Samuel. There is a movement behind the sketch pad and a small, pointed, gamine face appears. I am confronted by a pair of intense blue eyes. They widen, staring at me. In the background, I am aware of a voice, Mrs Thornton's, informing me that Pixie is a very good artist, and is doing her portrait.

But Pixie doesn't speak. And I can't. Mrs Thornton waits, then says, 'Oh – do you two already know each other?'

Pixie's face disappears back behind her sketch pad, leaving me to answer. I shake my head dumbly. Mrs

Thornton gives a sniff, as if she's trying to detect a bad smell in the room. Then she departs to organize the tea.

I'm feeling breathless. I would like to move over to the window for some fresh air. But that is where Pixie is. The faint scratching of her pencil suddenly stops. She looks up.

'I'm sorry.'

'Sorry?'

'I'm being rude,' she says.

'Rude?' I sound like a parrot. I feel like a parrot, ogling her.

She smiles. My solar plexus is electrified. 'To hell with this,' she says, dumping the sketch pad on the floor.

I watch her uncurl herself, stretch, and get up. She turns her back to peer at the view through the window.

'One should be outside on a day like today. Not stuck indoors, trying to make acquisitive nostrils appear aristocratic on paper.'

I wonder what Mrs Thornton would have to say about Pixie's description of her nostrils. Hesitantly, I ask, 'Can I see your drawing?'

She gives a little shake of her head. 'No one is allowed to see it until it is finished.'

'Not even Mrs Thornton?'

'What a beautiful butterfly.'

'What?' I say.

Her hand beckons. I practically leap over to the window. But the butterfly has gone; a bright flitting speck swallowed up by the blue sky. I stand next to her. An inch separates us. She has her nose pressed against the glass. We look at the garden, but I don't see it. I feel as if I'm choking. I risk a sideways peep and find her eyeing me askance.

'I'm sorry, I can't remember your name.'

'Sam,' I say hoarsely.

'Sam.' She rubs her nose on the window. 'Sam.' She is smiling. Then she is gone, like the butterfly. Taking her sketch pad over to the other side of the room, she settles herself in a chair and frowns at her drawing.

Mrs Thornton comes in, followed by the African maid carrying a tray. I remain at the window until the tea is poured. Then I sit where Mrs Thornton has placed my cup. I'm afraid to pick it up. The china handle is too small to hook a finger through, and my hands aren't steady. I wait until Mrs Thornton engages Pixie in conversation, before taking a sip. It is a mistake to glance in Pixie's direction. Our eyes meet. Tea slops into my saucer. Mrs Thornton's acquisitive nostrils twitch disapprovingly at me. Pixie hides a smile behind her own cup.

I decide I'm making a fool of myself and Pixie isn't really my type. I resolve to leave as soon as I've drunk my tea. Fifteen minutes later, I'm still there. Mrs Thornton has refilled our cups. She is babbling away to Pixie, but her voice is simply background static. With dread, I'm anticipating the moment when Pixie will get up and go, and I will never see her again. The moment comes. Pixie stands up. Mrs Thornton stands up. I stand up. Then Mrs Thornton turns to me.

'Samuel, perhaps you wouldn't mind giving Pixie a lift home to Hillbrow. She doesn't have a car, and it will save me a trip.'

And so here she is, sitting beside me in the Mini. I want to impress her with my driving. But I haven't been driving for very long, and her knees are disturbingly close to the controls. After grinding the gears several times, I tell her the synchromesh is on the blink.

'Really? Yours or the car's?' she asks drily, and offers me a cigarette.

I shake my head.

'It's very nice of you to give me a lift. I hope I'm not taking you too far out of your way. Where do you live?'

'In Saxonwold.'

'Saxonwold?' She makes a whistling sound, exhaling smoke.

'What's wrong with Saxonwold?' I ask defensively.

'It's rather posh, isn't it?'

'Well, I'm not posh.' I can feel myself reddening.

'No.' She sounds amused. 'You don't have a private school accent.'

'My father was left the house in a relative's will. And some money. He never earned a fortune himself. He was a botanist.'

'Was?'

'He's dead,' I say gruffly.

'I'm sorry.'

'It's okay. He died quite a while ago.'

'Were you close?'

I shrug. 'He was a nice guy.'

'You're lucky.'

'Lucky?'

'Hey, mind that dog!'

I hoot, hitting the brakes. The dog steps back on to the pavement, and sits down. He looks like Jock: the same colour, the same goofy expression. I lose track of what we've been talking about.

'And your mother?' Pixie asks. 'You know, I saw her recently in *The Woman in a Dressing Gown* at the Alexander Theatre. I thought she was brilliant in the part.'

I thought she was too. But I don't want to spend the journey talking about my mother's theatrical successes. So I keep my trap shut.

'I seem to remember reading somewhere that she is married to an impresario. He must be your stepfather then.'

'No.'

'He isn't?'

'Being married to my mother doesn't make him my father.'

'I see,' she says.

I'm aware of her eyes studying my face. I'm aware of the pink splat of a squashed insect on the windscreen. I'm aware of her fingers toying with the lighter in her lap.

'What about your folks?' I ask.

'My mother died last year. My father . . .' she pauses,

drawing on her cigarette and exhaling smoke through her nostrils. ' . . . He's still alive, as far as I know.'

'As far as you know? Don't you have any contact with him?'

No answer. I glance at her. She is staring out of the window. I can only see the back of her head. I love the way her hair curves round behind her ear. I make myself concentrate on the traffic.

We have now joined the Johannesburg-Pretoria main road, and are approaching Wynberg Industrial Estate. A heavy pall of smog hangs over Alexandra Township, hidden in the valley on the left. Escaping tendrils of acrid smoke reach out like dirty fingers grasping at the traffic ahead of us. I roll my window up hurriedly.

Pixie turns round. 'It's a bloody disgrace!'

'What? The township? Yes, it is. But they have to live somewhere.'

'There, in that hell-hole? In corrugated-iron hovels without electricity, or running water, or loos? Why should black people have to live there? Why can't they live in Saxonwold, for instance?'

I regret having spoken. Her eyes are a menacing blue now. I shrug. She knows the facts as well as I do. Apartheid is Apartheid. You can't change the law. So what's the point in arguing about it.

We drive on in silence. It isn't comfortable. I try to think of something conciliatory to say, but I'm nervous of putting my foot in it again, or sounding banal. When we're stopped by a red traffic light in Louis Botha Avenue, Pixie retrieves her packet of cigarettes which have fallen on the floor.

'I take it you don't smoke?'

'I do. Occasionally. When I get the urge.'

'Have you got the urge now?'

I look at her, and she smiles. The red changes to green without my noticing it. A car behind us hoots. I let out the clutch too quickly, and the Mini bounces forward, shuddering.

Pixie laughs. 'Your synchromesh again, huh?'

'Perhaps a cigarette will help.'

She lights one and hands it to me. I suck on it deeply, savouring the slight dampness on the end from her mouth. I feel as if she has passed me a kiss. I feel forgiven. I feel exultant, until I realize the journey won't last much longer and I don't know how to ask her if I can see her again.

When we reach Hillbrow, Pixie gives me directions to her flat. We end up in a narrow, tree-lined back street.

'This is it,' she says, pointing at an older style block of flats straddling the corner.

The building predates the era of high-rise architecture; built of brick with peeling paintwork, it has clearly seen better days. I park on the yellow line outside the entrance, which is flanked by two concrete tubs containing dusty marigolds. Pixie retrieves her art materials from the back seat. I hold my breath.

'Would you like to come up for coffee?' she asks.

I bruise my shin on the steering column in my haste to scramble out of the car before she can change her mind.

The red-tiled vestibule smells of floor polish and stale cigarette smoke. Pixie's flat is on the top floor. There is no lift. We climb the three flights of stairs. My rubber soles squeak an accompaniment to the soft clatter of Pixie's sandals along the open corridor. Her door is the last one, right at the end. I hold her sketch pad for her, while she finds her key. As I follow her inside, something grabs me round the neck. I squawk, and discover I'm being strangled by the ropy tendrils of an exotic plant.

Rescuing me, Pixie says, 'I've been meaning to cut it back.'

'What is it? A Venus man-trap?'

'I don't know what it is. But it seems to grow about an inch a day.'

I look around and realize I'm not standing in a hallway; I'm standing in a jungle of potted plants.

'This is my garden,' explains Pixie. 'My front garden.
I have a back garden as well.'

'Where's that?'

'In my bathroom.'

I'm not sure if she is joking. But after fighting my
way through the foliage in the hallway, I'm at least
relieved to find there aren't any plants in the living-
room, only some comfortable-looking pieces of furniture, and a well-worn rug. I like the feeling in the room.
While Pixie throws open the windows, I inspect the
pictures on the walls. None of them are by her.

'Where are your paintings?' I ask.

'Mostly stacked up in the room I use as a studio.'

'Can I see them?'

She gives a non-committal shrug. 'Do you take milk
in your coffee?'

'Please. And sugar.'

'I hope I can find the sugar,' she says.

I understand the reason for her uncertainty when I
follow her into the kitchen. It would be difficult to
find anything in here. Every available surface contains
a clutter of culinary objects usually kept in cupboards.
There are cupboards, but in helping Pixie hunt for the
sugar, I discover them to be mainly half-empty.

'I doubt you'll find the sugar in a cupboard,' Pixie
warns me. 'I remember getting it out yesterday.'

'Where should I look?'

'Try the top of the fridge. I haven't checked there
yet.'

The sugar turns up, finally, hidden behind a pineapple
in the fruit bowl on the window sill. Pixie clears a little
space at the end of the table, and we drink our coffee,
sitting facing each other over a motley assortment of
condiments and breakfast cereal packets. I'm happy.
From what I've seen so far, my antennae tell me that
Pixie lives alone. But I need confirmation, and ask her
about the layout of the rest of the flat, hoping she will
give me a tour.

'Apart from the bathroom, there are three other

rooms along the passage. My bedroom, my studio, and a spare room which I'm hoping to let because I need the money. Do you know anybody who wants to rent a—'

'Me,' I say instantly.

'You?'

'Yes, me.' I explain that I'm starting a Bachelor of Arts degree at Wits University this year, and looking for somewhere to rent within walking distance of the campus. It's true enough. I have been seriously considering moving out of the house at some point in the near future. 'When could I have the room?'

'You'd better come and see it first. You might not like it.'

I like it. It isn't very large, but that doesn't bother me. Even if it had been the size of a dog kennel, I would still have been enthusiastic. The furniture is adequate; there is a bed, a wardrobe, a table, and space for a bookcase. And when Pixie mentions the rent, it sounds cheap to me.

'I'll take the room,' I say, joining her at the window.

'The view isn't up to much.'

'I like the view.' But I'm looking at her, not the view. She turns to face me. She half-smiles, then walks away.

'When can I move in?'

'Are you sure you—'

'Yes. Is tomorrow afternoon too soon?'

'Tomorrow? Crikey! . . . No, I guess that's okay. I'll be here all day. I've got to work on Mrs Thornton's portrait. Come on, I'll show you the bathroom.'

She wasn't kidding about her back garden being the bathroom. The room is a forest of ferns, and trailing creepers suspended in pots from hooks on the ceiling. It looks as though it will be difficult to get into the bath without being molested by a particularly rampant ivy.

'I hope that one isn't carnivorous,' I comment, backing out into the passage.

'If you're worried about your tender bits, I could

hang the ivy somewhere else, I suppose. But it's happy where it is.'

She is very close to me. The reaction in my midriff is so sharp, it's like a pain. I'm afraid to look at her. I point at the two doors further along the passage.

'Which one is your studio?'

'The door on the left. And by the way, that room is private. No one is allowed in there, except at my invitation. Okay?'

'Of course.'

I want her to trust me. I have to meet her gaze. Close up, her irises are prisms of grey, cobwebbed with clear blue. I'm immobilized, caught up in them, like a trussed fly. Everything else around me blurs. She tilts forward. My heart stops. Then I feel her hand on my head, ruffling my hair, as she brushes past me and walks on down the passage, back to the kitchen.

My hope that she will offer me some more coffee is dashed when she carries our empty cups over to the sink and adds them to the pile of washing-up. I take the hint, and pick up my car keys. She shows me out.

'Well,' I say, 'see you tomorrow then.'

'Yes,' she says.

I wait. ' . . . Bye. And thanks for the coffee.'

'Bye,' she says.

I don't hear the door close behind me, and sense she is watching me walk away. Glancing round, I catch her retreating inside quickly. Suddenly, I'm ten feet tall. My rubber soles aren't squeaking along the corridor; I'm walking on air. I fly down the three flights of stairs.

The Mini has been standing in the full glare of the sun; its interior is like a hot oven. The stale trapped air releases a faint piquancy of musky petals – Pixie's perfume. I keep the windows closed to preserve the scent, and drive home, dripping sweat and singing at the top of my voice. I know I'm crazy. I tell myself I'm pathetic, but I don't care – except that it's scary to feel so happy. I'm terrified it can't last.

* * * *

They are back. Nick's Mercedes is parked in the drive-way. I know where I'll find them at this hour of the day; out in the arbour, relaxing over a sundowner. I walk round the side of the house. My mother sees me and waves.

'Come and join us, honbee.'

'Have you got a cold beer?' I shout. Nick fishes in the ice bucket, and holds up a can. 'Okay. Then I'll join you.'

I choose to take the longer path past the fishpond, where Benjamin is aerating the surface of the water with a sprinkler. In his comical pointed hat, baggy overalls, and clumpy boots, he looks like a little black gnome, crouching among the painted plaster ones Nick keeps buying for my mother. Benjamin has been our garden boy for many years. He is now a very old 'boy', pushing seventy. Our housemaids have come and gone in quick succession because my mother can never get on with them. But Benjamin has been with us for so long, he is almost part of the family. He tips his hat when I greet him.

'Afternoon, Master Sam.'

'What you doing? Drowning the fish?'

He laughs. 'The madam told me to water them. I think, Master Sam, she thinks they must be thirsty.'

I raise my voice so my mother will hear. 'Tell you what, Benjamin, I think you should water the madam. I'll pay you fifty cents to go and sprinkle her.'

Benjamin puts on an expression of horror. 'Hauww! I can't do that.'

'I can hear you,' my mother calls. 'Don't you dare listen to him, Benjamin.'

'Come on, Benjamin, let's do it, hey!'

I grab the sprinkler. He grabs it back. My mother shouts to him to turn it on me. I start to run. He chases me for a few yards, then gives up, laughing and wheezing. We're all laughing, apart from Nick. The best he can manage is a somewhat forced smile. Ignoring

17

him, I saunter up to my mother and plant a kiss on her cheek.

'Howdy, pardner,' I say.

'Howdy, pardner.' She squeezes my hand. 'You're in a good mood. Where've you been?'

'For a drive. I borrowed the Mini, in case you didn't notice.'

'We noticed.' Nick scowls at me. 'I hope you didn't bring it back with an empty tank like last time.'

He is wearing his kingfisher-blue shirt with a flowery tie. His colour schemes always strike me as a loud shout of self-applause. I look him up and down deliberately slowly.

'You're developing a paunch, Nick. Too much good living, I reckon.'

'I'm not,' he says indignantly.

'Are you, Nick?' Now I've got my mother worried.

While she investigates Nick's middle, I help myself to a Lion ale, and one of her menthol cigarettes. I notice her lighter is a new gold one. I suspect the inscription – 'From a Secret Admirer' – is one of Nick's little jokes.

Nick used to be dedicated to his career, until he married my mother and chucked it all in, to dedicate himself to her career.

'Nice lighter,' I comment, flicking the top open and shut.

'Don't break it,' growls Nick.

'Yes, don't break it.' My mother snatches the lighter from me. 'It's precious. It's a present.'

'Who from, Debs?' I've been calling my mother Debs for some years. She likes it. She claims being called Mum made her feel prematurely old.

'From one of my admirers,' she retorts coyly. 'But tell us what you've been up to, darling.'

'I've found myself digs.'

'Digs?' She appears genuinely startled. 'What do you mean?'

'You know. Digs. A room. To rent. Near varsity. I've

arranged to move in tomorrow, if that's all right with you?'

They both stare at me. I observe an ant crawling up the side of Nick's glass. I wonder if I should say something about it. Then I notice the look on my mother's face.

'You don't seriously mind, do you, Debs?'

'Of course she bloody does,' Nick mutters into his glass.

'I think you've just swallowed an ant,' I tell him.

'. . . Debs?'

'Yes?' She assumes her brave expression. 'I don't know what to say. It's a bit sudden.'

'It isn't that sudden. We've talked about it before. Remember? You thought it was a good idea.'

'I'm sure I didn't say it was a good idea.'

'Well, you didn't disagree with me when I said it was.'

'How much is the rent?' Nick snaps at me.

I pretend not to hear him. 'So what do you reckon, Debs?'

'How much is the rent?' repeats Nick.

'Yes, how much is the rent?' asks my mother.

'Chickenfeed,' I tell her, because I'm not prepared to discuss the financial details in front of Nick. I roll my eyes in his direction.

My mother understands, and gives a little nod. Then she puts on a performance of looking for a cigarette.

'I thought I had a couple left in my cigarette case. But it's empty. Do you have any on you, Nick?'

'You know I've given up,' he says grumpily.

My mother uncrosses her legs. 'Then I'll have to go and . . .'

That brings Nick instantly to his feet. 'You sit! You're supposed to be resting. I'll fetch them for you.'

'Oh, you are a Nickypoo darling,' she coos, and blows him a kiss. 'You'll find a new packet on the dressing table.' She and I watch him stride away towards the house. 'He is sweet,' she says.

'I don't know about that. But he is handsome,' I admit.

'I'm so lucky,' she sighs, 'having two handsome men in my life. Only now I'm about to lose one of them.'

'You're hardly losing me, Debs.'

'Aren't I?' She is still staring after Nick. 'I hope he isn't starting to go bald. It's such a shame men lose their hair. Other male animals don't. If I ever meet God, I'm jolly well going to have a word in His ear about it.' She rearranges herself in her chair. 'Anyway, tell me all about this room now.'

I explain only as much as I feel she needs to know. She agrees the rent is reasonable.

'I suppose we can afford it,' she says. 'After all, there won't be the expense of feeding you here.'

'Exactly.'

'Though money is quite tight at the moment.'

'You shouldn't keep it in the drinks cabinet.'

'Don't be a clown,' and she smiles. In her pleated, pink dress with matching hair-slides and arm bangles, she looks half her age this afternoon. I'm tempted to tell her so, but I don't; she receives enough compliments from Nick. 'What about your allowance? I expect you'll need a rise.'

'I might manage without one.'

'I doubt it. You're so unworldly concerning money and the other practical necessities of life. Just like your father.'

I shrug. 'He made out. So will I.'

'And me? How will I make out without you?'

'You don't need me, Debs.' I grin at her. 'You've got Nick.'

She pouts coquettishly. 'Yes, I've got Nick, but I'll miss my honbee. Darling, you know if you aren't happy, you can always come back home.'

'Thanks.'

I pat her knee. She squeezes my hand.

'You will visit us, honbee?'

'Of course. And you must visit me.'

20

She perks up. 'That might be fun.'

'What'll be fun?' Nick has re-entered the stage. He pushes in between us with his offering of cigarettes.

I grab my unfinished can of beer, and back off. My mother notices my retreat.

'Where are you going, honbee?'

'To pack.'

I blow her a kiss. She blows me two back. When I reach the end of the path, I turn. The scene in the arbour could be straight out of *Gone With The Wind*. A magnificent sunset sky forms a romantic backdrop. Golden shafts of light filter through the foliage, providing a soft focus. The hero has his arm round the heroine. She is smiling up into his face. They look very happy. I feel I won't really be missed. The play will go on without me. I exit, slinking off into the house.

2

'Oh. It's you,' Pixie says.

She looks at me. She looks at my luggage on her front doorstep. I feel a tightness in my chest. I'm afraid she's going to say she has changed her mind about letting me move in.

'Is this all you've brought?' she asks.

'There are a few more bits and pieces in the car. But I didn't pack very much. I can always go back for whatever else I need later.'

She smiles. At least I know now I am welcome. I feast my eyes on her like a hungry Spaniel.

'Do you want some help with those things?' she asks.

'No, I can manage.'

But she helps me anyway. In my room, there are flowers in a glass on the table. And the bed is freshly made up. I'm a little overwhelmed; I hadn't expected her to go to this trouble.

'I've put a clean towel out for you in the bathroom,' she says.

'Thanks,' I manage to croak.

'Would you like a cup of tea?'

'Please.'

I fetch the rest of my belongings from the Mini, which my mother has lent me for a few weeks. Then we drink coffee (Pixie couldn't find the tea), sitting on my bed and surveying my possessions.

'What do you want to arrange about food?' Pixie asks. 'Do you want to chip in for provisions each week and we'll eat together, or would you rather fend for yourself?'

'I'd like to chip in,' I tell her.

'Okay. You'll have to sort something out for yourself tonight though. You'll find left-overs in the fridge.'

The bubble is about to burst. 'Won't you be here this evening?'

'It's a friend of mine's birthday. We're going out to dinner.'

I stare at the dregs in my cup. They are a dark, murky colour; not enough milk. I hadn't noticed before. Friend could mean girl-friend, I tell myself.

Pixie slithers off the bed. 'I must bath and change. I'll leave you to it. If you need anything, just shout.'

I smoke a cigarette. Then I start unpacking, as I can't just sit and do nothing. I hear Pixie singing in the bath and, less audibly, in her bedroom. I hear the doorbell ring and then – a man's voice in the hallway. Ten minutes later, Pixie appears and invites me for a drink in the living-room.

She is a vision in white: white cotton slacks, white turtle-neck top, and cork-heeled white sandals. Her washed fluffy hair gleams like a golden aura round her radiant face. I can't stand to look at her because she is sparkling for him, not me.

Him. His name turns out to be Russ, and he is tall

and lanky and gingery blond, with a freckled, friendly face, and cobalt eyes that look as if they'd shine in the dark like a cat's. If I didn't resent him so much, I would like him. As it is, I find it difficult to be even civil. I gulp down my glass of wine, excuse myself, and return to my room.

I'm lying on the bed, when Pixie gives a little knock on the door. 'Sam? We're going now.'

'Bye,' I say gruffly.

'What?'

'I said "Enjoy yourself," ' I shout.

'Thanks.'

Her footsteps recede down the passage. She and Russ leave, laughing. The front door slams. Only then do I realize she hasn't left me a key. I'm trapped in the flat for the evening.

In a sudden rage, I finish unpacking, throwing my clothes haphazardly into the wardrobe, with my portable radio tuned to Lourenco Marques station and turned up as loudly as possible. Once the room is in some sort of order, I carry the radio into the bathroom, and have a long hot soak in the tub. That uses up half-an-hour. But it is still early; there are hours to kill before bedtime.

The left-overs in the fridge reveal themselves to be the remains of a fish pie, and a bowl of soggy cooked carrots and peas. I hate fish pie. I would settle for a sandwich, only I can't find any bread. I can't even find milk for a cup of coffee. The kitchen is in a worse state of chaos than the previous day. I'm momentarily consoled when I discover some wine in one of the glasses in the living-room. I polish it off. The bottle, unfortunately, is empty.

I walk back along the passage, past my bedroom. Pixie's studio door is closed. I hesitate; I had promised I wouldn't go in there. But my curiosity is stronger than my conscience. I convince myself that a quick peep from the doorway won't amount to breaking my word. Nothing happens when I try the handle. The door is

23

locked. Pixie obviously felt unable to trust me. I'm upset by that, despite having just proved her misgiving to be justified.

The door to her bedroom is ajar. I peer in, but I can't see anything; it's too dark. I fumble for the light switch, and nearly jump out of my skin. The sudden illumination reveals a young coloured boy, staring at me from across the room. I think I've disturbed a burglar. Then I realize it is only a painting on the wall. A life-size oil portrait. The boy is naked, apart from a pair of shorts. I understand why I thought he was alive. He looks alive; all the more so because the picture contains no setting. There's just the boy, standing alone, against the white wall, observing me with dark soulful eyes. I feel a tingle up my spine. It's uncanny. His eyes seem to be looking right into me. I want to look away, yet I can't. I snap off the light. Even though I have now made him disappear, I can still sense him staring at me in the darkness.

I creep back to my own room, undress, and climb into bed with a novel. After reading only a couple of paragraphs, I give up. The boy's face is haunting me from the page. I feel compelled to go and have another look at the painting.

From the doorway, I scrutinize the canvas for a signature. There isn't one, though instinct tells me it is Pixie's work. I would like to go closer, but I'm afraid Pixie would somehow know if I entered her bedroom. I feel uneasy even standing in the doorway. I squint up at the boy. His chiselled little face is grave, yet his mouth bears the semblance of a smile – a small, pensive, all-knowing smile. That is partly what is so disconcerting about him; he has the features of a young boy and the countenance of a wise old man.

Back in bed, I find it even more difficult to concentrate on my novel. Switching off the lamp, I lie wide-awake in the dark, listening for the sound of Pixie's return. It is after midnight when I hear the front door open and close, and footsteps in the passage – a single pair of footsteps. They pause at my door, then tiptoe on quietly. I smile to myself. She has come home alone. There is hope in that. Hugging the pillow, I curl up on my side under the sheet. I can sleep now.

* * * *

I am woken in the morning by Pixie shaking my shoulder. There is a crisis. Apparently Russ has just rung her to say that her horse has been injured. I didn't even know Pixie had a horse.

'Will you drive me there?' she says.

I squint at her groggily. 'Where?'

'To Linbro Park. Russ can't come and collect me because he has to wait for the vet to arrive. Will you?'

I am conscious of the fact that under the sheet I am starkers, and I have an erection. The semi-transparent, clinging nightie she has on doesn't help my state. My brain won't function properly.

'When?' I say stupidly.

'As soon as possible. Now! Please!'

She sounds and looks desperate. I feel mortified. She is in distress, and I am consumed with lust.

'Of course. Just give me a few minutes,' I rasp, 'to get dressed.'

She flies out of the room. I grab my gown, dash into the bathroom, and splash cold water all over myself as a penance.

The drive to Linbro Park is a nightmare. It is rush-hour, and Louis Botha Avenue is a conveyor belt of cars and lorries and buses. Pixie keeps urging me to go faster. I can't. We become caught up in a snarl. To try and take her mind off the hold-up, I get her to talk.

'Where do you keep your horse? At a riding stable?'

'No. On Russ's smallholding. But he isn't a horse, he's a pony.'

'What's the difference?'

'There's a lot of difference. Ifu is a Basuto pony. Why doesn't that bloody car in front move?'

'Ifu? That's an unusual—'

'I just hope the cut isn't too deep.'

'Cut?'

25

'Russ says he has a bad gash above his eye.'

'How did it happen?'

'Russ doesn't know. Ifu lives out in the field. I think he might have blundered into the fence during the night, and in a panic to get free, hit his head on a post with a nail sticking out, or something. He's pretty old now and half-blind. That's why I'm worried about him.'

'I'm sure he'll be all right,' I say reassuringly.

Her eyes moisten. She turns her face away. If I could make the Mini fly for her, I would.

The traffic is even worse on the narrow, winding Modderfontein Road through Lyndhurst. We get stuck behind a bus. But at last we reach Edenvale Hospital and the turn off to Linbro Park. I put my foot down. Not for long. Once we're past the neat houses and gardens of Lombardy East, the tarmac runs out. Open countryside stretches away to the left, with the smog of Alexandra Township visible in the distance. I have to change down to third, and then second gear, to navigate the dirt lanes of Linbro Park; they're gouged with deep dongas and I fear for the Mini's sump. We turn left and right several times before Pixie points at an unkempt narrow gateway.

'We're here. This is it.'

The meandering, rutted driveway takes us past an overgrown orchard on one side, and a large fenced field on the other. At the top of the drive, the house reveals itself to be small and dilapidated, its walls and windows half-smothered by some sort of frothy, flowering vine. From the front end, juts a verandah. I drive round the back and park next to a red Peugeot.

'That must be the vet,' Pixie says, and she is out of the Mini and running, before I've switched off the engine.

I'm prevented from following her by two Alsatians, who suddenly appear from nowhere. I have to submit, nervously, to being sniffed all over. Apparently, I pass as a friend. They wag their tails, and accompany me in the direction Pixie has taken, along a path between outbuildings containing rows of pottery and a kiln. Now I know what Russ does for a living.

The path peters out at a gate into the field. On the other side of the fence is an open shelter. Craning my neck over the gate, I glimpse the back end of a brown-coloured pony, lying on a thick bed of straw. Pixie and Russ, and a short stout man, presumably the vet, are in a huddle over it. As I lift the latch, Russ glances round.

'Don't let the dogs in.'

I drop the latch smartly. The Alsatians paw the gate, whining. Pixie frowns at me over her shoulder.

'Shut them up. They'll frighten Ifu.'

I don't know how to silence them; they aren't my dogs. I retreat along the path, and call them. They ignore me. But once I start to run, they hare after me joyfully. I take them back to the house, and sit on the verandah step, and throw sticks for them. Russ appears with the vet. He sees him to his car, then comes over to me.

'I was wondering where you had got to, Sam.'

'I thought I'd better keep the dogs out of the way.'

'Thanks. And thanks for bringing Pixie. You're a pal.'

I'm not a pal. I resent him for having the woman I want. Gruffly, I ask, 'How's the pony?'

'Not too good, I'm afraid. He's suffering from concussion, the vet says.'

'Is that serious?'

'At his age it is. Between you and me, what worries me is how Pixie is going to take it if he doesn't pull through. She's had him a long time, you know.'

'How long?'

'She was given him when she was a young girl, living on the farm in Natal. But he's more than just a horse to her.'

I watch the Alsatians romping on the grass. 'I know.'

'You do?'

'I know about losing a best friend.' I'm thinking of Jock.

'She's told you?' He sounds surprised.

I squint up at him. 'Told me about what?'

27

'About Bo... about what happened in her childhood?'

'No,' I say, and wait, expecting him to explain further. He shrugs. 'Best forget I mentioned it.'

'Why?' I feel annoyed. I want to know. 'Can't you tell me?'

'Nope,' and he grins. 'Pixie doesn't like talking about it much. She'll tell you if she wants to. Hey! I smell coffee. Great. I see Mercy has got breakfast ready for us on the verandah. You're probably starving like me. Come and tuck in.'

I am ravenous. I haven't eaten since lunch the day before. I polish off a bowl of cereal, and help myself to some toast.

'Try the home-made jam,' Russ suggests. 'But I wouldn't recommend the marmalade. It tastes a bit—'

'What's wrong with my marmalade?'

An outsize African woman has appeared in the doorway connecting the verandah with the house, and is glowering at Russ. He laughs.

'You weren't supposed to hear that, Mercy.'

'I have ears,' she informs him tartly. 'So what's wrong with my marmalade?'

'I think it's gone off,' he says.

'Gone off? Gone off where? To Durban? Here, bring me some. Let me try.'

Russ obligingly takes her the jar. She dips in a finger, licks it, and pulls a face.

'Poison. This one I'll give to my daughter's *tsotsi** husband. I'll say it's medicine for his stomach.' Tucking the jar under her arm, she turns her attention on me. 'Who's this, Russ?'

'This is Sam,' he says.

She inspects me up and down suspiciously. 'Is he a new friend for you?' she asks Russ.

'No. He came with Pixie.'

* tsotsi – rascal

28

'He's not your friend? He's Pixie's friend?' she says, as if she doesn't believe him.

'That's right,' and he laughs amiably. 'So you don't have to interrogate him, Mercy.'

'Okay, if he's not your friend. If he's Pixie's friend, it's okay. He can stay to lunch. Where's Pixie now?'

'She's with Ifu.'

'That horse!' she snorts, and departs.

Russ grins at me. 'Ifu once bit her on the bum. She's never forgiven him.'

'Doesn't she ever smile?'

'Not if she can help it. It would spoil the effect.'

'Of what?'

'Her sense of humour. It's very dry.'

I would call it very impertinent. She wouldn't last ten minutes in my mother's house. 'She's lucky you put up with her,' I comment.

'I'm lucky she puts up with me,' he retorts.

End of discussion. We carry on eating in silence, until Pixie arrives. Russ pours her coffee and butters her some toast which she only nibbles at. She says she isn't hungry. She and Russ talk about Ifu. When Russ puts his arm round her and gives her a cuddle, I stand up and fish my car keys out of my pocket.

'Thanks for the breakfast, Russ.'

'Hey, you aren't leaving now, are you?' he says.

'I might as well.'

'Don't feel you have to rush off. I've got to make a delivery of pottery to a shop in Rosebank shortly, but I shan't be away long. Why don't you stick around, and make yourself at home?'

I look at Pixie. I feel it is up to her; if she'd like me to stay, I will.

'Do you have to go?' she asks me.

'I guess not,' I say, and sit down again.

During the morning, the condition of the pony improves. He gets back up on his feet, and manages to drink a little water. Lunch is therefore a happier affair than breakfast. Mercy dishes up a steaming stew, wearing the air of a hospital matron on a ward round, doling out a laxative.

'This is a surprise, Mercy,' says Russ. 'I thought you said we were only going to have cheese and bread.'

'The cheese can keep. I had to use up the dogs' bones. They were taking too much room in the fridge.'

I peer more closely at my portion. Russ catches my eye and winks.

'Don't worry,' he assures me, after Mercy has gone, 'there weren't any dogs' bones in the fridge. At least I don't think there were.'

The stew tastes all right. I have a second helping. We all do. The dish is empty when Mercy reappears. She complains crossly that we haven't left the dogs any.

'I'm sorry we haven't left you any either,' Pixie apologizes to her.

'Me? Eat that? You think I'm mad. I cooked it. What you want for pudding, Pixie?'

'You mean we have a choice?' asks Russ.

'No. Just fruit salad,' she says, and waddles away to fetch it.

After coffee, Pixie excuses herself, and returns to her vigil in the pony shelter. Russ has to make another delivery of pottery. I'm left to my own devices. Under the trees at the end of the lawn, I discover a hammock, and climb into it for a snooze.

As I'm dozing off, I suddenly remember the last time I slept in a hammock. It was when I was about ten. I was with my father on a field trip in search of rare orchids. We were having a lot of fun together, he and I. I felt closer to him than I did at home, where he spent most of his time ensconced in his study, preoccupied with his work and unapproachable. Out here in the wilds he was different; more relaxed and cheerful; and treating me as a buddy rather than a son. I was glad my mother had refused to come with us. The outdoor life didn't appeal to her, and she couldn't have coped with sleeping rough under the stars. She would have spoilt our fun. I said as much to my father one evening when we had settled down in our hammocks deep in a forest. To entertain him, I pretended to be my mother, reacting hysterically to the night sounds around us. I believed I was being very amusing. However, my father didn't laugh. In fact, he was so quiet, I thought he couldn't be awake. But when I shone my torch on his face, the beam showed a trail of wetness down his cheeks.

'Turn that damn thing off,' he growled at me, 'and go to sleep.'

In the morning, he was his usual self again. And I never really understood his sorrow that night. Until now. Now, lying in Russ's hammock, I think I finally understand how he felt. When you love somebody, and they don't need to be with you, it hurts.

While I'm snoozing under the trees, Pixie's pony dies. Russ wakes me with the news. It takes me a few seconds to orientate myself, and register what he is saying.

'Pixie?' I ask.

'She's okay. She seems okay. But she'd like you to drive her home. Do you mind? She wants to go straight away.'

That surprises me. I would have expected her to want to stay with Russ. I tumble out of the hammock.

'She wants me to take her home? Are you sure?'

'It's better if she isn't here. You know, there's the body to be disposed of, and—'

'Oh yes. Right. Of course. Where is she?'

'She's waiting in the car . . . Hey, hang on, you needn't run.'

I stop to let him catch up. He grasps my arm. 'Sam . . .'

'What?'

He looks me straight in the eye. It's disquieting. I suspect he's picked up how I feel about Pixie, and is about to issue me a warning or threat.

'Pixie likes you,' he says.

I tense my shoulders. 'I like her.'

He nods. 'Yes, I know. But she's special, Sam.'

'Meaning?'

'Meaning, I'm asking you to look after her. She does

give the impression of being very independent and strong, only underneath she is pretty fragile, like we all are. She might need a shoulder to lean on, for the next few days. You'll be there, won't you?'

'Of course!' I don't know how he could even ask the question, though I realize he doesn't know me very well.

'Good.' His face suddenly creases into a disarming grin. 'You're okay, Sam,' he says, and walks on to the car to say goodbye to Pixie.

He waves us off down the drive. I wait until we are bumping along the road before I look at Pixie. Her face is calm and composed.

'I'm sorry about Ifu,' I mumble inadequately.

She shrugs. 'We all have to die sometime. At least I don't have to worry about him any longer.'

'Yes.'

'How does this radio work?'

I switch it on for her. 'What would you like to listen to?'

'Anything light and cheerful.'

We listen to a request programme on Springbok radio station all the way home. It is rush hour again, but the return journey seems relatively quick, perhaps because we aren't in a desperate rush this time. At the flat, as I'm getting out of the car, I notice the two bottles of wine on the back seat.

'Where did these come from?' I ask Pixie.

'From Russ. Will you carry them? They're good wine, so don't drop them.'

I read the labels. 'They are. It's very nice of him.'

'He is very nice,' she says, with a wan smile.

While she is having a bath, I do the washing up. After that, I try and tidy up the kitchen a bit. Pixie is in the bathroom a long time. I start to feel anxious about her, and go and knock on the door.

'Are you all right?'

I hear the slap of water against the sides of the bath,

as if she has shifted suddenly. 'I haven't drowned.' Her voice sounds croaky; I suspect she has been crying.

'Well, would you like me to start making something for supper? Are you hungry?'

'No. But I could do with a drink. Will you open a bottle? I won't be long.'

I set a tray with the wine and glasses, and a packet of nuts I discovered in the cupboard under the sink when I was looking for the washing-up liquid. It is growing dark outside. I draw the curtains in the living-room, switch on the standard lamp, and sit and wait apprehensively for her to join me.

She comes in, wearing a turquoise cotton nightgown, and fluffy slippers. She looks – she looks, well, not like a princess exactly; more like a schoolgirl dragged out of bed for an unplanned midnight feast, as she surveys the room with big surprised eyes, staring through the floppy mop of her tousled hair. If she has been crying, there is no sign of it now in her face.

'You've made it nice and cosy in here,' she says. 'But the lamp's too bright. Let's have some candles.'

She finds the candles. I light them, and pour the wine. She kneels on the floor with her bottom in the air, searching through her records. Her bottom is delectable; so are the backs of her heels – which are all I can see of her for the time being. She puts on a selection of the Beatles' songs, and settles herself down beside me on the sofa.

We discuss the songs we're listening to. We discuss other songs we like. We drink wine. I have to hold my glass in both hands to keep it steady. When she is this close to me, I find it hard to concentrate, or even speak sensibly. We drink more wine and listen to more records. Then I remember I'm supposed to be looking after her.

'Are you getting hungry yet?' I ask her. 'Would you like something to eat now?'

She turns her eyes on me. They are smoky-blue in the candle-light. A small smile softens her mouth. 'You're sweet, Sam.' She reaches up and runs her hand over the top of my head. Then she gets up to change the record.

'Would you like something to eat?' I repeat stupidly.

'Nope. Let's dance,' she says. 'When someone dies, we should celebrate, not mourn. We only grieve for ourselves. It's selfish. We should be happy for them. No more suffering!' She shouts the last words almost desperately. I'm expecting this to be the moment when she might burst into tears. But she doesn't. She turns the volume up on the record player, and starts gyrating in time to the fast beat. 'Come on, Sam.'

And so we jive, energetically, wildly. Neither of us are altogether steady on our feet. We bump into the furniture, and trip over the rug, and laugh breathlessly at each other's clumsiness. But we keep on moving frenziedly, as if our very lives depend on it. When I glance at her swivelling face, the frenetic play of light and shadow across her features makes her expression look quite savage. My expression must look the same to her. Finally, she catches her foot in a fold of the rug, and almost falls; I manage to grab her in time.

'Are you okay?' I gasp.

She nods, wheezing. We're both out of breath. I hold on to her firmly.

'Are you sure you're okay, Pixie?'

'Yes, but I need some more wine.'

The first bottle is now empty. I open the second, and fill up our glasses. When I turn round, she is selecting another record.

'What are you putting on this time?'

'You'll see.'

It is a slow, smoochy number. I walk towards her. She comes to meet me, with her arms out. In a tight clinch, we move more or less in time with the music, our hips swaying together. Her head rests on my shoulder. I recall Russ telling me that she might need my shoulder to lean on. This isn't quite what he meant, I'm sure; but I refuse to feel guilty. I shut out any thought of him. I have a more immediate concern on my mind. The soft rubbing movement of Pixie's body against mine is having an embarrassing effect on a certain part of my anatomy. She must be aware of it. If she is going to push me away in disgust, it will be any second now. I silently count to ten. Then I whisper her name gruffly.

She lifts her face. Her eyes smile at me.

I kiss her. It is a little, testing kiss.

Her eyes are still smiling at me. Her lips remain slightly open.

I kiss her again, for a much longer time. Her tongue flirts with mine in her mouth. I crush her more tightly against me. But then she pulls back, freeing herself.

'The music has stopped, Sam.'

'It stopped ages ago,' I say breathlessly. 'Do you want me to turn the record over?'

'No, I don't think so. I think it's time to go to bed. Is there any wine left in my glass?'

I check for her. 'It's full.'

'Good. I might as well take it with me as a nightcap.'

After I hand her the glass, she leans up and strokes the back of her fingers down my cheek. 'You've been really kind and supportive today, Sam. Thanks.' She is already walking away, when she says, 'Can I leave you to turn off the record player and blow out the candles?'

The feeling of let down is so terrible, I'm struck dumb. I can only stare after her. The few seconds it takes her to reach the doorway seem to happen in slow motion. She is almost out of the room, before she looks back.

'I'll be warming the bed up,' she says. 'Don't be too long, will you?'

3

Morning. Waking up to warm woman flesh against mine. Warm woman. Woman. Pixie.

I raise my head and peer at her face. She is asleep. I'm glad. It means I can study her in secret, without her knowing. Her haystack of hair is all mussed up, sticking out in tufts over her ears. Round her eyes and mouth, faint little lines are visible; the ghosts of wrinkles yet to come. But it is difficult to imagine her old and wrinkled. Pixies don't age. And she does look like a pixie. If she were an actress, she could play an elf in pantomime, or Peter Pan, without any need for stage make-up.

Her mouth drops open, and she starts snoring. I press my forefinger against her lips. She wriggles the end of her nose, gives a little snort, rolls over on her side, almost on top of me, and continues snoring. She is too close now for my comfort. I want to kiss her. But I'm afraid to wake her. I'm afraid of how she will feel about me in the sober light of morning.

I decide to try and go back to sleep. I can't. I'm too lustful, while she is this close. Very carefully, I extricate my arm from under her neck, and shift myself away a little. She stirs and her eyes open.

'Hi,' I say.

She stares at me blankly. ' . . . What's . . . oh my God! My head!'

'Hangover?'

She groans, rubbing her temple. I brush her hand aside, and massage the spot for her. ' . . . Better?'

'That feels good . . . Mmmm . . .' She smiles. 'Haven't you got a hangover?'

'No . . . How's your head now? Still throbbing?'

'A bit. Don't stop. It's nice.' She snuggles in closer, and cuddles me. '. . . Hey, it feels like you're throbbing too. More than a bit.' She is amused.

I start kissing her. I start getting carried away by my own urgency.

Then: 'Ouch! Quick, move,' she says, pushing me off her.

'What's the matter?'

'My bladder. I need to pee. It's full.'

'Bloody hell!' I mutter. 'That's very romantic.'

She leaps out of bed. 'It'll be even more romantic if I burst before I get there.'

Now that she mentions it, I'm aware of my own bladder; I wasn't before. It's also full. I race after her down the passage. We wrestle and fight in the bathroom doorway, squealing like kids trying to reach the ice cream van first. She is more desperate than I am, and manages to slam the door in my face.

When I get back to the bed, she is lying with the sheet pulled right up under her chin. Her eyes are closed and her breathing is quiet and regular. I'm nearly fooled. Then one eyelid flickers, and I realize she is only pretending to be asleep. But she looks so demure; so self-contained. I am suddenly overcome by a feeling of nervous inadequacy, as if I'm about to sit an exam. My earlier urgency has left me. In its place is a terrible, vulnerable tenderness. I want to tell her I love her.

'Pixie?'

She opens her eyes. 'What?'

But I can't tell her. It's too soon. She won't believe me. I gaze at her dumbly. After a moment, she smiles.

'Did you know,' she says, 'that you've got irresistibly sexy ears? Come here, I want to nibble them,' and she lifts the sheet up for me to climb in.

*　　*　　*　　*

The phone rings. We are eating breakfast in bed. It is lunchtime.

'That'll be Russ,' says Pixie.

37

I almost choke on my mouthful of toast. 'Don't answer it,' I splutter.

'I must. I want to talk to him. Besides, he's probably worrying about me.'

She is already running across the room. I can't stop her. I retrieve her plate from the rumpled bedclothes and put it back on the tray.

The phone is in the hall. It is too far away to hear what's being said. But it bothers me that Pixie should want to talk to Russ, while she has another bloke in her bed. I know it's the sixties, and we're all supposed to believe in free love and uncommitted relationships. And maybe Pixie and Russ do. But I don't. I don't want to share Pixie with Russ, even if Russ doesn't mind sharing her. I toy with the possibility that I've misinterpreted their relationship; only I've seen all the signs of intimacy between them when they are together. It seems far more likely that I'm simply a diversion for Pixie in an hour of need.

I discard the remains of my toast, dump the tray on the floor, and light a cigarette. Pixie is still talking on the phone; I can hear the indistinct mumble of her voice. Leaning back against the headrest, I sit and blow angry smoke-rings at the ceiling.

Suddenly I'm aware of being watched from across the room. The young coloured boy in the painting is gazing at me sympathetically. I have an uncanny notion that if I get up and walk around, his eyes will follow me. It's unsettling. Irritably, I reorganize the pillows and sit sideways, so the painting is no longer in my immediate line of vision.

Pixie comes back bouncy and chirpy. She dives on to the bed, gives me a smacking kiss on the cheek, and starts wolfing down what's left of her breakfast, exclaiming that she is ravenous.

'Your toast has got cold,' I point out.

'I know. So has my coffee. If you were nice, you'd go and make me a fresh cup.'

'I'm not nice,' I say sullenly.

'No, you aren't nice. I told Russ you got me drunk last night, and seduced me.'

I stare at her, aghast.

'It's all right,' she says, tweaking my ear. 'I'm only teasing.'

'What did you tell him?'

'About us?' Her voice has sharpened.

'Yes.'

'Nothing.' She looks defensive. Colour tints her cheeks. Grimacing, she drinks her cold coffee. I glare at her. ' . . . Well, what did you expect me to tell him? Give him a blow by blow account of how we've been spending the morning?'

I feel too aggrieved to answer. I frown down at a small smear on the sheet. It might be butter from our toast; it might not be; but it seems to confirm I'm only a one night stand in her life. She is now pulling the bedclothes about with unnecessary energy.

'What are you doing?'

'Can I have my pillow?' She yanks it out from behind me. 'I'm tired. I'm going to have a snooze.'

She settles herself down, turning on to her side, with her back to me. I light another cigarette and glare morosely at the doe-eyed coloured boy. I find the portrait intrusive. I can't imagine why Pixie should have chosen to hang it directly opposite her bed.

'Did you do that painting?' I ask her.

'What?' she mumbles.

'The portrait of the coloured boy. On the wall. Did you do it?'

She nods her head slightly.

'When?'

She doesn't say anything.

'Who is the boy?'

'What?'

I breathe out irritably. 'The boy! Who is he? Someone you know?'

She mutters something that sounds like yes, and burrows her face more deeply into the pillow.

'When did you—'

'Please!' Curling her body up into a ball, she pulls the sheet over her head.

'What?' I ask.

'I'm trying to go to sleep,' she says in a muffled voice.

I lie back and stare at the ceiling. The afternoon sun has found the window and is filling the room with a sweaty radiance of heat. The air feels heavy and close, smelling stale from our cigarette smoke. Pixie is very quiet. I can't even hear her breathing. But then she makes a couple of funny little noises, like a prelude to snoring. I listen; it sounds as if she is struggling to catch her breath. I'm suddenly afraid she is short of oxygen under the sheet, and carefully lift it away from her face. Her eyelashes are wet.

'You're crying,' I say, shocked. 'Pixie, why? What's the matter?'

'Nothing,' she gulps.

'Is it me?'

She shakes her head. 'Can't I even cry in peace?' she says, and manages to smile.

She lets me hold her. I turn her round, so I can hug her properly. Her nose is dripping. I reach behind me for the box of tissues, and wipe it.

'Now blow,' I say, and she laughs. 'That's better.' I kiss her. 'Is it Ifu? Or something I said, or did?'

'No, it isn't your fault.'

I stroke her hair. 'What then? Tell me.'

'I don't want to talk.'

I kiss her gently all over her face. At first she doesn't respond. Then she does. I start to make love to her. I try to be very coaxing and slow. I try to contain my own need. But in the end, I can't hold myself back any longer. Afterwards, I feel she hasn't really been with me. She has retreated somewhere inaccessible inside herself.

Feeling dissatisfied, I watch her drift off to sleep. I don't understand her. I don't understand anything. I only know that the prospect of losing her is unbearably painful.

We are in the bath when Pixie informs me she has invited
Russ to supper. I am sitting behind her. She can't see
my expression. I stop scrubbing her back.

'Have you finished?' she asks.

I hand her the sponge. I feel *we're* finished. 'You
might have told me earlier,' I say.

'I forgot. But there's plenty of time yet. He isn't due
for an hour. Pass me the soap, will you?'

I fish around for it under the bubbly froth.

'Hey, you're tickling my bum,' she giggles.

'You're sitting on the soap.'

'So I am. I thought it was your toe. Here, I've got it.
I'll do your back now, if you can manage to turn round.'

'I can't,' I say brusquely. 'Just tell me what you expect
me to do this evening?'

'Do? Nothing. Nothing needs to be done. Russ is
bringing the supper with him. That's one of the reasons
he rang. Apparently Mercy, bless her, specially made me
a big pot of *bobotie* this morning because she knows
how much I like it. I hope you like it. Well, too bad if
you don't. That's what you're getting for supper.' She
lies back against me to soak.

'What the hell is *bobotie*? It sounds like baboon meat.'
I could believe anything of Mercy's cooking.

'You don't know what *bobotie* is?' She squints up at
me through her hair. 'My God, you are inexperienced.
It's a traditional Cape dish of curried mince with
almonds and—'

'What do you mean? Inexperienced?' I ask sharply.

'Aren't you?' She stares at me in a teasing manner,
like a cat eyeing a mouse it has caught. 'I should hope
you are, at your age.'

'My age?' I give an indignant snort. 'How old do you
think I am?'

'Eighteen.'

'I'm nineteen. Almost.'

She smirks.

'You think that's young. So how old are you then?'

41

'Twenty four.'

'Big deal!'

'Yes.' She chucks me under the chin. 'Which makes me the experienced, wicked, older woman.'

'You reckon?' I'm not amused. 'What's this all about, anyway? Are you trying to tell me I'm hopeless in bed? Is that it?'

'Hopeless? ... Hmmn ... No. No, I wouldn't say hopeless. You show promise. You do show a lot of promise.' And she stands up, and steps demurely out of the bath.

I lie back in the water, sulkily watching her towel herself. She looks round at me over her shoulder.

'I'm only teasing you, you know,' she says. 'Can't you take a little teasing?'

'No.'

Scooping up some water, I splash it at her. She dodges nimbly out of the way. I scoop up more water, but she escapes to the door.

'Come back here! Pixie!'

She sticks her tongue out at me. 'I'll leave you to mop up the mess,' she says. 'Don't play with your ducks too long. And don't forget to clean the bath. The Vim is on the shelf behind you.'

I dress up for dinner in my best pair of trousers and my brightest shirt. I suppose I'm being prompted by my male animal instinct to try and outshine my rival. I can't very well lock antlers with Russ, but I can at least attempt to make myself more strikingly noticeable to the female I'm battling to win from him. She notices. She says I look very nice; only this is before Russ arrives.

He turns up in a pair of old jeans and a faded check shirt. Nevertheless, he gets all her attention during dinner. She gives me no more than the odd glance and smile. And she keeps a more than respectable distance from me at all times. I understand. She doesn't want Russ to suspect anything. I understand, but I resent the implication. I don't much fancy the *bobotie* either. The flavouring is a bit too spicy and rich for my taste. I pick at my helping and fill myself up on the salad which Russ has also brought. He is the only one who seems totally relaxed. He talks to me. I respond more or less civilly, though I try to avoid meeting his direct gaze. It isn't easy. He is the sort of person who looks you straight and steadily in the eye when he is conversing with you.

We leave the dirty dishes on the table in the kitchen where we've eaten, and move into the living-room. Then Pixie suggests coffee, and disappears to make it. I sprawl on a floor cushion near the window. Russ reclines on the sofa.

'So!' he says. 'I hear the two of you had a skinful last night.'

I stiffen. 'Skinful?'

'Didn't you get tipsy? You were meant to. That was what the wine was for.'

'Oh. Yes, well . . .' I'm starting to feel very defensive. 'Thanks – for the wine, I mean.'

'Don't mention it.' He stretches out his long legs, and leans back comfortably, grinning at me. 'You know, you needn't be jealous of me, Sam.'

'Jealous?'

'I think you understand my meaning,' he says amicably. 'I'm trying to reassure you, that's all.'

'Why?' My face is reddening. 'What has Pixie told you?'

'About the two of you? Very little. But as Mercy would say, I have eyes.'

I decide to come clean. 'I feel a helluva lot for her,' I inform him challengingly.

He smiles. 'Good. I'm glad to hear it. I think Pixie feels quite a lot for you too.'

'Don't you mind?'

'Why should I? Pixie and I just have a very close friendship.'

'Friendship?' I want to believe him, only I'm not sure I understand his meaning of the word. 'That's not the way it comes across.'

43

'I know. People often assume we're a couple.'

'How come?'

'I suppose because we're openly affectionate with each other, so people—'

'No, I mean how come you are just friends? Are you involved with someone else?'

'I was, for a long time – until recently.'

'What happened?'

'He left me for another man.'

I gawp at him. 'Pardon?'

'You heard me correctly. I said he, not she. I was living with a man.'

'Oh . . .' I flounder. ' . . . You mean you're . . .?'

'Gay?' he says, smiling at me calmly. 'Yes. I'm gay.'

I feel as if an enormous weight has lifted off my chest. I also feel stupid. 'But you don't *look* gay,' I blurt out almost accusingly.

'Don't I?' He raises his eyebrows. 'How do you expect me to look?'

I shrug, shifting awkwardly, and busy myself lighting a cigarette. He watches me with an amused expression.

'Anyway, you can quit looking daggers at me over Pixie from now on, because there's no need. Okay?'

I nod. Then I manage to meet his gaze. 'And thanks – for the information.'

He sits up and slaps his knee. 'So, to change the subject, what do you intend doing with your B.A. degree once you've got it?'

'I'm thinking of going into journalism.'

'Here? In this country?'

'Probably. Why?'

'Do you believe in freedom of the press?'

'Naturally.'

'Then good luck to you, pal,' he says, and jumps up to take the tray from Pixie, who has just come in.

Russ stays fairly late. After he has gone, Pixie and I do the washing-up together. I'm feeling quite full of myself now I know that the woman standing near me at the sink, with her arms buried to the elbows in greasy

44

water, and her shaggy plumery of caramel hair hiding her face, doesn't belong to anyone else. She doesn't belong to me either. Not yet. But she will, because I love her, and because tonight I believe in the omnipotence of love.

'Hey!' – I prod her playfully – 'Why didn't you tell me Russ is gay?'

She gives me a sharp glance. 'Who told you he is?'

'He did, this evening.'

'So now you know. Pass me those glasses, will you?'

'Yes, I know *now*. Only I wish you had told me before.'

'Why? Do you fancy him?'

I flick her bottom with my drying-up cloth. 'Don't be ridiculous!'

'I'm not. He's very attractive. Do you fancy him?'

'Of course I bloody don't,' I say, rattled. 'I'm not gay.'

'In that case, why should I have told you? His private life isn't any of your concern.'

'Oh yes it is.' I open the cutlery drawer and drop in the knives I've just dried. 'It concerns me in that I thought you were involved with him.'

'I am involved with him,' she replies mildly. 'Caring about someone is an involvement. And Russ is a very close friend. In fact, he's probably my closest friend at the moment.'

I make a disgruntled noise in my throat. 'That's not what I mean, and you know it.' I pause because she has pulled out the plug, and the sudden gush and gurgle of draining water is deafening. I wait for the pipe to empty, then I say, 'I thought you were sleeping with him.'

'If I'm sleeping with him, why did I sleep with you last night?'

'That's what I was wondering.'

I grin at her. She eyes me quizzically as she dries her hands on the cloth I'm holding. 'I see,' she says. 'One swallow doesn't make a summer though, you know.'

'Meaning?'

'You don't really know me yet. And I don't really know you. Let's take this one day at a time. Right?'

I shrug. 'Okay.'

We walk down the passage together. I'm a lot less sure of myself now. I'm not even able to feel certain I'm welcome in her bed tonight. She stops at my bedroom door. My heart sinks.

She says, 'Do you mind if I use the bathroom first?'

'No. Go ahead.'

I wait where I am, for her to come out. She has changed into a nightie. My heart sinks again. She didn't wear one last night. Her expression doesn't seem very encouraging either. She looks at me. I look at her.

'Uh . . .' I scratch my nose. 'Uh . . . I'm wondering if there's room for me in your bed tonight?'

I hadn't intended to be comical, but she laughs.

'I could make room,' she says, 'providing you don't expect anything more than a goodnight kiss. It's late, and I'm tired. I really don't think I'm up to feeling frisky.'

'Me neither,' I assure her. I'm lying. Just gazing at her now has given me a very frisky feeling.

When I come to bed, I find her sitting up, gazing hypnotically at the portrait of the coloured boy. She must be lost in thought, because I seem to startle her. She jumps, and looks round with big eyes.

'Sorry,' I chuckle. 'Did I give you a fright?'

The room is only dimly lit. The bedside lamp behind her, casts her face in shadow as she continues to stare at me without saying anything. The whites of her eyes are huge. A cold tingle runs up my spine. She doesn't seem to be seeing me. I feel as if she is looking right through me at something – a ghost or presence behind me. I glance nervously over my shoulder. Then she switches the lamp off, and the room is plunged into blackness. I fumble my way into bed.

'What is it? Pixie? What did you see?'

'Nothing.' There is a catch in her voice. Her lips

brush my cheek. 'Goodnight,' and she turns over on her side, with her back to me.

I lie very still, listening for sounds in the room. The whole flat is unnervingly quiet. I can't even hear Pixie breathing; but after some time has passed, I conclude she is asleep.

Then: 'Sam?' she whispers. 'Are you awake?'

'Yes,' I mumble.

'Can't you sleep?'

'No.'

'Me neither.'

She rolls over towards me. I hold out my arms, and she snuggles in close, like a small kitten wanting to be stroked.

'That's better,' she murmurs. 'Much better.'

I stroke her hair. Then I start caressing her. She doesn't respond. This time she is asleep.

'Damn!' I mutter. But I don't really mind. It's good just to be holding her like this. It makes me feel she is mine, even if she says one swallow doesn't make a summer. With her scent in my nostrils, I finally drift off myself.

4

Wednesday. A magical day. A bewitching day. The sky is serene lake-blue, with only a few blobs of clouds lapping harmlessly at the horizon. Beneath our hired rowing boat, the lake is reflective sky-blue, with a fractured sun starring the ripples of our wake. We are drifting weightless, above and below a reversible sky.

Between the sky-lake above and lake-sky below, is the world. And the world, for me, is Pixie, sitting in the stern of the boat, wearing a floppy floral sunhat, T-shirt, and shorts; dabbling her fingers in the water, and smiling like a schoolgirl playing truant. She is supposed to be working on Mrs Thornton's portrait. I am supposed to be doing some preparatory reading for my university course. Instead, we are spending the morning at Zoo Lake. I know what we are doing there. We are on honeymoon. I haven't told Pixie that. It is a preposterous notion. We only met four days ago. And she hasn't even said yet that she loves me. But it is, nevertheless, a glorious day for a honeymoon.

I row to the island in the middle of the lake and steer in under the trailing branches of a weeping willow. The green tresses of leaves enclose us in a secluded dusky cove.

'Playing Robinson Crusoe, are we?' says Pixie laconically.

'Don't you like it? It's a little private hideaway.'

'From what?'

'The ducks.'

'For what?'

'What do you mean, for what?' I was going to kiss her, but I don't now. She is right. It's too obvious a ploy. And it isn't really romantic. Under this tree, probably countless frustrated couples, with nowhere else to be alone, have come and pawed each other desperately.

We row on round the island. Then Pixie takes a turn at the oars. She is more proficient at it than I am.

'You've obviously had a lot of practice,' I say.

She smiles. 'A fair amount.'

'Here?'

'Sometimes.'

'Then you know that willow tree well?'

'Quite well.'

'Of course, I was forgetting,' I say a bit sourly, 'you're the experienced, wicked older woman.'

She smacks the oar down into the water, splashing me. In contact with my skin, the lake water is not a clean mirror image of the cerulean sky. It is slimy, and smells of decaying algae and duck shit. I'm drenched.

48

'You look like a frog,' says Pixie, laughing.

'Thanks a lot!'

She kisses me. 'You smell like a frog. We'd better take the boat back, and get you cleaned up. Then I'll stand you to lunch in the restaurant.'

I borrow Pixie's comb, and have a wash in the gents. As it is a weekday, the restaurant isn't very busy. We sit at a table outside in the sun, so that my clothes can dry off. We look slightly scruffy, I suppose, and out of place among the smartly attired, middle-aged housewives from Rosebank, and Saxonwold, and other surrounding suburbs, who are gossiping over their pots of tea. The two at the nearest table eye us disdainfully.

Pixie grins at them. 'Isn't it a lovely day to be unemployed?'

They glare through her haughtily, as if she doesn't exist. The African waiter arrives to take our order. Pixie jokes with him, drawing more glares from the next table.

The menu offers a fairly wide selection. I choose just a salad. In Pixie's company, I can't think about food. All my senses are tuned into her, feeding off her presence, and I forget about the need to eat.

'Is that all you're going to have?' Pixie asks me.

'Yes. I'm not very hungry.'

'I am.'

She casts a glance at our neighbours. In tightly-corseted tones, they are now complaining about 'the dirty hippie cult' and the effect it is having on the moral standards of society.

'Mind you,' Pixie says, raising her voice, 'salad should be good for your gonads. I mean, look what it does to rabbits.'

I nudge her foot under the table. 'You're wicked!'

'*I'm* wicked? *You're* the one who pulled my knickers off in the boat.'

The women glower at her, call for their bill, and leave. Pixie grins, gloating like a mischievous elf.

'How did you acquire your name?' I ask her. 'I presume you weren't christened Pixie.'

'No.'

I wait for her to explain. She doesn't. 'So what's your proper name then?'

'Priscilla.' A guard has come down over her face instantly, like a camera shutter closing. 'But don't call me that. I don't like it. It isn't me.'

'I agree. Pixie suits you better. But you still haven't told me how you got the nickname.'

'Does it matter?'

'No,' I say touchily. 'Not if you don't want—'

'Someone special who was very important to me thought I looked like a Pixie, that's all.'

'Oh.' I feel a stab of jealousy. Toying with my glass so I don't have to look at her, I ask, 'How long ago was that?'

'A long time ago.'

I glance up to check her expression. Her face is impervious. 'So you were only little. Yes?'

'Yes,' she says.

'Was it . . .' I hesitate. ' . . . Russ mentioned that you grew up on a farm in Nat—'

'When did he tell you that?' she asks sharply.

'He only mentioned it. The other afternoon after Ifu . . .' I break off, as she flinches. Quickly, I say, 'I've been wanting to ask you – what was the farm like?'

'Like a farm.' She glances past me, then all around, as if searching for a diversion.

Russ was right. She clearly doesn't want to talk about it. Out of consideration for her feelings, I know I should change the subject, but I'm still feeling jealous.

I play with my glass again. 'Well . . . whoever the someone special was, he was right about calling you a pixie. He, or she,' I add hopefully.

'He.'

I'm aware of her fiddling with her napkin. We're both avoiding looking at each other. She must know I'm waiting for her to elaborate.

Finally, she says, as if she's admitting it reluctantly, 'Actually, sometimes you remind me of him.'

'Who was he?' My voice is tight. 'A boyfriend?'

She makes a non-committal gesture.

'I'm more handsome though, aren't I?'

It is meant to sound like a joke, but it doesn't. It falls flat anyway. She is gazing at me now, unsmiling.

'I was only kidding,' I tell her.

'I know.' Her face relaxes suddenly. She sort of grins. 'I'm trying to decide if you are handsome.'

'Yes? . . .' I leer. ' . . . No?'

'You have nice front teeth,' she says. 'Oh good, here comes our food. I'm famished.'

We talk very little during the meal. Pixie concentrates on eating. I concentrate on her. I find it fascinating the way she uses her knife and fork, and butters her roll, and chews and swallows her food. Every movement she makes, tantalizes and absorbs me. I could sit watching her like this for hours; except that I keep wanting to touch her.

I contain myself until after the waiter has cleared away our plates, and brought our coffee. Then I stretch over the table, and take her hand.

'What would you like to do this afternoon?'

'Depends on the choices.'

'Well . . . we *could* go to the zoo.'

'No. I hate zoos. They're animal prisons.'

'We *could* go for a drive.'

'We could. Yes.'

'Or we could go home.'

'And do some work?'

'Yes, and do some work. Or . . .'

Her eyes tease mine. 'Or what?'

'Just or,' I say, caressing her fingers.

She smiles. 'I like the feel of or.' Her mouth puckers into the shape of a kiss. 'Orrr,' she sighs, making it sound the most erotic word in the English language.

'That's settled then. Let's be off,' and I scrape my chair back.

'Yes . . . Oh no, do you see what I see?'

I follow the direction of her gaze. She's ogling a plate on the table behind me.

'Chocolate gateau,' she says, licking her lips. 'I didn't notice that on the menu. I absolutely love chocolate gateau. I must have some.'

I slump back in my seat, shaking my head. Woman! She is Eve. She is a temptress. She is a puzzle. She is Pixie. She is beautiful. She is my love. She is a mystery. She is a stomach.

I watch her devour her cake with relish. Then we pay the bill, and go home to or.

*　*　*　*

Thursday. It is a scorcher. The sky today is an inverted, vitreous blue bowl, balanced on the rim of the earth, glassily reflecting the sun's radiance. The pavements in Hillbrow sizzle underfoot like hot plates. The trapped air is pungent with exhaust fumes, and sweaty odour from the crush of pedestrians. We've run out of almost everything in the flat, so we have to buy a load of groceries this morning. But we try to get through our shopping list as fast as possible.

Back in the flat, the temperature is warming up like an oven. Our faces are glistening wet, our clothes sticking to our skins.

'We can't work in this heat,' I tell Pixie.

'But I've got to do Mrs Thornton's portrait, and you have university preparat—'

'To hell with Mrs Thornton. To hell with university.'

'But I need the money,' she protests.

'To hell with money.'

'Right,' she agrees unexpectedly. 'To hell with it all.' Her eyes light up like blue flares. 'I know what I'd love to do.'

'What?'

'Drive into the country and have a picnic.'

I grin smugly. I feel omnipotent; even the weather is abetting my secret intention to turn this whole week into an unofficial honeymoon.

We throw some food and cold drinks into a rucksack,

hop in the Mini, and head out of town, making for the Magaliesberg Mountains. Only after we have turned off the highway and left the traffic behind, do we breathe more easily, sniffing the succulent mountain air through the eddies of dust the Mini's wheels kick up from the dirt road. We don't really know where we will end up. Pixie has never been to the Magaliesberg before, and I have only come here once with my father, when I was too young to remember much about it.

On impulse, we follow a track snaking up a steep, rock-littered slope. The track peters out at the bottom of a higher ridge. We abandon the Mini, and scramble up a tortuous path.

And there it is, suddenly, in front of us: a hidden kloof, carved out of the flank of the mountain, with clear spring water trickling down a buttress of rock into a deep shady pool. Pixie stands beside me, moon-eyed, drinking it all in. I decide the spot has been created specially for us. Today I believe in a benevolent God.

I clamber down to the pool, sliding some of the way on my bottom. When I look back, Pixie is standing where I left her; a small dark silhouette against the blaze of sky. I call, but she doesn't answer; so I don't wait for her. I strip naked, and dive in. The water is freezing cold; it is like plunging out of a sauna into snow. The shock takes my breath away. I thrash about numbly, gasping. At some point, I look up. Pixie is now sitting on the ledge of rock just above the pool. She has taken off her clothes, and is staring down. I splash water up at her.

'Come on! Jump!'

The mountain echoes my voice. I laugh. Pixie shakes her head, and the mountain laughs hollowly. It is suddenly eerie. Something is wrong. I haul myself out of the pool, shivering.

Pixie makes no movement as I approach. Her eyes stare at me as if I'm a ghost.

'I'm going to throw you in,' I threaten half-heartedly.

When she doesn't respond, I pull up. Her unsmiling

gaze travels over my nakedness. I wasn't self-conscious before; I am now. Hugging myself, I crouch down beside her.

'We forgot to bring a towel,' I mutter.

She stretches out and touches my face, still without saying anything. I'm dumbfounded to realize the shine in her eyes are tears. But I don't even try to speak because her fingers are pressed over my lips, exploring their outline, and because something in her expression stops me. She seems totally absorbed in her sense of touch, like a blind person. I crouch, almost spellbound, while her hands move slowly down over my body. Then she stretches out her arms to me.

She takes me into her, and holds me there in stillness. It is a new experience for me. I feel no urgency, no striving. I feel no awareness of self apart from that of man, joined with woman, as we begin to move together unhurriedly on a gradual undulating wave of sensation that becomes all encompassing. It is endless, until she cries out, and the wave breaks in my chest. I flow out of myself into her, and she cries again; or perhaps it is an echo from the kloof.

We lie fused, in quietude. Then I become aware of the hardness of the rock under my elbows, and shift slightly.

'Don't!' Her arms tighten round me. 'Sshh!' and she presses my face back down, cradling it between her breasts.

I listen to her heartbeat. The only other sounds are the trickling of water, and the faint, shrill, violin bowing notes of distant crickets.

A sudden loud rustling in the thick undergrowth nearby makes us both start. We glance round in time to catch a glimpse of brownish fur bounding back out of sight.

'A hare?' I ask.

'A duiker.' She stares intently at the spot where the animal disappeared. 'A young duiker.'

'Surely not?'

'A duiker,' she insists, and for some reason it makes her smile. Relaxing, she closes her eyes again. The smile lingers at the corners of her lips as she dozes off.

She mumbles briefly when I ease myself out of her, though she doesn't wake. A light breeze has sprung up, fanning some of the heat out of the air. But the sun is still fierce. I move the rucksack so that its shadow falls over her face, cover as much of her as I can with her bits of clothing, dress myself, and go for a walk.

On my return, she is sitting waiting for me, with our picnic spread out on the rock. Ominous, crenellated black clouds have appeared over the crown of the mountain. We eye them anxiously as we eat. Within minutes they curtain the sun, and rumble threateningly overhead. The background serenade of cricket song suddenly stops. We heed the warning, grab up our belongings, and make a run for it, back to the car.

We get there just in time. A heavy barrage of rain blots out the landscape. We sit huddled in the front of the Mini, listening to the drumming on the metal roof. The path to the kloof has become invisible – as if it never existed. Pixie is shivering in her sleeveless cotton blouse and shorts; neither of us thought to bring jerseys with us. I put my arms round her. She smells of brushwood, and moss, and salty dried sweat. She smells of healthy appetizing woman. I press her against me. It is quite dark inside the car, and dark outside – a false twilight in the storm.

'What happened back there?' I ask in a reverent tone.

She looks up at me out of glow-worm-light eyes. The rest of her features are shadowy and indistinct, like an under-exposed photograph. 'To us, you mean?'

'Yes.'

'We made love,' she says, almost inaudibly.

I grin. 'Really?'

'Yes, *really*.' She turns, breaking free of my hold, and stares at the water streaming down the windscreen. 'It was special. But let's not talk about it. Okay?'

I fiddle with the key in the ignition. The drumming

over our heads is easing. I switch on, and the engine clears its throat, coughs, and comes to life. I rev it a few times. Then I switch off. Pixie is wiping at the condensation on her side window.

'I'm in love with you,' I say to the back of her head. Her hand stills. 'I know.'

I can't see her face, though it seems that is all she is going to say. I restart the engine, and flick on the head-lamps. She looks round.

'I'm in love with you too,' she admits.

It is a portentous moment. I feel like leaping out and dancing in the rain. But in the faint illumination from the dashboard, her expression is spectral and solemn. We gaze at each other.

'Well, what are we going to do about it?' I ask finally.

'Do?' She gives me a Mona Lisa smile. 'Return home. Have a hot bath. Eat some supper. Get into bed. Sleep. Wake up in the morning. Go on living.'

'Ask a silly question . . .'

'Yes.'

The downpour has stopped as suddenly as it started. I set the car in motion and steer cautiously through a steamy mist back to the main road.

* * * *

Friday. We wake to the sound of soft fingertips of rain strumming on the window panes.

It rains all day. Love dictates. We stay in bed all day, oblivious to the life outside: Mrs Thornton waiting for her portrait; the university waiting to receive me as a student on Monday; people waiting to cross our paths. None of them exist. The outside world doesn't exist today.

Only the two of us exist: me – Sam-Man, and she – Pixie-Woman. I understand now, the story of Adam and Eve, as a love story. But the Bible got it a bit wrong. It forgot to mention that Eden is a flat on the third floor in Hillbrow, and the Garden is in the bathroom and the hallway.

We play together in Eden all day, have a bath together

in the evening, make supper together, and eat it together in bed. Then the serpent pops up. It's all my fault. The Bible got it wrong again. In our story, it is me, not she, who is tempted by the serpent to taste of the sour fruit of knowledge. I start to feel niggled by the ever-watchful presence of the small coloured boy on the wall opposite. Tonight, for some reason – perhaps the reflection of light from the lamp, his smile seems more pronounced, as if he's feeling happy for me. I draw up my legs and twist round to face Pixie.

'Mind the tray!' She makes a grab for our wine glasses. 'What are you doing?'

'He's putting me off my food,' I grouse humorously. 'Who?'

'Him.' I gesture with my head. 'Over there.'

She looks at the painting. Narrowing her eyes, she studies it. I study her profile, wishing *I* could draw *her*.

'I would much rather have a picture of you up there, wearing only shorts,' I tell her.

'Well, I wouldn't,' she says.

'He seems to be grinning at me,' I complain. '. . . Hey, can I have my wine back?' I put out my hand, and wait, then take the glass from her without her appearing to notice.

'Perhaps he is.' She leans back to drink, smiling as though at some private meaning.

'Who is he?'

'Bokkie.' As she says it, her face looks soft and glowing.

I have a sudden hollow feeling in the pit of my stomach. 'Bokkie? Bokkie who?'

'Just Bokkie,' and she holds out her glass for me to refill. I top up mine as well.

'Where do you know him from?'

'*Knew* him.' A little frown furrows her forehead, turning her smile into a grimace. She swallows some wine. 'He's dead.'

She pulls a cigarette out of the packet lying between

us. Lighting it for her, I look into her eyes, and see pain in them.

'How did he die?' My voice sounds as hollow as I feel.

'He shouldn't have! He was special! But he died!' It all comes out in a rush. She is curled up now, hugging her knees.

'Special?' I remember our conversation over lunch at Zoo Lake two days ago. 'So *he* was the one who gave you the name Pixie?'

'Yes,' she says in a constricted whisper.

I stare at her. Her eyes appeal to me mutely over the top of her knees. It's obvious that she really doesn't want to talk about it any longer. She looks close to tears. I pick up her plate and hold it out.

'Better eat,' I say gruffly. 'Dinner's getting cold.'

She only picks at her food. So do I. We both seem to have lost our appetites. I take myself off to the bathroom.

Standing at the basin, I inspect my face in the mirror. In view of what Pixie said at Zoo Lake, I'm supposed to remind her of Bokkie. I can't see any resemblance, myself. I don't want to see any resemblance. It's true that my eyes are chocolate brown. And my hair is also dark and quite curly – but it's not that curly. And my skin isn't dusky; it is very white when I'm not suntanned. *I* certainly don't *look* coloured.

Special, she called him. What could be so special about a small coloured boy? I'd rather not think about it. I wet my palms and try to slick my curls down. Then I make two cups of coffee and carry them back to the bedroom.

Pixie is sitting cross-legged on the carpet under the window, sketching. All I can see of her are her elbows, and knees, and her ruffled mop of amber hair. She looks up; and it is like the first time we met. An electric charge rips through my solar plexus. Everything blurs in the background, and I can't hold the cups steady as I cross the room. I put them down next to her, while I try to catch my breath.

She discards the sketch pad to drink her coffee. I sneak a sideways look at it. The page is covered with drawings of a small antelope: standing, peering through foliage, lying down, bounding over scrub. She catches me looking, and closes the pad.

'Don't! Let me see,' I plead.

She shakes her head. 'It's no use. I can't really draw any more.'

'Rubbish! Those sketches are beautiful. Let me have—'

'Oh, I can draw a duiker,' she says. 'That's easy. I've drawn so many; it's almost like automatic writing now. But I don't seem able to do anything original these days.'

'You do portraits.'

She laughs cynically. 'Yes, I can do pretty portraits of rich pampered women, who expect me to make them look twenty and beautiful, when they are forty and fat. But that isn't what I want to paint.'

I crouch down in front of her. 'What do you want to paint?'

She gazes at me with the soft liquid eyes of the duiker she has been sketching. Gently, she touches the side of my face.

'You're so sweet, Sammie,' she says. 'Why is your hair damp?'

'What do you want to paint?'

She shrugs. 'Pictures that are exciting and new and—'

'Well, why can't you?'

'I don't know. I seem to have lacked the necessary inspiration for a long time.'

I grasp her shoulders. 'Then I will have to inspire you.' I'm in deadly earnest, but she laughs. I shake her. 'I mean it!'

'Yes.' She smiles. 'Perhaps you will inspire me.'

'I love you,' I say fiercely.

She puts her arms round my middle and squeezes me. 'Me too,' she sighs.

We clutch each other tightly, rocking back and forth from our waists. We must look ridiculous, but who cares. Behind Pixie's head, the shower of raindrops striking the window resemble confetti. In my chest, the pressure of happiness is almost unbearable. We are Adam and Eve secure again in our Eden. All is well. The serpent has slithered back into the shadows.

*　*　*　*

Saturday. The rain has cleared. After breakfast, we return to the world outside. It is a world washed free of drabness and dust and debris and stale odours. A world sparkling with dewdrops, glistening and steaming with sunshine. A world smelling of wet cement and soggy bark and pungent petals.

My Pixie-woman is like a little girl this morning. She takes my hand and skips through puddles on the pavement, laughing. As we cross the road she stops, holding up the traffic, to peer in delight at a rainbow mandala of spilt petrol on the wet tarmac. She smiles at all and sundry. Everyone smiles back at her.

We walk to The Wilds park. Pixie kicks off her sandals, and dabbles her feet in a pond, squinting up at the lurex threads of waterfalls seaming the craggy contours of the ridge above. Then she dances away from the path, leaving a silvery snail-trail of toeprints behind her in the damp grass.

On the way home, she stops and jokes with a young African male servant, who is clipping the front hedge of one of the smart properties in Houghton. I disapprove of her familiar manner towards him. She weaves a crown from the leaf clippings and places it on his head. When she tries to do the same to me, I push her hand away, and start to walk on, leaving her to catch up.

The incident casts a shadow on the gaiety of our morning. Neither of us refer to it, but it has left a tangible tension between us. We don't touch each other or speak, except in monosyllables, the rest of the way back to the flat.

We're barely through the front door, when Pixie announces it is time we cleaned the flat, and thrusts a broom at me. I'm flabbergasted, refusing to believe she has to do her own housework. I've seen the other flats being serviced. She informs me coldly that she has a private agreement with the black cleaner responsible for the top floor of the building. Apparently, he is trying to take his Matric by correspondence course, so she has told him she will clean her flat herself to give him extra time for his studies.

I've never done housework in my life, and I don't intend to start now – especially as it isn't necessary. 'You're crazy!' I explode. 'You're paying for your flat to be serviced in your rent. It's insane to pay for it, and then do it yourself.' I thrust the broom back at her.

Her face flushes with suppressed fury. 'If that's how you feel about it,' she says heatedly, 'I'll manage on my own. But you can bloody well clean your own bedroom. I'm not going to do that, as well as everything else,' and she shoves me aside to reach into the hall cupboard for some dusters.

I stamp off to my bedroom and slam the door behind me. The room feels alien and airless. Since the night of my arrival, I haven't been in here, except to change my clothes. Throwing open the window, I lean out and take some deep breaths. The view is depressing: a narrow concrete courtyard, flanked by grimy brick walls and the curtained windows of other flats. For the first time, I feel homesick for my old bedroom in Saxonwold with its view of my mother's carefully cultivated rose garden, and the bird bath and bird table, where the sparrows and starlings used to splash themselves and fight over their breakfast offerings.

Tomorrow is my birthday. I haven't told Pixie yet; I didn't want to make a big thing of it in advance. I was hoping, though, that we would celebrate it together in some way. Now that prospect isn't looking too likely. I only hope my mother will remember. She hasn't rung me since I moved out; but then, I haven't rung her either.

Casting my eye round the room, I notice dust on all the furniture. Resentfully, I wipe all the visible surfaces with a wad of tissues – I don't bother with the floor; it looks clean enough. Then I sprawl on my bed, and listen to Pixie clattering objects and singing loudly in the bathroom. She moves into the passage. It sounds as if she is down on her knees, polishing the parquet. I start to feel guilty and go out, and offer somewhat ungraciously to help.

'Do you mean it?' she says, frowning at me from under her hair. Her expression is hostile, but the effect is spoilt by a blob of polish on the end of her nose. She looks like a querulous clown. I think she looks beautiful.

'Yes,' I say more contritely. 'Have you another tin of polish?'

'No. But you can go and clean the living-room,' she says, and waits for me to shift so she can wipe the bit of floor I'm standing on.

I sweep diligently. Then I dust everything I can reach. I'm brushing crumbs off the sofa, when I become aware of Pixie standing in the doorway watching me.

'What are you doing?' she asks wooden-faced.

'I've swept the floor. Now I'm dusting . . . Why, what do you think I'm doing?'

'You should dust first, then sweep, to save yourself the bother of having to sweep up again.'

I take her point as I survey the litter of crumbs at my feet. 'Damn!' I mutter.

Her smile is only brief, but it looks friendly, like a flag of truce. 'You've obviously never done any house-work in your eighteen years of existence,' she says.

'Nineteen. I'm nineteen tomorrow.'

'Tomorrow? Your birthday is tomorrow?' I'm aware of her eyes boring into my back as I carefully rearrange the cushions. 'Why didn't you tell me?' She sounds cross again.

'It's no big deal.'

When I turn round, she has gone.

A few minutes later, the phone rings. I let Pixie answer it. 'It's for you,' she shouts.

It's my mother. She asks me how I am, tells me she and Nick have been very worried about me because I haven't been in contact; then, in the next breath, tells me she has been rushed off her feet all week, rehearsing for her new play. Finally, she says she must see me tomorrow as it's my birthday, and invites me to have lunch with her and Nick and the American impresario they are picking up at the airport in the morning.

'No thanks,' I say bluntly. 'I'll pass on lunch. Impresarios are a pain in the belly button.'

She giggles. 'I won't tell Nick that. What about supper then? Oh... hang on a minute, honbee.' There is a mumble in the background. Nick is obviously hovering as usual.... 'Honbee? I'm so sorry, Nick has just reminded me that we've been invited to a *braai** at Richard's house in the evening.'

'Richard who?' I ask.

'Richard Broom, you know, the director. We have to go. But you could come with us, if you like. I'm sure Rich—'

'No thanks,' I cut her off. 'Actually, I've got plans for the evening.'

'Oh... You're going out, are you?'

'Yes.'

'Somewhere nice?'

'Yes,' I say.

She waits for me to be more forthcoming. I stay silent.

'... Oh... well, I'm glad, honbee,' she says in her brightest voice. 'In that case, perhaps Nick and I could pop in on our way to the airport in the morning, and give you your presents.'

'Fine. If you can manage it,' I say in my brightest voice.

* braai – barbecue

63

'We can't stay long, but we must see you on your birthday ... You sure you're all right, honbee? You are happy there?'

'Very,' I tell her.

'Good. I must dash. Nick's pulling a face at me, and pointing at his watch. We have to gobble some lunch and get back to rehearsal.'

'Have fun!'

'Miss you,' and she makes kissing noises down the line.

'Me too,' I say, but she has already replaced the receiver.

Pixie is working in the kitchen, with the radio on loudly. The door is closed. I take that to mean she wants to be alone, and meander down the passage into her bedroom in search of a cigarette.

The sun is beaming through the window like a spotlight, illuminating the room as if it is a stage-set. It looks like a stage-set to me suddenly. A stage-set in a romantic farce, with the bed unmade and littered with clothes and sections of half-read newspaper. A pair of Pixie's knickers are hanging on the doorknob, as though they've been placed there intentionally by a stage hand to raise a laugh from the audience. I remember lines from a school production of *As You Like It*:

All the world's a stage, And all the men and women merely players: ... And then the lover, sighing like furnace, with a woeful ballad Made to his mistress' eyebrow.

That's me – the woeful lover. What a joke! Flopping down on the bed, I stretch out on my back. Perhaps old Will Shakespeare was right. Perhaps all of life is just a joke; a stage production created by a bored god to entertain himself in eternity. We play a part and then we snuff it like my father, like Jock, like that little guy, Bokkie, on the wall there. He's looking awfully solemn in the sunlight, as if he's sorry his role in the production didn't last very long. It bugs me that I still don't know

64

how he died, or why, or what part he played in Pixie's life.

He bugs me. I close my eyes so I don't have to look at him.

The next thing I know, Pixie is shaking me: I must have dozed off. She is crouched over me, holding a plate on which is a chocolate cake, decorated with icing and a single candle.

'Happy Birthday!' she says, plonking the plate down on my middle.

I squint past her, trying to orientate myself. The room is golden with the rays of sunset. Pixie's fair hair looks as if it is alight. 'But it's not my birthday yet,' I say confused. 'It's still Saturday.'

'I know,' she grins. 'Only I want you to admire the cake now, while it is at its best. It's the first cake I've ever baked and it's a bit wobbly. I think it might collapse in on itself any minute.'

The smell of warm chocolate and icing under my nose makes me realize how empty I am. I haven't had any lunch today, and I'm suddenly starving.

'It's a beautiful cake. Can we eat it now?'

'That's the idea.' She produces a knife.

'Aren't you going to light the candle first, and let me blow it out?'

'I can't light it. It's the only candle I could find, and it hasn't got a wick.'

Very carefully, she inserts the knife. Immediately, gooey mixture squelches out of the sides of the cake, and the icing subsides in the middle. She looks dismayed. I find her expression very funny. I kiss her. Then I dig my finger into the mixture and taste it. She follows suit. We agree that it tastes all right. We agree that we like half-raw cakes. She fetches two spoons and we gorge ourselves. Then she puts on a tape of jazz music and we lie back, bloated, and sticky, and giggly; like small kids who have overeaten at a children's party.

Pixie asks me about my phone call. In relating the gist of the conversation between my mother and myself,

65

I allow my hurt to show. But if I'm bidding for sympathy, I don't get it.

'You're lucky she isn't the clinging type,' is Pixie's only comment.

'Why? Did your mother cling to you?' I ask her.

'No.' She blows a smoke ring. 'The problem with my mother was that she was too submissive. She never really stood up for herself – or for anyone else – against my father. It was a bit pathetic. I don't know how she could be like that. I would never let any man take control of my life and treat me as if I'm no more than his possession.' She is looking at me; I feel she is warning me.

'I don't think I like the sound of your father,' I say.

She pulls her mouth in tightly. Disparagingly, she says, 'Old Gerrit the *regtig boer*.* A dyed-in-the-wool Calvinist platteland Afrikaans farmer. A God-fearing man. Only his god is racist and cruel and revengeful and irrational.'

'Your father is Afrikaans?' I'm suprised, even though I know Pixie's surname is de Jager. 'What about your mother? Was she Afrikaans too?'

'No. English.' She stubs out her cigarette, and immediately lights another. 'My mother was a pampered banana girl, brought up on a sugar plantation in Natal. Her family disapproved of her marrying an Afrikaner. They felt he was beneath them. They were prejudiced too – no better than him. But they provided their daughter with a farm when she got married, as Gerrit had no money.'

'A sugar farm?'

She smiles without humour. 'It was supposed to be. Only Gerrit refused to plant sugar. It was his way, I suppose, of getting back at his English in-laws. He would have made money out of sugar. It was the right sort of terrain for it. Instead, he insisted on sticking to the traditional farming methods he had been brought up with in the Free State, and planted mealies and ran

* regtig boer – true farmer

66

a few cattle and some sheep and pigs, and made very little profit, especially after he started hitting the bottle.' She shakes her head suddenly. 'Crikey! Why am I getting into all this? What started it?'

'Don't stop,' I say hurriedly. 'It's fascinating.'

She looks at me uncertainly, as if she's trying to make up her mind about something. Shaking her head again, she says fondly, 'You should be a priest, Sam.'

'Why?'

'You'd make a good father confessor.'

I snort. 'No, I wouldn't.'

'Yes, you would. You have very deep soulful eyes,' she says teasingly. 'And such long sexy lashes.'

'Cut it out,' I growl, embarrassed. 'Don't change the subject. You haven't finished telling me about your family.'

'There's nothing more to tell.'

'There is. You haven't mentioned any brothers or sisters.'

'There aren't any to mention,' she says.

'How come? Didn't your parents want more kids?'

'Gerrit did. He longed for a son. But my mother had a weak constitution. She was quite ill when I was born. After that she couldn't conceive.'

She gives a little shiver and rubs her arms. They are covered in gooseflesh.

'I'm cold,' she says, and gets up to close the window.

I'm dying to ask her about Bokkie now; but I sense it isn't the right moment. She is standing with her back to me, hugging herself, and staring out at the view. The last rays of sunset have faded from the room. In the insipid half-dark of dusk, her slim hunched figure seems smaller and frailer. I see her as a little girl, gazing out of a farmhouse window at the encroaching night. A lonely, unhappy little girl, living with parents who don't sound very warm and loving to me. I feel I want to protect her fiercely from whatever pain she went through as a child.

'Pixie?' My voice is husky. 'Come back to bed.'

She starts, as if she has been miles away, lost in a daydream. Looking round, she says, almost apologetically, 'I think I'd like a hot bath.'

I go and run the water, and climb in, and lie back to soak, while I wait for her to join me.

* * * *

In the middle of the night, I am jolted awake by the noise of Pixie talking in her sleep. Her speech is slurred, but it sounds like she's crying: 'Don't hurt him! Don't hurt him!'

I touch her shoulder gently. 'What are you saying?'

'Run!' She shudders. 'Please! Run!'

Her body starts jerking and twitching, like a dying animal. I stroke her face.

'Pixie, wake up. You're having a nightmare.'

Her eyelids flutter open. But her gaze is blank. 'All right,' she mumbles. 'You'll be all right. Meet me there.'

'Where?'

She gasps, and stares up at me, startled. 'What is it?'

'Don't panic. You were having a nightmare, that's all.'

'Was I? Did I wake you up? I'm sorry.'

'It doesn't matter.' I hug her. She presses herself close to me, and tucks her face under my chin. 'What were you dreaming about?' I ask.

'Don't remember,' she mumbles drowsily. 'Sshh, let's go back to sleep now.'

* * * *

Sunday. Day of sun. My birthday. Day of rebirth. Pixie gives me breakfast in bed, and then herself. She is the best birthday present I've had in nineteen years. Better even than the racing bicycle my father gave me when I turned twelve, I tell her.

'And did you unwrap the bicycle in bed too?' she enquires drolly.

'You bet. But it wasn't as passionate as you.'

'I was never given a bicycle,' she says. 'I was given a pony instead.'

'Ifu?'

'Yes.' She sits up, and thrusts her feet on to the floor.

68

'Where are you going?'

'To wash the breakfast dishes. Then to wash my hair and doll myself up to be presentable to your mother.'

'Blimey!' I leap out of the other side of the bed. 'What's the time? I forgot she was calling in this morning.'

Pixie smirks at me from the doorway. 'I'm going to tell her I've seduced her little ewey lamb.'

'Good. I don't care if she knows about us. I will introduce you as my sugar-mommy.'

'Bloody cheek!'

She grabs an egg shell off the tray she is carrying, and throws it at me as she leaves the room. I duck, and the shell smashes on the portrait of Bokkie. A trickle of egg yolk slides down his cheek like an infected tear. I wipe at it with the sleeve of my gown.

'Sorry about that,' I apologize to him, and he grins at me, I swear. His presence doesn't bother me today. Today I feel at peace with everyone and everything.

My mother finally arrives, dressed in a brightly spotted silk outfit with gossamer gauze sleeves. Brilliant as a butterfly, she flutters into the living-room and down the passage to see my bedroom.

'It's a bit small,' she comments. Her gaze focusses briefly on the neatly-made bed. I have the uncanny notion she can tell it hasn't been slept in. 'Still, I don't suppose you spend too much time in here.'

'What do you mean?' I'm trying to look innocent, but my ears are burning.

'Presumably, you have the use of the rest of the flat,' she says, and picks a hair off my sleeve. It is dark and wavy – one of mine, fortunately. My mother carries it over to the waste-paper basket and drops it in with a little flourish. 'Where's Pixie?'

'Somewhere around. In the bathroom, I think. Where's Nick?'

'He's sitting in the car because we had to double park. We're running late as usual, and I promised I'd only stay a minute.'

69

We hear the loo flush as we go back down the passage. Pixie appears. I introduce her to my mother, who inspects her, smiling carefully so as not to get lipstick on her teeth.

'So you're Pixie,' she enthuses. 'I've heard so much about you.'

'Not from me,' I assure Pixie, and laugh intentionally. 'It must be your fame as an artist spreading.'

My mother giggles self-consciously. 'Well, I *have* heard you're a marvellous artist,' she ad libs, and slants her eyes up at the walls. 'But where are your paintings?'

'They're hidden away,' Pixie tells her.

'Oh.' My mother manages to make the vowel sound carry ambiguous significance.

'Would you like a cup of tea?' offers Pixie.

'That's really very sweet of you, but my husband is waiting in the car. We're on our way to Jan Smuts Airport to meet someone. Another time, perhaps.'

'Any time,' smiles Pixie.

'My word, what a lot of plants you have in here,' my mother remarks, wafting ahead of us into the hallway. She fishes in her bag, and decorously arranges an envelope, and a card, and a small wrapped parcel on the telephone table. 'You can open these when I've gone, honbee.'

'Thanks Debs.'

I kiss her on the cheek. She cuddles my hand between both of hers.

'Look after my darling boy for me, won't you?' she asks Pixie. 'See that he eats properly.'

'I will,' promises Pixie.

'And please come and see us soon, honbee.'

'I will,' I promise. 'Bye Debs. Have fun.'

She blows me kisses halfway along the corridor. At the end, she turns and gives a little gracious bob and a wave, as if she's taking a final bow to an audience.

'That's my mother,' I say, closing the front door.

Pixie sniffs the air in the hall. 'I like her perfume; it

must be French. I like her. She would be fascinating to paint.'

'You told me you didn't enjoy doing portraits,' I say accusingly.

'I don't; not when they have to be crappy chocolate box moonlight-and-rose-petal pictures to please the sitter. The way I'd want to paint your mother would be different. It would be a challenge. I'd somehow success-fully have to capture so many beguiling images of her as an actress playing many roles.'

'On stage, or off?'

'Both. The quest would be to discover the real Deborah Mane on canvas.'

'Good luck!' I scoff. 'I can't help you. I've lived with her for nineteen years and I still don't know who the real Debs is. How about some lunch now? I'm hungry.'

Over our sandwiches at the kitchen table, Pixie is unusually talkative on the subject of art, and what the purpose of painting should be. She's all lit up and ani-mated, as if she has been given a stimulant. In a sense, she has been, I realize; and I can't help feeling a bit miffed that it is my mother and not me, who has inspired her.

As soon as we've finished eating, she jumps up, announces that she has to go and do something in her studio, and rushes away. I pour myself another cup of coffee and open the presents my mother left.

The tag on the small parcel claims it is from Nick, but the handwriting is my mother's. I tear the wrapping off to reveal a leather wallet, inscribed with my initials. I already have a wallet which my father gave me shortly before he died. I don't want a new wallet. Ungratefully, I cast it aside, and slit open the envelope. Inside are keys, and a fifty rand note wrapped up in a scribbled message from my mother:

Dear honbee, I'm giving you the Mini for your birthday. I feel it is time you had your own car. You won't have any excuse now for not coming to visit us!!! The money is for you to spend on a birthday celebration. Lots of love and kisses, Debs. P.S. The keys are the spare set for the Mini.

Whooping, I tear down the passage, and bang on the studio door. 'Pixie!'

There are noises of something being knocked over and then feet scurrying, before the door opens a fraction, and Pixie sticks her nose out. 'What?' she says, frowning.

'Look!' I show her my mother's message. She reads it.

'That's great,' she says.

'And . . .' I dangle the fifty rands in front of her. 'Fancy a slap-up meal out tonight?'

'Great,' she says.

'You could sound a little more enthusiastic,' I complain.

'I'm delighted. We'll celebrate later. But I'm busy right now.'

'Doing what? Can I come in?'

'No,' she says.

'Well, how long will you be?' I ask, peeved.

'I don't know. As long as it takes,' and she closes the door in my face.

I hear the key turn in the lock, and realize there's no point in standing there any longer.

Disgruntled, I go to my room and try to sort out what I'll need to take with me to university in the morning. I pack my briefcase. Then I lie on the bed with a book: *An Introduction to Nineteenth Century English Literature*. It's boring. I discard it, and fetch a pile of old, tattered, women's magazines stashed away in a cupboard under the kitchen sink. They are more fascinating. I read all the articles and learn, among other things, about premenstrual tension. I wonder whether that is what's wrong with Pixie this afternoon.

She emerges, finally, after dusk, looking very pleased with herself; although she still won't tell me what she has been up to. She is in a teasing, playful mood; but

I'm not. I'm still smarting from her having locked me out of her studio, as if she didn't trust me not to open the door and barge in.

As we're leaving the flat to go out to dinner, Pixie suddenly stops. 'I've forgotten my bag. You carry on. I'll catch you up,' she says, and dashes back inside.

I'm not thinking very clearly. I reach the bottom of the stairs before my brain registers that she had her bag under her arm as she opened the front door. I climb back up the stairs, and meet her at the top. She smiles guiltily.

'Was I long?'

I shrug. I suspect she had wanted to check up on something in her studio and had used the bag as an excuse, so I say nothing.

Despite the candle-lit table, and the zealous attention of the Italian waiter, the meal is not a great success. The food is over-cooked and over-priced, and the champagne makes Pixie sleepy. She yawns over her chocolate blancmange pudding.

'Would you like some coffee? It might wake you up,' I suggest.

She shakes her head. 'Let's go home now. We can have coffee there.'

But back in the flat, she stops me entering the kitchen. 'Forget coffee,' she says, taking my arm. 'Let's go straight to bed.'

I'm all for that idea. I practically drag her down the passage.

'Don't put the light on. Just get undressed, and climb into bed,' she says.

I do as I'm told. But when I reach out for her in the dark, she pushes me away.

'Wait!'

Her bedside lamp clicks on. I look at her. She looks at me, then at the wall opposite. On her face is a funny smug smile. I turn my head.

The portrait is gone. In its place is a new painting. A landscape. I recognize it instantly. It is our secret kloof

73

in the Magaliesberg. The waterfall is there, and the pool, and the rock on which we made love. I gaze spellbound. Every detail is so real, I fancy I can feel the sun beating down on the rock, and hear the water trickling and the crickets chirping in the grass.

Pixie's lips brush my cheek briefly. 'Happy Birthday, Sam.'

I find my voice. 'You painted this? Today? For me? This is what you were doing in your studio this afternoon?'

'Yes. Do you like it?'

'And you hung it up in here when you said you had forgotten your bag?'

She laughs. 'I had to find some excuse to do it while you were out of the way. But do you like it?'

'I love it! It's . . . it's brilliant!'

'No, it isn't brilliant. But it isn't that bad either, even if I say so myself.'

'There's only one thing missing. The duiker.'

'Look more closely,' she suggests. 'You'll find him.'

I jump out of bed and stand in front of the painting. She is right. In the undergrowth, a little pointed buck's face is peering out at me shyly, with gentle liquid eyes. When I move to one side, the eyes seem to follow me.

I step back to take in the whole scene. I'm mesmerized. I don't know how long I stand there. Finally, I look round. Pixie has gone to sleep. I switch off the lamp, and ease myself carefully under the bedclothes, so as not to disturb her.

I'm awake for ages because of the tightness of emotion in my chest. I feel the painting has more significance than merely a birthday gift. I feel it has exorcised a ghost. I feel . . . well, I guess I feel Pixie is truly mine now, and I'm choked with elation.

5

The honeymoon is over. I am now an undergraduate student, with a lot of reading to get through, essays to write, tutorials to prepare for, and end of year exams to start worrying about. Pixie is an artist again, drawing and painting in her studio all day while I am at university. For the time being, she has given up doing 'bread-and-butter' portraits, and is concentrating on building up a portfolio of new work. I am chuffed because she is drawing me in a series of studies – to keep her eye in, she says. She sketches me in the bath, washing up, studying, lying in bed, sitting on the sofa, reading, listening to the radio, scratching my ear. She is going to call the series *Sam*. I think it should be called *The Lover*, but she says that is too sentimental.

'What's wrong with being sentimental?' I ask.

'Nothing,' and she gives me a smoochy kiss to prove it. 'Only we're talking about art here, not romance.'

I don't agree with her. The drawings aren't purely descriptive art; I see her love in them, as well as her skill. I think they are very good. She lets me look at them, though she won't show me what else she is doing. 'I'm experimenting with a new approach to painting,' is all she will say.

We are happy. We have very little money, but it doesn't matter. We live simply and don't go out much. Russ visits us; and sometimes other people drop in, though not often. Pixie seems to have few friends, and I have lost touch with mine from my schooldays. And I haven't formed any new friendships at Wits. I've made no effort to get to know the students in my tutorials and lectures.

University is not my life. It is a place I have to go to each day, but I can't wait to return to the flat. Pixie is my life. I would probably skip half my lectures to be with her, were it not for the fact that she locks herself up in her studio during the day and won't be disturbed.

My mother's new show opens and promises to be a modest success. It is an American farce. My mother has the star role, playing a glamorous widow being wooed by half a dozen men of different ages and backgrounds and nationalities. The part could not have suited her better; she is in her element having all her leading men fawning at her feet.

I take Pixie to the first night performance. Afterwards, there is a party backstage which is noisy and boisterous. Everyone is in high spirits, except Nick; he looks a bit down at the mouth. I suspect he feels threatened by all the male competition in this particular production. I almost feel sorry for him.

There is no chance to talk to my mother alone until people start leaving. After saying goodbye to a group of well-wishers, she glides over and draws me aside from the conversation Pixie is having with a set designer.

'Did you *really* enjoy the performance, honbee?' she asks in her anxious voice.

'Yes. It was fun. And you were a natural, Debs.'

'You don't think I seemed a tiny bit old for the part, do you?'

'Never.' I smile into her eyes. The humidity in the room has diffused her thick make-up, revealing a small delta of wrinkles at the corners of her lids. She looks tired tonight, and middle-aged. I kiss her on the forehead. 'You, Debs, will never be too old to play glamorous parts, even when you are eighty.'

'Eighty?' she says, horrified. 'I hope I don't live that long. Honbee, you must promise to have me shot if I ever become old and feeble and ugly.'

'I will. I'll send you straight to the knackers,' I promise.

'Is Pixie enjoying herself?' she asks, casting a glance in her direction.

'I think so.'

'You two seem to be becoming very fond of each other.'

Before I can answer, Nick suddenly pops up like a Jack-in-the-box.

'Excuse me,' he butts in, 'but Richard is waiting to have a word with you before he leaves, darling,' and he takes my mother's hand to escort her across the room.

She goes willingly, pulling an apologetic face at me over her shoulder, and mouthing something silently which I can't interpret. I decide it's time Pixie and I went home, and fetch our coats from the cloakroom.

'My mother was asking if you were enjoying yourself,' I say in the car.

Pixie winds down the window and sticks her head out for some fresh air. It is past midnight. The streets are dark and deserted, and eerily quiet. Johannesburg city is like a giant cemetery at this hour of the night; office blocks and department stores resembling monolithic headstones, inscribed with blank glass commemorating the lust of daytime commerce. Pixie sighs.

'Soulless city,' she remarks.

'I was thinking the same thing.'

She smiles at me, and leans back, clasping her hands demurely in her lap. She is dressed up in a slinky trouser suit, made of pale blue silky material. I would rather she had worn a skirt that would have shown off her legs. But she looks alluring to me, whatever she wears.

'So, *did* you enjoy the evening?' I ask.

'I'm glad we went. The performance was good.'

'And the party?'

She hesitates. 'I'm not really crazy about social gatherings,' she admits. 'People are never real at parties. They wear masks.'

'Especially actors.'

'No, everybody does. In a sense, actors are more

honest than other people at parties. At least actors admit they are actors.'

I shift into a lower gear as we begin the long steep climb up to the summit of Hillbrow. 'Would you like to be a hermit then?' I say jokingly.

'I wouldn't mind.'

'And exist all on your own, even without me?'

'No. You'd be there,' she says. 'We'd live in a cave, and I would paint on the walls, while you hunted for our food.'

'Sounds okay to me.' I press her knee. 'Who needs other people?'

'Stop the car!' she exclaims suddenly.

Reacting to the urgency in her tone, I swerve into the kerb, and brake. We are both thrown forward. Before I can recover, Pixie has her arms round me and is kissing me passionately.

'What's . . .?' I gasp for air.

'I love you, Sam.' She kisses me again, on the cheek this time. 'And thank you.'

'For?' I grab at the handbrake as I realize the Mini is rolling backwards.

'For making me happy,' she says, settling back in her seat. 'You can drive on now.'

I gaze at her speechlessly. She smiles.

'Don't look at me with your bedroom eyes,' she says huskily. 'Wait until we get home.'

Yes, we *are* happy at this time; Pixie-woman and me, living in our cave in the concrete cliffs of Hillbrow. But it doesn't last.

* * * *

Two weeks later, I come back from university to find someone in the living-room with Pixie. A woman in her fifties, smartly dressed, with short grey hair, an ample figure, and an Oxford English accent.

'This is Cecily,' Pixie says, 'an old friend of mine. We're having a drink. Grab a glass, Sam, and join us.'

I perch on the edge of a chair, nursing my wine and observing Cecily, while she and Pixie continue the conversation I had interrupted. They're talking about painting. I gather from what is said, that Cecily owns an art gallery in Durban and wants to exhibit Pixie's latest work.

'But I haven't anything ready yet,' Pixie tells her. 'And, anyway, I'm not sure you'll like the stuff I'm doing now.'

Cecily laughs, grinds out her cigarette, and pulls a new one from her packet. As she lights it, her eyes size me up. 'You know, Sam, Pixie has been saying that to me since she was fourteen years old.'

'Saying what?' I can feel myself bristling for some reason.

'That I won't like her paintings.' She leans across to Pixie, and pats her hand. 'But I always do, sweetie. I've always liked everything you've painted, haven't I?'

I catch Pixie's eye. She seems embarrassed. 'You might not this time,' she replies.

'She always says that too,' Cecily informs me. 'Have you seen these new paintings, Sam?'

I wish I could say yes. I shake my head. 'Only the drawings. They're great.'

'Are they?' Cecily gives me another sharp look.

'He would have to say that,' cuts in Pixie. 'The drawings are all of him.'

'Are they?' Cecily says in a higher octave. There is a short awkward pause, before she laughs chestily. '. . . Well, let's see them then. And the paintings too.'

Pixie jumps up. 'If I have to show you, I need some more wine first. I'll fetch another bottle.'

'I'll fetch it,' I offer. I don't want to be left alone in the room with Cecily. I'm developing a strong feeling of antagonism towards her.

When I return they are both suddenly silent, which makes me think they've been talking about me. Pixie half-empties her glass almost as soon as I've filled it, and holds it out for a top up. I'm afraid she is going to become drunk; so obviously is Cecily because she snatches the glass from Pixie's hand.

'That's enough Dutch courage,' she says firmly. 'You can have the rest after we've seen the paintings. Come along now, sweetie, let's not delay the agony any longer.'

Meekly, without protest, Pixie allows herself to be walked out of the room on Cecily's arm. I follow in the trail of smoke from Cecily's cigarette. The force of her will is overpowering; I feel as though I'm being sucked along in the slipstream of a steam engine.

While Pixie is unlocking the door of the studio, Cecily turns to me.

'I never give Pixie advance warning of when I'm coming up to Johannesburg,' she explains. 'That way, she doesn't have time to hide what she's been working on, or think up some plausible excuse as to why I can't have a look at it. I know I'm a bully, but without bullying, Pixie's extraordinary talent would never see the light of day.'

'You are a bully,' Pixie tells her fondly.

I have been allowed into the studio once before briefly. It was in a shambles then. It is in even more of a shambles now. The bare floorboards are multi-coloured with dried splashes of paint, and strewn with discarded paper and other litter. Two tables are jampacked with pots, and jars, and tubes, and paintbrushes, and rolls of paper, and rags which look as if they've been used to mop up after a grisly murder. A couple of easels stand near the window, and in one corner are several huge untidy piles of sketch books and canvases and boards. Framed canvases lie stacked up against the skirting board with their backs to the room. Only one painting is on view; the portrait of Bokkie, which is balanced on its side on the floor in a far corner. Cecily goes straight to it, and turns it the right way up.

'I'm glad you haven't got rid of our Bokkie,' she says. 'I still think he is one of the very best of your early endeavours. Didn't you paint this in your Matric year?'

'Yes,' mutters Pixie. She is down on her knees, thumbing through the contents of a huge portfolio under the nearest table.

'Golly! You know, you were even more talented than I realized at the time.' Cecily looks round at me. 'I was Pixie's art teacher at her boarding school. When she is famous, I'll be able to claim I discovered her.'

Pixie grunts. 'You won't want to after this,' she says, dragging out a painting.

She puts the painting on an easel. We all converge, and stand in a row, staring at it.

'Mmm! . . .' says Cecily.

I don't say anything. I'm trying to figure out what the painting is about. Swirls and streaks and curves of vibrant hot colours cover the paper in a formless turmoil of movement.

'Very interesting,' says Cecily. 'You've gone abstract, sweetie.'

'No, not abstract,' Pixie corrects her. 'I'm attempting to paint the inner landscape, rather than the outer, and objectify feelings and sensations, that's all.'

She replaces the painting with another. Cool pale colours merge into darker hues in intertwining waves which peter out into motionless black at the centre of the paper.

'Mmm! . . .' says Cecily.

'What is this one called?' I ask Pixie.

She hesitates, looking diffident. ' . . . It's . . . well, what do you *feel* it is.'

I'm aware of feeling empty, and also light-headed from the wine. Glibly, I say, 'I *feel* it is suppertime.'

Immediately I've spoken, I regret it. I can see that I've hurt Pixie, although she puts on a smile. Cecily scowls at me.

'Plebeian!' she growls. 'Trust a man to think only of his belly. Sweetie, don't—'

But Pixie has removed the painting, and closed the portfolio. 'I've shown you enough for now,' she decides firmly. 'It is suppertime. Come along to the kitchen and I'll make us something to eat.'

I'm conscious of the dark melting brown eyes of the

Bokkie portrait staring after us with sad compassion, as Pixie marches us out of the studio and locks the door.

The meal is a constrained affair. Cecily and I don't speak directly to each other. Pixie keeps the conversation going on the subject of food and recipes and other neutral topics. After we've cleared the table, Cecily manages to persuade Pixie to take her back into the studio. I would like to see the rest of Pixie's paintings, and ask contritely if I can come too.

'No,' Pixie says, and ruffles my hair in passing. It is the first time she has touched me since I got home. 'You can wash up, and would you mind changing the sheets on the bed in your room for Cecily? She's staying the night.'

They remain in the studio all evening. I sit in the living-room, and try to make a start on *Paradise Lost* which I'm supposed to have finished reading before my English tutorial tomorrow. It is hard going. I cast it aside, and go and have a bath. By now it is quite late. Dressed for bed in a clean pair of pyjamas and a dressing-gown, I knock on the studio door and ask them if they'd like a hot drink.

The two of them emerge and join me in the kitchen. They are both bright-eyed and quite merry. I suspect they have polished off the second bottle of wine we had opened earlier. Over her mug of Milo, Cecily looks at me mellowly, and starts asking me about my university course.

I turn to Pixie. 'It's time I was in bed. I have an early lecture in the morning.'

'Off you go then.' She gives me a little peck on the lips. 'I probably won't be long, but I'll try not to disturb you.'

'Aren't you tired?' I was hoping she would come with me.

'No,' she says, smiling.

Cecily laughs wheezingly. 'You must excuse us, dear boy. Pixie and I haven't seen each other for ages, and we have a lot to catch up on.'

I don't appreciate being called dear boy. I barely manage to say goodnight to her civilly.

When Pixie comes to bed an hour or more later, I pretend to be asleep. In the morning, I take myself off to university before either of them have stirred. By the time I get back home in the late afternoon, Cecily has gone.

My room stinks of her strong tobacco and perfume. An ashtray next to the bed is overflowing with squashed cigarette ends. It is easy to get rid of that, and air the room. It is less easy to get rid of the seed of suspicion that has been sown in my mind.

Pixie has a hangover and bad period pains, and is clearly not in the mood to discuss anything. Common-sense tells me to let the matter rest for now, but I'm not inclined to wait. As neither of us feel up to cooking a meal, we eat toasted sandwiches on our laps in the living-room. Pixie switches on the radio, and finds a station playing music.

'Do we have to listen to that?' I ask irritably.

'Why? Don't you want to?'

'I think we should talk.'

'What about?'

I get up and turn down the volume. 'About Cecily.'

'What about Cecily?'

I take a deep breath. 'For a start, did she like your paintings?'

'She wants to exhibit them in her gallery,' Pixie says blandly. 'She thinks they will sell well.'

'Do you agree?'

She shrugs, and chews her toast.

'You don't seem terribly enthusiastic.'

'I'm not sure.' Depositing her plate on the floor, she draws her feet up under her on the sofa, and rests her head back. The colour seems drained out of her face. 'I'm not sure I want to do anything with them,' she says tiredly, 'except burn them.'

'You can't do that!' I exclaim in horror. 'You can't just burn three or four months' hard work.'

'I can, if I must. And start again.'

'You can't!'

She looks at me expressionlessly. 'Why should you care? The paintings didn't mean anything to you, did they?'

'They . . .' I flounder. ' . . . I think they're very colourful and clever.'

'Exactly!' she retorts. 'Colourful and clever.' Closing her eyes, she lets out a deep resigned sigh.

Guiltily, I say, 'I don't dislike them. I just prefer your figurative work. You're so good at drawing people and places and – but I'm not the art expert. Cecily is. And she evidently finds them very exciting or she wouldn't want to exhibit them.'

'Cecily isn't infallible.'

'No,' I agree with feeling. 'All the same, you obviously think a great deal of her.'

I hadn't meant to sound bitter, but I do. Pixie's eyes open a fraction, revealing two slits of reptilian blue that stare at me like a cobra.

'I think we'd better drop this discussion now.' There is a warning hiss in her voice.

'Why?'

'Because you've made it abundantly clear that you dislike Cecily, and I happen to owe her more than anyone I know.'

'Owe?' I ask carefully. 'In what sense?'

Pixie doesn't answer. She tilts her head forward and rubs her forehead, grimacing, as if she's in pain.

'In what sense?' I insist. 'Do you mean in terms of your art?'

'No. I mean in terms of my life. Have you got a cigarette? My packet's empty.'

I light two and hold one out. But she doesn't seem to notice it. She is sitting curled up now, hugging her knees, and frowning at the floor. I lay her cigarette in the ashtray and wait, sensing that she is trying to decide whether to say more.

After a few moments, I prompt, 'Well, go on then.'

'Why didn't you take to Cecily?' she asks, turning her frown on me.

'She wasn't exactly very amenable to me, was she? In fact, I got the strong impression she doesn't approve of men.'

'You did, did you?' She smiles stiffly.

'From the way she acted, I think she loves you,' I say sourly.

Pixie looks at me with exasperation. 'Of course she loves me. And I love her. She's given me more than I can ever repay. She's been like a mother to me, and a mentor, and the best friend – the *only* real friend I had at the most difficult time of my life. I don't know many people who would have taken on board a strange, suicidal, skinny, moody, teenage girl, and provided her with a home to go to during the school holidays and love and affection and support and encouragement and a reason to live. Cecily did. And she—'

'Hang on!' I interrupt. 'I don't understand. You had a home to go to. The farm.'

'No, I didn't. I couldn't go back there.'

'Why not?'

'I *just* couldn't!' she says emphatically. She's all worked up. There is a strange wild look in her eyes that is almost frightening. 'The point is, Cecily was the mainstay of my life from when I was fourteen until I left art college. I'll always be grateful to her for that. I know she can be a bit bristly and bossy, but it's only her manner. She has one helluva big heart, and I won't hear a word against her. All right?'

I shrug. It isn't all right, as far as I'm concerned. But I don't want to say anything to upset her further while she is in this mood. Her unsmoked cigarette has excreted a long grey turd of ash. I stab at it with the still burning filter end. Then I watch Pixie rub her temples with her fingertips.

'Where does all this leave *us*?' I ask tersely.

'I don't know where it leaves *you*,' she says, rising

awkwardly. 'But I've got a headache and a sore tummy and I'm going to bed. You can do what you like.'

I sit and brood over what she has told me, as well as what she hasn't told me. I feel as if I'm trying to put together an emotional jigsaw of her past and I can't, because there are vital pieces missing which she won't give me.

I'm too uptight to go to bed. Kicking off my shoes, I stretch out on the sofa and spend the night there, sleeping fitfully on the lumpy cushions.

In the morning, Pixie tells me she missed me when she woke up early and I wasn't in bed with her.

We're having breakfast. Pixie is perched on the edge of the kitchen table, drinking coffee. She looks small and sad and vulnerable in her nightgown, with her bare feet hooked round the table leg, and her hair in tumbled disarray. I'm overcome by guilt at having made her so miserable. I want to grab her and hug her tightly. But I'm afraid to; I'm afraid that in the sudden overwhelming force of my feeling, I might squeeze too hard and break her bones.

'Promise me you won't burn your paintings,' I croak.

'Okay. I won't,' she says meekly. 'I'll parcel them up and send them off to Cecily. If she thinks she can sell them, well and good. Who cares? We need the money.'

'Will you paint today?'

'Probably. I don't know what.'

'Inspiration will strike.'

'Yes,' she says, sounding unconvinced. 'But I hope you don't have too many lectures this morning.' Reaching out, she prods the tip of my nose with her finger. 'You look tired, my Sam.'

I grab her hand and kiss it. 'I love you, Pixie.'

'Me too, very much,' she says comically.

'Me too, very much is all that matters.' I jump up and hug her. 'Everything will be all right, you see.' Holding on to each other, in that moment, I believe it.

But the next time Russ visits us, I make a point of

accompanying him to his car when he leaves, as it is the only chance I have to talk to him alone.

Following him down the stairs, I ask, 'Do you know Cecily?'

'Yes,' he says. 'Why?'

'How long have you known her?'

'Jeepers. I don't know. A long time. Why?'

'How long?' I make a quick calculation in my head. 'Ten years?' That was when Pixie would have been fourteen.

'Probably longer,' he says. 'I met Cecily when she was living in Johannesburg. Then she got a teaching job in a boarding school in Natal, and we lost touch; until she rang up out of the blue a couple of years back and asked me if I would let a friend of hers, who was moving up to Johannesburg, keep her pony on my small-holding.'

'So that was how you met Pixie?'

'Yes.' He pauses on the landing, and looks round at me. 'She's a great character, isn't she?'

'Who? Pixie?'

'No. Cecily. Pixie mentioned she was here a few days ago on a flying visit.'

I wait for him to start down the next flight of steps before I ask my next question. I find it easier to talk to his back than have to meet that disconcertingly direct gaze of his. 'Is Cecily gay, Russ?'

He laughs. 'You gathered that, did you? Well, she's quite open about it.'

His long legs are leaping the stairs two at a time. He's almost at the bottom. It's now or never.

'Were she and Pixie ever . . . I mean, have they been, at some point. . . .' I'm getting my tongue in a twist. I don't know how to put it without being too explicit.

He stops on the last step, and turns to face me. I stop too. His expression is intimidating.

'I understand what you're trying to ask,' he says. 'But I don't understand why you're asking me. You should ask Pixie, if it's bothering you.'

'It isn't bothering me,' I lie. 'I just thought I'd – but anyway, Pixie won't talk about the past,' I finish lamely.

'She's right. We all talk about the past too much. We live in the past instead of enjoying the present.'

'Maybe,' I say grudgingly. 'But I think Pixie won't talk about the past because it's too painful for her. Especially what happened to her when she was fourteen.'

'Aahh, yes.' He nods, eyeing me more sympathetically. 'Bokkie, you mean. So you know about Bokkie then?'

'I know he died. But I don't know how, or what he had to do with Pixie.' I take a flying leap down the last six steps. 'Will you tell me?'

'Sorry, pal, I can't help you there,' he says, walking on. 'If Pixie hasn't told you, she must have a reason.'

'What?'

'Perhaps she doesn't feel she can trust you enough yet to understand.'

'Thanks a lot,' I say, offended.

He grins, holding the front vestibule door open for me to go through first. We emerge into the sunshine. Russ's old battered Morris Estate is parked on a yellow line. He checks the windscreen.

'My lucky day. No ticket,' he comments.

Climbing in, he coaxes the engine into spluttering life, and winds down his window. I lean my fists on the rusty sill.

'Before you go, Russ, tell me something – do you think I resemble Bokkie?'

He laughs. 'Don't flatter yourself, Sam. Bokkie was an extraordinary little guy, from all accounts. If he had been born in the East, he would probably have been recognized as an Enlightened Being and brought up as a Buddha.'

'I haven't a clue what you're talking about,' I complain, frowning.

'You wouldn't. In this Godforsaken country of ours, anything Eastern – including Eastern religious concepts, is considered to be the work of the devil.' His mouth twists into a sarcastic smile. 'We live in a very Enlight-ened land.'

I step back on to the kerb as he lets his foot off the clutch and the Morris rattles forward phlegmatically.

'You need a new car,' I shout after him.

He sticks his head out of the window. 'No, I don't. The hooter still works fine.' As he drives off, he gives it a blast that makes me jump out of my skin, and a cat on the pavement opposite run for its life down the nearest alley.

* * * *

Things are different after Cecily's visit. A note of dissen-sion has crept into Pixie's and my relationship. It isn't obvious. But it is there, like a night shadow that is felt rather than seen. Pixie's painting is going badly. She is dissatisfied with whatever she produces each day, and usually tears it up, or paints it out to start over. I'm under pressure with my university workload, having put off doing essays and other projects, and now trying frantically to meet deadlines at the last minute. We still have our moments though; especially at the weekends when we can spend time together relaxing, and I'm able to believe we are as happy as we were before.

Pixie says she loves me. Whenever I ask her, she says she is happy. Only sometimes, in the middle of the night, she cries out in her sleep. It wakes me, though it doesn't wake her. I lie in the dark beside her, feeling unnerved, as she sleeps on peacefully.

One evening, in a grumpy mood, I tell Pixie that she shouldn't be so friendly with the African domestic, Solly – he's the one who is supposed to clean her flat, and is studying for his Matric. She has just been up to his room, on the roof of the building, with a couple of books she has borrowed for him from the public library.

'Why not?' she asks, narrowing her eyes warily like a cat.

'You're too familiar with him.'

89

'Too *familiar*?' Her voice has sharpened to a razor-edge. 'What exactly do you mean?'

'You know what I mean,' I say sullenly.

'No, I don't.' She plants herself in front of my chair, and stands with her hands on her hips, glaring down at me. 'Explain yourself.'

I'm beginning to regret having spoken. Pixie's sponsorship of Solly's education has been a bone of contention between us from the beginning. I still resent the time we have to spend cleaning the flat each week. But I don't want to have a row. It's nearly bedtime, and I have some preparation to do for a tutorial in the morning.

'I just think you should be a little more formal towards him,' I tell her, and I open my folder of lecture notes and pretend to start reading them, in the hope that she will go away.

'Formal, as in superior, you mean?' She snaps the folder shut, and chucks it on the floor. 'What you're saying is, I should call him "boy", and make him call me "madam", and treat him not as a man at all, but as a faceless, sexless, inferior who is only there to do my dirty work for me.'

I've never seen her so angry. I feel she is over-reacting, and bend down to retrieve my notes which have scattered across her feet. She kicks them out of reach.

'I'm not a racist, Pixie,' I say, glowering up at her.

Her eyes stare into mine. For a long frozen moment, she doesn't do anything. But her eyes change; the fury in them gives way to a look of cold resignation that makes me feel hollow and sick inside suddenly.

In a flat neutral voice, she says, 'That, I think I find hardest to accept – a racist who doesn't even recognize he is a racist,' and she walks out of the room.

Automatically, I gather up all my muddled notes and put them back in order. I'm struggling to get to grips with what has just happened. To me, it seems like a storm in a tea cup; a row which blew up out of one resentful remark. Yet there was something in Pixie's tone and manner and expression that has left me with a sense of foreboding. I get up to go to the bathroom, and notice Pixie's bedroom door is closed. It never has been shut before, at any time. A slither of light is visible underneath. I knock softly.

'Pixie? Can I come in?'

No answer. I turn the handle; the door is locked.

'Pixie?' I'm worried now. 'Are you okay?'

A bedspring squeaks. Then: 'Yes,' she says. The word sounds muffled, as if she has her face pressed into the pillow.

'Can I come in?'

'No,' she says more clearly. 'I want to be alone tonight.'

I haven't slept in my own room since the night I moved into the flat, months ago; and the bedlinen hasn't been changed since Cecily's visit. A slight smell of perfume on the sheets recalls her memory, provoking my resentment. I lie and curse her, blaming her for things being different between Pixie and me. Feeling angry helps; it relieves the awful hollowness deeper within.

Pixie doesn't appear in the morning. Her door remains firmly shut. I listen outside it, and can't hear any sound at all. I don't want to go to university, but there seems no point in sitting around in the flat either.

All morning, as I drag my feet from one lecture room to another on the campus, I'm plagued by a presentiment; a niggling sense that something traumatic is about to happen. I start to get anxious about Pixie. My anxiety builds up into a panic by lunch time. Abandoning my coffee in the canteen, I almost run to the car park, and drive home as fast as I can.

Pixie's bedroom door is ajar. Just inside the room, a broken mug is lying on the floor, bleeding brown liquid that could be coffee or tea. With my heart in my mouth, I step over it, and peer round the door at the bed. Pixie is sitting propped up against pillows, wearing a nightie, and clutching a bottle in her hand – a wine bottle. On her lap is an open exercise book, but she isn't looking at it. Her eyes are closed. Tears have left wet streaks down her face, yet she isn't making a sound. That is what is most harrowing of all – the utter silence and stillness of her grief. She could be dead, except that I can see she is breathing.

'Pixie!' I rasp.

She gives no sign of having heard me. But when I reach the bed, and touch her shoulder, her eyes open briefly. Their gaze is unfocussed and vacant, like the eyes of someone in a coma. I realize she is very drunk; the bottle in her hand is empty. I remove it, and grasp her fingers.

'Pixie, what's the matter?'

She shakes her head without opening her eyes again. Her face is pallid and desolate. 'I'm dizzy,' she mumbles, slurring her words. 'I'd better lie down.'

I help her slide down on to her back. She won't let me take the exercise book. She clutches it between her hands, and as I pull the sheet up to cover her, she rolls over on her side on top of the book. I draw the curtains, and clear up the mess of the broken mug. Pixie is breathing noisily through her mouth. She starts snoring. Lifting the sheet, I carefully extract the exercise book from under her. She doesn't even stir.

I wait anxiously until the stertorous sounds she is making settle down into a quieter, regular breathing rhythm; then I retreat to the living-room with the book. Collapsing shakily on the sofa, I frown down at the dog-eared red cover with its black printing. STERLING EXERCISE BOOK. NAME: SUBJECT: CLASS: Next to NAME is written **Pixie de Jager (Private!)**. Next to SUBJECT – **The Story of Bokkie.** Next to CLASS – 1963. 1963 is five years ago. Pixie would have been nineteen then – my age, and an art student at college.

Suddenly I'm reluctant to lift the cover. It isn't guilt that holds me back, so much as trepidation at what I am about to discover. Balancing the book on its spine, I riffle through the edges of the pages with my finger. There are a lot of pages, and every one of them is filled from top to bottom with Pixie's small compact handwriting. It is obviously quite a long story. On the inside back cover, I discover a note, written in bold lettering:

To whom it may concern,
This story is private, and not for publication until
I am dead. Although I have written it as a story, it
is not fiction! It is a true account of the life of a
boy called Bokkie. It is also a true love story.
P. de J. 1963.

Trembling, I put the book down, and go and make myself a coffee, and gulp it in the kitchen. Then I check up on Pixie. She is still dead to the world, and likely to remain so for some hours.

Arranging myself more comfortably on the sofa, I take a deep breath, and open the book at the first page, and start reading.

6

The Story of Bokkie
by Pixie de Jager

The story begins in 1944 with the discovery of an abandoned new-born baby in some bushes at the side of the main road near a farm in Natal – the de Jagers' farm. The de Jagers have just had a baby daughter, Priscilla. Gerrit de Jager is deeply disappointed, having prayed for a son. The abandoned baby is a boy.

Gerrit, a devout member of the Afrikaans Dutch Reformed Church, believes the boy has been sent to him by

God – as a sort of divine apology for having made a mistake with the first delivery. He calls the boy his 'Bokkie' (baby buck) because it resembles a fawn with its pointed little face, velvety dark eyes, and delicate skinny limbs. The baby is very ill and weak and anaemic. There is some doubt that it will survive. Gerrit postpones informing the police and takes charge of the baby's nursing himself. The baby survives. As its anaemic condition improves, its skin darkens to a distinct brown, and tiny tufts of soft crinkly hair start to grow on its scalp. Gerrit's Bokkie is revealed to be a coloured baby. Gerrit is bitterly shocked and disillusioned; he feels betrayed by his God. The baby is summarily handed over to Florence, the African kitchen maid, to bring up.

Florence's duties include being nanny to Priscilla. The two babies play together in her charge. By the time they are toddlers, they have become inseparable friends. Priscilla shares her toys with Bokkie, and her picture books. Together, they learn to read. In a fairy story, Bokkie finds a picture of a pixie who looks like Priscilla. He begins calling Priscilla Pixie. She likes the name and adopts it for herself. Everyone else continues to call her Priscilla.

When Pixie turns seven, her parents send her to the local village school. Bokkie is given the job of driving her to and from school in the donkey cart. Pixie isn't happy with this arrangement. It makes her feel guilty every time she gets out of the cart at the school gate, knowing that Bokkie can't come into the classroom with her because the school is for white children only. She keeps asking her father to buy her a pony so that she can ride to school on her own. He keeps saying he will look out for a suitable one for her, and then doesn't seem to do anything about it.

It is Bokkie who finally finds Pixie a pony. He turns up with it out of the blue one day, and explains he got it from a man who was going to shoot it because it had been lame for quite a while and was useless. The pony does have a very swollen and inflamed front leg. But Bokkie wraps herb poultices round the inflammation, and within a week the swelling subsides and the leg is completely healed. The pony is only a youngster and unbroken as yet. Bokkie climbs on its back without any tack, and talks to it gently. The pony seems to understand him. It does whatever he asks it to do without protest.

Once Gerrit is convinced the pony is safe to ride, he buys Pixie a bridle and saddle for it. She and Bokkie name the pony Ifu (Zulu for cloud) because Bokkie says clouds are light on their feet like the pony, and float across the sky without leaving any footprints on it.

At school, Pixie is mixing with other white children for the first time. After a while, their racism and her parents' attitudes start to rub off on her. She suffers a conflict: she can't involve Bokkie in her new life; she daren't even mention her friendship with him to any of her classmates. Temporarily, she resolves her conflict by rejecting Bokkie as her friend. But it leaves her feeling guilty, so she tries to avoid him altogether. Bokkie makes it easier for her by keeping out of her way.

He takes to wandering off on his own for hours at a time. When anyone asks him where he has been, he says he's been to school with the animals and birds and trees and flowers. People laugh at him, but their laughter is uneasy; there is a deep look in his eyes that suggests he knows something they aren't capable of understanding.

Bokkie *is* a strange little boy. Everything is alive to him, including rocks and stones and the earth under his feet. He can't bear to see any suffering; he even tries to avoid stepping on ants in his path. He refers to all creatures as his friends, and won't eat meat. Whenever an animal is slaughtered on the farm, he runs away and hides, hugging himself with his face screwed up in pain – as if he is feeling the knife on his own body.

The African farm labourers have children, a few of them the same age as Bokkie. But they don't play with him. He isn't one of them. He isn't black. He is a half-caste and enjoys certain privileges they don't have; living with Florence in a room in the farmyard; whereas the labourers' families are housed in mud huts in a compound far away from the white farmer's dwelling.

Bokkie is a misfit on the farm, not only because of his in-between colour, but also because of his strangeness. The African children have seen him stroke poisonous snakes without being bitten, and rescue a vicious stray dog from a wire trap they had set which had cut into one of its paws as it struggled to escape. The dog had licked Bokkie's hand while he tended its injury, and then slunk off docilely. The children are afraid of this strange power in Bokkie. When he approaches, they scream, '*Tokoloshe*'*, and throw stones, and then run away as fast as they can.

Pixie too, is discovering herself to be a misfit in her own peer group. Her new friendships don't make her happy. She finds herself missing Bokkie's company more and more, instead of less. One day, in a depressed mood, she talks about Bokkie to a girl she considers to be her best friend. The word is passed around. Pixie is called a '*kaffir-sussie*'† and ostracized.

Rejected herself, Pixie now knows what Bokkie must have felt when she turned her back on him. Full of remorse, she seeks him out, and tearfully asks if he will be her friend again. Bokkie looks at her. Then he takes something from his pocket and puts it in her hand. It is a heart-shaped stone.

From that moment on, Pixie carries the stone with her everywhere. She hates school now, and the stone gives her courage to get through the long mornings in the classroom and in the playground. There is one other source of comfort – the art period on Wednesdays. Pixie discovers she can draw better than anyone else in the whole school. She decides she wants to become an artist, and starts drawing and painting everything in

* Tokoloshe – demon
† Kaffir-sussie – Kaffir sister

sight. Her mother is pleased that her daughter has a talent and buys her art materials. Gerrit is pleased too. He hangs Pixie's paintings up on the wall in his study, and shows them off proudly to visitors.

Every day, after lunch, except when it is raining, Pixie takes her sketch pad and her school satchel – loaded with textbooks and paints, and goes outside to meet Bokkie waiting for her in the farmyard. Drinking his coffee on the stoep, Gerrit watches their small figures disappearing into the distance across the valley pasture-land, with Bokkie leading the way and carrying Pixie's satchel and sketch pad. He smiles. His daughter is going to be a famous artist one day. It is good that she wants to practise drawing as much as she can. And he doesn't have to worry that she will come to any harm when Bokkie is with her. He knows about Bokkie's strange powers. They worry him at times in terms of his religion. But on the other hand, they are useful as a protection for his daughter against any dangers out in the veld. He has told Bokkie to look after Priscilla, and he knows he will.

What Gerrit doesn't know, however, is that Pixie and Bokkie have a secret place they go to on the farm. It is a little shallow creek, tucked away in a tight fold of the hills. The creek is completely enclosed by thick jungly mamba-infested bush – a deterrent to all but Bokkie, who views snakes not as adversaries, but as friends. Pixie manages to forget her own fear of snakes when she is with Bokkie. Nevertheless, she always holds her breath as she creeps behind Bokkie along the hidden path he has tunnelled through the entangled vines and creepers and thorny branches of bushes.

But it is worth getting scratched arms and legs to reach the secluded glade of the creek, with its clear rock pool fed by trickling water from a hidden spring in the hillside. The creek is the refuge of small wild animals and birds. It is also Bokkie's and Pixie's refuge. They are happy here. They can be themselves.

In summer, they strip off their clothes, and swim

naked in the crystal cold water of the pool, and lie on the flat rock above it to dry off in the sun. In winter, the spring water is too cold to tempt them; but the creek is sheltered in the groin of the hills, and the surrounding bush acts as a wind barrier, so that even on the chilliest days they can sunbathe on the rock. They share the sandwiches Pixie brings with her, and the wild fruit Bokkie provides.

Then Pixie gets out her textbooks and they work. It is Bokkie's school time. Pixie teaches him everything she has learnt in the classroom that day. She teaches him to do sums, and how to discover the countries of the world on a map, and how to use a dictionary, and what the Bible has to say about God. Bokkie is very interested in what the Bible has to say about God. But he has difficulty understanding God as the Father.

'If God is the father of people,' he says, 'then there must be father gods of trees, and sheep, and butterflies, and monkeys, and everything else as well.'

'No. The Bible says there is only one God,' Pixie tells him firmly. 'And we are made in His image.' She doesn't know what that means. Neither does Bokkie.

'If there is only one God, then He can't be a man,' he says.

'He isn't. He's God.'

'Where is He?' asks Bokkie.

'In heaven.'

'Where's heaven.'

'I don't know.' Pixie points at the sky. 'Up there somewhere.'

Bokkie squints up through the leaves. Then he looks at Pixie with his disconcertingly deep gaze. 'I don't think God is up there. I think God is inside me. When I close my eyes I can see God inside me.'

He closes his eyes, and goes very still. A little shiver runs up Pixie's spine; it always does when Bokkie goes very still. It is as if he disappears somewhere inside himself. He doesn't even seem to breathe when he is that still.

'What do you see?' she asks nervously.

'Gold. A gold light.' He opens his eyes. He gazes at her. 'I see a gold light in you too. And in that tree and in that bird and . . .' He is gazing around as though he sees a gold light in everything. Smiling, he shuts his eyes and goes still again.

Pixie grabs her sketch pad and starts drawing him. She is always drawing him. She also draws the little wild creatures that come to drink at the pool, and the monkeys that turn up punctually at tea-time. Pixie has several sketches of Bokkie with monkeys sitting on his shoulders and his head and his knees, eating the fruit he has brought them. All the feathered and furred visitors to the creek let Bokkie feed them from his hand, though they keep a wary eye on Pixie. Sometimes she feels jealous, without knowing whether she is jealous of Bokkie's extraordinary empathy with animals, or jealous of the way he strokes and talks to them lovingly. She doesn't understand her own feelings. She only knows that Bokkie means more to her than anyone or anything else in her life.

For several years, the creek remains Bokkie's and Pixie's secret hideaway; a place where they can be happily alone together without interference from the outside world. They call it their 'house', and begin to believe that their daily sojourns there will be able to continue indefinitely.

But the innocent beliefs and hopes of childhood are never allowed to last very long. Soon after her twelfth birthday, small round buds of breasts start to make themselves visible on Pixie's flat chest. Gerrit notices, and tells his wife gruffly that the time has come for their daughter to stop being so friendly with Bokkie. She agrees with him. It is also about time, anyway, that Bokkie started earning his keep on the farm, Gerrit grumbles, and decides to find something for Bokkie to do the next day. But the morning brings more pressing problems to contend with, and he forgets.

Several days pass. Then Pixie unwittingly provokes

99

Gerrit's unresolved conflict of emotions concerning Bokkie. She refuses to eat her mutton chop at lunch. She says she doesn't want to eat animals any more. She says animals are people too, and if people are made in the image of God, then so are sheep.

Gerrit explodes in sudden fury. He knows immediately who has been infecting his daughter with such heathen notions. Purple in the face, he leaps up and slaps Pixie for being blasphemous. Then he tells his wife to keep her at the table until she has eaten every scrap of meat on her plate, and storms out to find Bokkie.

He doesn't have to go far. Bokkie is in the yard, waiting for Pixie to finish her lunch so they can set off to their hidden creek as usual. Trembling with rage, Gerrit grabs Bokkie by the scruff of the neck and shakes him violently.

'*Bliksem!** *Duiweltjie!*'† he yells. 'From now on, you stay away from my daughter. You hear? I don't want you anywhere near her. Understand?'

Bokkie stares up at him out of huge frightened eyes. He can't speak because all the breath has been squeezed from his lungs, and his heart is hammering wildly in his throat. Gerrit shakes him again.

'You understand?'

Bokkie nods, gasping for breath. Gerrit's hard grimy nails are biting into the back of his neck.

Gerrit calms down a little, relaxing his hold slightly. 'It's time you did some work and started to pay for your—'

'Baas? . . .' Florence is running towards them from the kitchen, wringing her hands. ' . . . What's wrong? What's Bokkie done, Baas.'

'I won't have him hanging round the little missus any longer, Florence,' Gerrit snarls at her. 'It must stop. So must all the sissy nonsense he gets up to. From now, he must work for his food, like all the other kaffir boys

* Bliksem – Scoundrel
† Duiweltjie – Little Devil

on the farm. He's old enough. I've been too easy on him. No more. He's just a blerry sissy, man. Look . . .' He pinches Bokkie's skinny arm. ' . . . Where's the muscle, hey? You must make him eat meat, Florence.' Gerrit grins suddenly. 'I know what. We'll get him some meat, now, hey, Florence. Go and fetch a chicken and a kitchen knife.'

Florence hesitates, glancing from Bokkie to Gerrit and back in consternation.

'Go on! Hurry up!' Gerrit growls, and she scurries off, too frightened of him to disobey his orders.

Gerrit leers into Bokkie's shocked face. 'Today, you will learn a first job on the farm. Today I will teach you how to be a man and kill a chicken.'

Bokkie doesn't say anything. His small body is rigid in the pincer-like grasp of Gerrit's thick fingers. He stares at Gerrit without blinking, and there is something in his dark expressionless gaze that makes Gerrit avert his eyes, and scratch himself uncomfortably, and shuffle his feet while they wait in the hot dusty yard.

When Florence returns, Gerrit tells her to give Bokkie the squawking chicken and the knife. Bokkie looks at the chicken. Then he looks at Gerrit. Shaking his head, he clasps his arms firmly behind his back.

Gerrit's rage builds up in him again. Keeping a stranglehold on Bokkie with one hand, he makes Florence wrap her apron tightly round the chicken like a strait-jacket, and truss up its legs with the strings. Then he takes the chicken from her and shoves it between his thighs, pinioning it as in a vice.

'Now the knife,' he snarls, snatching it. ' . . . Now give me your hand,' he shouts at Bokkie.

Bokkie shakes his head. His face has blanched almost as white as the chicken's feathers. Florence starts weeping.

'Please, Baas. Please don't make him, Baas,' she begs.

'Go back to the kitchen,' he orders her. 'This is between him and me. So *voetsek*!'*

'Please, Baas,' she wails.

'*Voetsek*!' He waves the knife at her threateningly.

She backs off. Hiding her face in her hands, she turns and flees.

Gerrit slides his hand down Bokkie's arm to the elbow and yanks it. Bokkie cries out in pain and pitches forward. If he tries to struggle free now, he will break his arm. Gerrit presses the knife handle into Bokkie's other hand, and squeezes his own fingers round Bokkie's so Bokkie can't drop the knife. Then he forces the blade down on the back of the chicken's neck, and starts sawing.

It is not the quickest way to kill anything. The chicken swivels its head desperately, making terrible noises. Blood starts to spurt everywhere. But finally the head is severed. Gerrit lets go of Bokkie's hand, dips his fingers in the blood gushing from the raw neck stump, and smears it over Bokkie's cheeks. Then he releases him.

'Now I have made a man of you,' he says. 'Next time, you will kill a chicken on your own.'

Bokkie stands, staring at him mutely.

Gerrit starts to feel uncomfortable. His anger is gone. In its place is a sour sensation in his stomach. He is aware of how dry his throat is, and how much he needs a brandy. The body of the chicken is still pinioned between his thighs. He lets it drop to the ground and steps back out of the pool of blood.

'You can clean up this mess,' he says gruffly. 'And give the chicken to Florence. Tell her she can have it.'

For a few moments more, Bokkie continues to look at him. Then he turns round slowly and, very straight-backed, walks away across the yard.

'Hey!' Gerrit shouts. 'Where do you think you're going? Come back here.'

Bokkie carries on walking. Florence, who has been

* Voetsek – Go!

viewing the scene through the pantry window, comes flying out of the kitchen and hares after Bokkie, crying. She grasps his arm, but he shakes her off, and strides on determinedly, leaving her behind. She and Gerrit watch him go through the gateway, and start down the dirt farm track that leads to the main road. His little figure diminishes until it disappears finally behind a line of trees.

Florence falls to the ground and beats her head with her palms. Gerrit shuffles shamefacedly into the house to pour himself a stiff drink.

Bokkie hasn't returned by nightfall. Pixie discovers from Florence what happened out in the yard. Tearfully, Florence acts out the whole traumatic drama in emotional and minute detail, demonstrating every action taken and every line of dialogue – including the noises of the dying chicken; so that Pixie is made to feel as if she was there herself.

'I'll kill him! I don't care if he is my father. I'll kill the bastard!' she swears. But she means it only in the heat of the moment. Once she has cooled down a little, she is all too aware of her own helplessness as a child to do anything, except hate Gerrit with every fibre of her being.

Bokkie doesn't return the next day, nor the next, nor the next. Pixie saddles up Ifu and searches for him, visiting all his favourite haunts on the farm. She braves the dark overgrown tunnel through the bush to their creek, treading fearfully with eyes darting about, imagining every rustle of leaves or snapping of a twig to be a mamba. But Bokkie isn't at the creek. Pixie doesn't find a trace of him anywhere on the farm, though she keeps searching each day hopefully.

After a week has passed, Gerrit organizes a search party. He sends all his black labourers off to scour the countryside. He has Florence drive his wife in the donkey cart to the nearest farms, to find out if Bokkie has turned up at one of them. And Gerrit himself climbs into his battered old pick-up, and trundles up and down the local roads and byways, stopping to ask anyone he meets if they've seen a young coloured boy aged twelve. But he doesn't go to the police; Gerrit doesn't believe this is a matter for the cops. And anyway, Bokkie's birth was never registered, so how could the Law trace someone who officially doesn't exist? – as he gruffly explains to Pixie when she hysterically insists Bokkie's disappearance should be reported to the authorities.

The concerted search for Bokkie proves fruitless. There hasn't been a single sighting of him in the entire neighbourhood. It is as if he has disappeared off the face of the world. Weeks pass, and Bokkie starts to be forgotten by the people on the farm, except for Pixie and Florence – and possibly Gerrit who has taken to shutting himself up in his study in the evenings with a bottle of brandy. His hangovers in the mornings do nothing to improve his general irascibility.

Finally, as the weeks turn into months, even Pixie stops looking for Bokkie. But she won't accept that he is dead. She sustains a belief that one day he will turn up again, and everything will be all right. Her faith keeps her going. She finds consolation in her art, though her pictures at this time are dark and disturbing – dead trees silhouetted against a black sky, or soldiers killing each other in battle with pools of blood on the ground. Gerrit doesn't like them. He won't look at them. Pixie leaves them lying around where he can't help but notice them. Her paintings are cathartic, but they have also become a form of revenge on Gerrit.

Then, one day Bokkie does turn up again, as suddenly and silently as he left. Everything is not all right, though. There is a marked change in him. He is withdrawn. He is also mute; he can't, or won't talk – not even to Pixie. Outwardly he looks the same, but he seems somehow to have aged way beyond his years. When you peer into his eyes, you feel as if it isn't a small boy looking back at you, but a little old man.

Gerrit drives Florence and Bokkie, in the back of his pick-up, to the non-European hospital, which is a long distance from the farm. The doctors there examine Bokkie, but can find no physical cause for his muteness. So Florence takes Bokkie to consult the local witchdoctor. After spending a few hours alone with him, the witchdoctor informs Florence in an awed voice that there is an ancient wise spirit inside Bokkie, and she mustn't worry, he will talk again when he is ready to.

Bokkie's bed in Florence's room remains empty. Bokkie now sleeps on a blanket in the tractor shed next door. Before dawn each day, he slips away into the darkness and doesn't return until dusk. Pixie tries to discover where he goes to. In the afternoons, she rides around the farm looking for him. He is never at the creek; he is never anywhere else either.

But, eventually, she does discover where he is spending the daylight hours. It isn't on the farm. It is in a sort of no man's land – a steep rugged krans cresting the bushy brow of a hill, which marks the boundary between the de Jagers' and the next farm. The krans is the playground of monkeys. One late afternoon, riding along the path below the hill, Pixie spots a diminutive dark figure sitting on a ledge of rock near the summit. At first she thinks she is seeing a monkey; the figure is too high up and too far away to be distinctly visible. But when she shades her eyes and stares hard, she realizes it is Bokkie. She waves. He doesn't wave back, though she is aware he is watching her.

After that, Pixie gives up on him, and withdraws into her own loneliness. Her school holidays start. The first morning, in a desolate mood, Pixie packs up her art materials and sets off on Ifu for the creek; driven by the need to escape her own unhappiness in the farmhouse, rather than any expectation of finding Bokkie at their former refuge. She is taken completely by surprise, therefore, to see him sitting on the flat rock above the pool in the glade. He isn't alone. He has his arm round a young duiker, which is feeding out of his hand. Her appearance startles both of them. The duiker flees, darting away across the clearing in graceful zigzagging bounds before disappearing into the bush. Bokkie frowns at her.

'You frightened my friend,' he reprimands her gruffly.

Pixie's jaw drops. 'You spoke! Bokkie! You can speak!'

He shrugs, as if it isn't of any great importance and stretches out on his back. Cushioning his head on his forearm, he stares up at the sky. 'Did you come here to draw?' he asks.

Pixie lets go of her satchel, and clambers up the rock. She feels suddenly very angry. All the bottled-up emotions of months burst out of her in a furious rush of words. 'Is that all you can say? Don't you care about— don't you realize how worried I've been about you and hurt and—'

In mid-flow, she breaks off as he turns his gaze on her. She isn't prepared for the look of forlornness in his eyes. It cuts her to the quick. Remorsefully, she kneels beside him and touches his elbow.

'Bokkie, please tell me,' she pleads, 'what happened to you? Where did you go when you ran away from the farm?'

'I went to look for my mother.'

He sits up. Hugging his knees, he unexpectedly starts sobbing. The noise of his crying is like a dam bursting inside his small slender body; a dam of grief pent-up so long that its release is uncontrollable. Pixie doesn't know what to do. She holds him and waits helplessly, wanting to cry herself. At last the spasms subside. Bokkie sucks in air and gives a long shuddery sigh. It is over. He has emptied himself out. Weakly, he rubs his face dry on his shirt. Pixie hands him her hankie so he can blow his nose.

'You didn't find your mother?' she asks as gently as possible.

Bokkie looks at her. His face is calm now. He points at the ground. 'She is my mother,' he says.

Pixie doesn't understand. 'Do you mean your mother is dead, and buried?'

He shakes his head. The crying has polished his eyes;

there is a deep dark shine to them. 'You can go to a lot of places looking for something,' he says, 'but you won't find it.'

'Find what?' she asks.

'Why people are cruel, and hate, and hurt, and kill things.'

'I'm sorry,' Pixie blurts out guiltily. 'I'm sorry about my father. I'll never forgive him.'

Bokkie shakes his head. 'Nobody understands,' he says sorrowfully, and from the way he is looking at her, Pixie knows he means her too. 'That's what's sad. You have to be able to be very quiet inside, and then you know.'

'What? Why people are cruel and—?'

'No.' A small tentative smile briefly touches the corners of his lips. 'Why animals can be happy even when they are empty and hungry and alone because they can feel God inside them. But people can't feel God inside them. They think God is outside – in the sky or somewhere. If they could really feel God inside them, then they would be able to see that God is inside everything else as well, and they would be kind.'

Pixie remembers Bokkie saying before that he could see God inside himself as a golden light. She shuts her eyes and tries to see a golden light. She can't. She tries to feel God inside her. She can't.

'What does God feel like?' she asks.

When Bokkie doesn't answer, she peers at him through her lashes. He has gone very still, as he used to do; sitting cross-legged, with his hands folded, and his eyes closed. The sun has bronzed his body the same warm brown as the rock supporting him. He looks like a statue. Pixie's fingers itch to sculpt him. She fetches her pad and tries to sketch his serene expression. But she finds it difficult to concentrate; she keeps wanting to reach out and touch him. Frightened by the new intensity of her feelings, she creeps away to the pool.

Stripping, she wades in, welcoming the numbing effect of the cold water. After thrashing about for a while, she looks up. Bokkie is no longer where he was before. Having removed his clothes, he is now sitting right on the edge of the rock, directly above her. She splashes water up at him.

'Jump!'

He shakes his head, without taking his eyes off her.

'If you don't jump, I'll come and throw you in,' she threatens.

He doesn't smile, or say anything, but continues staring at her intently.

'Don't you want to swim?'

His gaze travels over her nakedness. 'No,' he says, in a funny thick voice.

Self-consciously, Pixie gets out, collects her clothes, and joins him to sunbathe. They lie side-by-side on their stomachs. They have lain this close together hundreds of times in the past. But this time it is different. Pixie can't relax. Her heart starts thumping whenever Bokkie shifts slightly, or lifts a hand to gently brush off an ant crawling over his flesh with tiny ticklish feet. She pretends to be an ant, and walks her fingertips lightly down his back. His hand comes up and connects with hers. His head twists round. He looks surprised, then he smiles.

'Do you love me, Bokkie?' she asks shakily.

'Yes,' he says, before the words are even out of her mouth.

'Then promise you won't leave me again.'

He nods. And that's when it happens. Somehow their faces come close together, and they kiss clumsily and shyly. He touches her hair and strokes it very softly, as if he is stroking a wild animal. Then, trembling all over, he jumps up, keeping his back turned, and pulls on his clothes.

'We must go now,' he says gruffly, and he bounds off the rock and runs to wait for her at the entrance to the path through the bush.

After this day, Bokkie starts spending more time on the farm. He plants vegetables on a stony patch of spare land that isn't being used for anything. The soil isn't arable, but Bokkie's vegetables grow as if by magic. Within a few months, he is supplying everyone on the farm with all the fresh greens they can eat. He always plants extra rows of everything for his furred and feathered friends. Gerrit cannot understand how Bokkie manages to cultivate such succulent produce on ground that is virtually arid sand. It defeats all the logic of Gerrit's lifetime of farming experience. He says nothing to Bokkie. He and Bokkie avoid each other.

Whenever it is possible, Pixie and Bokkie meet secretly at the creek. They no longer get undressed in front of each other, however; or swim naked. Pixie swims in a bathing costume, Bokkie in his shorts. It isn't something they talk about, but they would just feel self-conscious and shy, having no clothes on when they are together now. Their relationship has changed. Something significant has been declared between them, causing them to view each other in a new light – a light that makes the leaves shine brighter, and the grass, and the sky, even on the dullest day. They hold hands as they lie on their rock; sometimes they kiss and cuddle. They give each other presents, small love tokens. Bokkie never arrives at the creek without a flower to put in Pixie's hair.

He is eating more now that he is growing his own food, and his skinny adolescent body is filling out with lean compact muscle that delights the artist in Pixie; though she doesn't draw very much these days – at least not while she is with Bokkie. She considers their stolen time together too precious to spend on her own preoccupations. But she likes to sit and feast her eyes on him, while he plays with the wild animals that inevitably turn up when he is there. The shy young duiker has become a regular visitor. Bokkie goes down on all fours and gambols with it. The first time he did it, Pixie couldn't help laughing because he looked ridiculous, running about on his hands and feet with his bottom sticking up in the air. Mockingly, she called him a monkey. But he didn't react to the jibe. He didn't even realize he was being ridiculed.

'I'm not as clever as a monkey,' he said solemnly. 'They know which roots and berries and leaves are poisonous. I don't, or didn't, until I learned from them.'

Bokkie is different to most other people. He believes animals aren't inferior to humans, so you can't insult him by calling him one. While she is with Bokkie, Pixie feels different in herself too, and happy. But when she is away from him, she becomes depressed and full of fear. She is in love and can't tell anyone; she is terrified of anyone finding out she loves a coloured boy. She begins to doubt the rightness of her feelings for Bokkie. Until she sees him again, and all her doubts and fears disappear.

A year passes. It is a Sunday in early summer. Bokkie and Pixie are at the creek. They are lying on their rock, holding hands. Pixie is studying Bokkie covertly out of the side of her face. He looks as if he could be asleep, except that he is wearing a blissful smile. After a while he sighs, and blinks, and gazes up at the sky. It seems to take a moment for his eyes to focus, as though he is returning from somewhere far away inside himself. Pixie feels a little cold tingle up her spine, and squeezes his hand.

'Where did you go, Bokkie?' she asks timorously. 'To God?'

He breathes in and out slowly. 'We don't die,' he says in a strangely husky voice that doesn't sound like his own. 'Not really die.'

'How do you know?'

'I *know*,' he says.

'How?'

'When the sun sets, and it grows dark, where is the sun?'

'It's still there, somewhere in the sky, only we can't see it.'

He looks at her. His eyes seem very big, and bottomlessly black like the sky at night, with little stars of reflected light in them. 'What happens to the sun is what happens to us when we die,' he says.

Pixie shivers. 'I don't want to die. Not ever.'

'Never ever ever!' And he grins, and is a boy again. A happy boy who grins a lot these days.

'I'll be like the princess,' decides Pixie, 'the one in the picture book who sleeps forever until—'

'The frog prince comes along and kisses—'

'That's a different story. It's not the frog who—'

'I'd rather be a frog than a prince,' he says, and croaks. Then he kisses her, like a frog, with his mouth stretched wide and his lips pressed tightly together.

'Yuk!' Pixie pushes him away, giggling.

A second later, a sudden deafening shout from the bush near the entrance to the creek makes them both jump in fright. As they clamber to their feet, they see a figure charging towards them across the clearing, waving its arms. Recognizing Gerrit, for a moment, Pixie thinks he must be being chased by something. Then she notices the fury on his face and, as he starts yelling, she is gripped by terror.

'Run!' she gasps, shoving Bokkie. 'Run!'

But Bokkie stands his ground. 'You run,' and he pushes her. 'I'll hold him off.'

She pushes him back hysterically. 'He's not after me. He's after you. Run! Quick! Run!'

They are wasting valuable seconds. Gerrit is now only fifty feet away. The noise he is making, and the insane murderous look in his eyes, freeze Pixie's blood. She falls to her knees, sobbing. ' . . . oh God, please! . . . He'll kill you. RUN!'

But still Bokkie doesn't run. Pale-faced and trembling, he jumps in front of Pixie to protect her, as Gerrit reaches the bottom of the rock. Gerrit pulls up, panting. Swearing at Bokkie in Afrikaans, he starts unbuckling his belt.

'You little kaffir bastard!' he bellows. 'I'll flay you alive for messing with my daughter.'

Pixie is suddenly galvanized into action. Grabbing a stone, she springs to her feet.

'If you hurt Bokkie, I'll kill you,' she threatens. She is shaking so much she drops the stone and has to bend to pick it up again.

That is when Bokkie runs. Leaping down from the rock in one bound, he dodges past Gerrit, and hares off through the glade; with Gerrit in furious pursuit, roaring at him to come back. Bokkie could have escaped at this point, but he chooses to flee in the wrong direction, away from the path through the encircling barrier of bush. Afterwards, Pixie realizes he must have done it on purpose, to give her a chance to escape. It is a senseless self-sacrifice as Pixie has no intention of leaving Bokkie to fend off Gerrit on his own. Searching desperately for a stick, she finds a broken branch under a tree, and sprints after them, screaming.

But she is too late. Bokkie has been forced to run in a semi-circle along the edge of the bush, ending up back at the base of the rock where Gerrit, cutting across in a straight line, has him trapped. Before Pixie can get there, Gerrit starts laying into Bokkie with his belt, whipping him frenziedly on the head and face and shoulders. The violence only lasts a matter of seconds. But to Pixie, it seems to be being played out in slow motion, as she races towards them. Reeling under the blows, Bokkie staggers back, trips, and falls sideways, crashing his head against the sharp corrugations of the rock face. The sound of the impact reverberates in Pixie's ears like a pistol shot, as Bokkie's knees give way under him and he pitches forward. By the time she reaches him, he is lying in a crumpled heap on the ground. There is a deep gash in his left temple. At first she thinks he is dead, then she realizes he is still breathing.

After a moment, he opens his eyes. They have a vague unfocussed gaze. He doesn't respond to her voice. He doesn't seem to see her kneeling over him. His eyes stare blankly past her, up at the sky. He must be seeing something though, because his lips part slightly in a faint tranquil smile. Then his lids droop and close, and he lapses into unconsciousness.

Gerrit is standing a few feet away, clutching at his chest. His face, blotchy purple a minute ago, is now ashen. Pixie screams at him.

'Do something! He's badly hurt. Do something!'

Avoiding looking at her or Bokkie, he shakes his head – as if he doesn't want to believe her.

'I'll kill you!' Pixie snatches up the branch she has discarded, and throws it at him with all her strength. It hits him on the arm. He doesn't even flinch. He seems stupefied. 'Do something!' she shrieks.

'What?' he says finally.

'Get help. Fetch a doctor. Hurry!'

He nods and starts to shamble off.

'Oh, for God's sake, *please* hurry,' Pixie sobs, and he breaks into a stumbling run.

Once he has gone, Pixie is suddenly numb and calm, as if she has become detached from herself and can't feel anything at all. She sits, cradling Bokkie's head in her lap. He looks peaceful. He looks like he is asleep. His breathing is slow and slight, but regular. She is reassured by this, and watches the gentle rise and fall of his chest, experiencing a sense of awe at the miracle of the breathing process. She thinks she is only imagining the interval between each breath is growing longer. Closing her eyes, she prays fervently.

When she next tries to feel for his pulse, she can't find it. He has stopped breathing. Numbly, she stares down at the shuttered eyelids with their fringe of curly lashes. She is conscious of a sudden peculiar stillness, as though everything around her has paused in its activity to honour the dead. Minutes pass. Then there is a slight movement – a shadow shifts on the periphery of her vision. Startled, she glances round; fearful, yet also half-hoping to see a ghost – Bokkie's ghost, returning from wherever he has gone to reassure her. In the twilight zones of the undergrowth, a small pointed face with large dark eyes gazes back at her. It is Bokkie's friend – the duiker. Pixie wills it silently to come closer. It sniffs the air, nervously indecisive.

'Bokkie's gone away. He's left us,' she tells it gruffly.

At the sound of her voice, the duiker pirouettes round in panic, and bounds off into the shadows. Pixie too now experiences a sudden panic. Bokkie has gone; the duiker has gone; she is sitting all alone in an isolated spot, nursing a dead body. For an instant, she is tempted by a desperate impulse to jump up and run after the duiker. Instead, she steels herself to lower Bokkie's head carefully on to the ground; before letting out a wild howl and fleeing down to the pool to try and wash the blood stain off her shorts.

Splashing in the shallows, she is suddenly convinced Bokkie is alive. With her heart hammering, she sprints back to where she left him. The only signs of life are the flies buzzing and settling in his head wound, and on the red weals caused by Gerrit's belt. She lifts his fingers. They are cold and stiff. The numbness inside her reasserts itself. She swats uselessly at the flies; then she remembers the towels she brought in her satchel. She fetches them, and very carefully lays them as a shroud over Bokkie's body.

Dimly, she is conscious of how much time must have passed. It bothers her briefly that Gerrit should have been back by now with a doctor; until she remembers there is no longer any need for a doctor. She puts that thought out of her mind in order to try and concentrate on what she has to do next. But there doesn't seem to be anything to do next, except wait. Flopping down, she hugs her knees under her chin and sits, staring vacantly into space.

When Gerrit returns, he is alone. Wordlessly, Pixie watches the reactions on his face: fear, as he lifts the towels covering Bokkie; then sudden unexpected anguish. Sinking on to his knees, he bursts into tears.

'*Ag nee, my seuntjie,*'* he snivels. '*Ag, nee!*' Pressing Bokkie's hand between his huge fists, he rocks back and

---

* Ag nee, my seuntjie – Oh no, my little son

forth, blubbering. 'I didn't do it. I didn't kill him. He fell. *You* saw,' he sobs, glancing round at Pixie pleadingly.

She says nothing; just stares at him with eyes like blue ice.

Gerrit pulls himself together, and mops his face. Lifting Bokkie into his arms, he sets off, stoop-shouldered, and dragging his feet. Pixie follows a short distance behind. Gerrit has left his pick-up at the top of the grassy slope leading down to the creek. He lays Bokkie's body in the back, and ropes it to the sides to prevent it sliding about too much on the journey home. Pixie refuses to climb in the cab with Gerrit. She climbs in the back with Bokkie, and cushions his head on her lap. The rough track they have to follow is pitted with pot-holes. Pixie sits, watching Bokkie's body being bounced and jiggled – giving the impression he is alive and struggling to free himself from his bonds.

When they finally reach the farmyard, Florence is waiting. She heaves herself over the back end of the pick-up, and throws herself on the corpse, weeping and wailing. Pixie hangs about until Bokkie's body has been carried into Florence's room, where she knows it will be safe. Then she saddles up Ifu, and gallops all the way to the police station, with the intention of having Gerrit arrested for murder.

The sergeant on duty and a young constable accompany Pixie back to the farm, following patiently behind Ifu in their police van. Pixie wants to show them Bokkie's body, but Gerrit appears and they talk to him first. He tells them he caught Bokkie trying to rape his daughter and they are immediately sympathetic. Hysterically, Pixie accuses him of lying.

The policemen go and inspect the body, and reach their own conclusions. They regard Pixie with abhorrence. Their pity is directed at Gerrit, for having a daughter who obviously likes nigger boys. They inform him that he's saved them a lot of bother. They say that if he had laid a charge against Bokkie instead of dealing with him in his own way, Bokkie would have been brought to trial and hung. But that would have involved the police in hours of paperwork and what not. They and Gerrit then discuss what to do about the body. When Gerrit explains that Bokkie was an abandoned baby and his birth wasn't registered, the sergeant is relieved. It means he won't have to bother with paperwork at all.

'So the piccanin was a non-person,' he concludes. 'Officially he never lived; therefore, officially he never died either,' and he winks at Gerrit. 'Just bury the corpse, man, and that will be the end of the matter as far as we're concerned.'

They shake hands. Gerrit then takes the two men into the house for a brandy. Pixie runs off into the veld, feeling small and puny and powerless, and so choked with outrage and grief that she has to explode. She climbs to the top of the nearest hill and bawls her lungs out at the empty sky. Finally, she falls asleep in exhaustion. It is dark and chilly when she wakes up. From her vantage point, she can see the lights of the farmhouse in the valley below. Shivering in her shorts and T-shirt, she waits until her parents' bedroom light goes out. Then she creeps down the hill.

The back door is never locked at night. Pixie feels her way through the dark kitchen into the passage, and sees a soft glow of lamplight coming from Gerrit's study. She tiptoes up to the doorway. Gerrit is sitting slumped over his desk, nursing his head in his hands. Next to his elbow are an empty bottle of brandy, and a box of ammunition. His shotgun is resting against the edge of the desk. Pixie stares at the leather belt round his middle. In her mind, she sees Gerrit unbuckling the belt, as she and Bokkie cower on the rock above him. She remembers the rage in his voice and she remembers the expression in his eyes. And she realizes this is her chance to kill him. Rushing forward, she grabs the shotgun, and backs off out of reach, pointing it at him.

Gerrit looks up. He tries to focus on her, but he is terribly drunk. His vision is either too blurred to notice what she is holding, or he doesn't care. He struggles to speak.

'You've come back.' The words are heavily slurred. He makes an attempt to grin. 'I knew you would. I told her . . . your . . . mother not to . . . worry . . .' Swaying, he topples back in the chair. 'I've been waiting for . . . Go . . . bed now.' His head is wobbling. It drops forward on his chest. His eyes shut.

Pixie lays the gun down, and dives to the open window to be sick. But she hasn't eaten since breakfast; there's nothing to come up. She retches ineffectually. When she turns round, clutching her stomach, Gerrit has pulled himself upright. Hanging on to the chair arms for support, he squints towards her, rheumy-eyed.

'I had to do . . . Protect my little girl. I followed . . . I saw . . . I saw . . . He tried to kiss her. I . . . had to . . . Oh God . . . Almighty!' He begins whimpering like a baby. Tears stream down his face, as he blabbers on incoherently in Afrikaans about God letting him down, even though he'd always believed in Him, and read the Bible, and gone to church and said his prayers every night.

It is as if he doesn't see Pixie standing there, and is talking to himself. He doesn't even seem to notice when she runs past him and out of the door.

In her bedroom, Pixie frenziedly stuffs some clothes and other belongings into a rucksack. On her way out through the kitchen, she grabs some food, and a canteen of silver cutlery which she hopes she will be able to sell as she doesn't have any money. Saddling up Ifu in the dark, she mounts and rides off in the direction of the main road. She doesn't know where she is going. She doesn't care what happens to her. She only knows she cannot stay on the farm. It is after midnight, and exactly a week before her fourteenth birthday.

7

I close the notebook.

Dusk has invaded the living-room. I hadn't noticed, or been aware that I was having to strain my eyes to decipher the last handwritten pages of *The Story of Bokkie*. My body is cramped and achy from sitting still for so long. Stiffly, I get up, and draw the curtains and switch on the lamp. Then, tucking the notebook under my arm, I tiptoe to the bedroom. In the shadows of semi-darkness, I can distinguish Pixie's shape under the sheet. But I can't tell if she is asleep. Without bothering to undress, I climb in and hug her.

'What's the time?' she mumbles.

My throat is swollen and tight. 'I don't know,' I rasp.

'I feel terrible. I'm drunk.' Her hand clasps mine. '... I'm sorry.'

'Can I get you anything?'

'No,' she moans. 'Just keep holding me. It stops the room spinning.'

'Pixie,' – I swallow painfully – 'I read your notebook.'

She turns her face away.

'I'm so sorry,' I gulp.

'For what?'

'For what happened to Bokkie. And to you.'

She struggles to sit up, and falls back, clutching her forehead. 'Where is it?'

'The notebook? It's ...' I feel around on the edge of the bed for it, and hold it out. '... Here.'

'I shouldn't have kept it,' she says. 'Tear it up.'

'No,' I protest. 'You don't mean that.'

But she does mean it. She won't wait until she is sober. She makes me destroy it, page by page, in front of her. After I've thrown all the bits on to the floor, we lie and hold each other in the darkness. I try to stop thinking about the notebook now, only I can't; even though I won't be able to read it again, every word of the story is indelibly engraved on my mind.

'My love.' I caress her cheek. 'Will you tell me something? Where did you go when you left the farm that night on Ifu.'

'I didn't get far. The police found me and brought me back.'

'And then?'

She moves my hand up to her forehead. 'What do you mean, and then?'

'Did you run away again?'

'Yes. And the police brought me back, and advised my parents to send me to boarding school. I agreed to go, on the condition I could take Ifu and keep him near the school, and not come home in the holidays.'

'So that's when you started staying with Cecily. Have you never returned to the farm since?'

'Only once, briefly, last year, for my mother's funeral ... Oh God!' She clamps her hand suddenly over her mouth. 'I think I'm going to be sick.'

I manage to get her to the bathroom in time. She is in there, with her head down the loo, for ages. But afterwards, she feels better, and sits up in bed and sips black tea, and nibbles the toast I've made. Her cheeks are very sallow though. I'm still worried about her.

Intercepting my gaze, she smiles contritely. 'I must look a mess.'

'You don't,' I lie.

'Well, you look a bit blurry to me,' she says. 'I think I'd better put my head down again.'

I tidy the bed, and tuck her in, and switch off the bedside lamp.

As I'm going out the door, she calls, 'Sam?'

'Yes?'

Her face is a pale moth on the dark pillow with two

black spots on its wings – her eyes. 'It's over, Sam. The past. I want to forget about it.'

'Good,' I say.

'And Sam . . .' her voice flutters. 'I *do* love you.'

'Good. You can go to sleep now,' and I walk down the passage with the tightness back in my throat.

*   *   *   *

But it isn't over. Even if Pixie says she wants to forget about the past; I can't. Not now I've read the notebook and know the full story. I thought I had exorcised a ghost in the bedroom when the portrait of Bokkie was removed. But now the ghost is inside me. I'm haunted by vivid mind-pictures of the little boy who loved animals and found God in everything; and the little girl who loved him; and the man who killed him because he couldn't find God in anything, not even himself, and so believed in a god who reflected his own fear and resentment and anger. I try not to think about it all, but I'm not able to forget. And I believe Pixie isn't able to, either.

The first thing she does, once she has recovered from her hangover, is go out and buy a vegetarian cookery book. She spends hours poring over it, and experimenting with recipes. The results are very palatable. After a week of nut roasts, bean casseroles, shepherd's pies made out of soya mince, and various egg and cheese dishes, I admit I haven't missed eating meat at all and agree to take it off our shopping list.

My mother is horrified when I casually mention to her over the phone that I have become a vegetarian. She claims my brain cells will atrophy if I don't include animal protein in my diet, and rushes in the next day with a carrier bag full of packets of ProNutro and vitamin pills. It is a flying visit as usual. Nick is waiting in the car downstairs to whisk her off to the South African Broadcasting Corporation to record a radio play.

Russ's reaction is more positive. Pixie invites him to dinner, and he has three helpings of her spicy stir fry with cheese noodles; after which he declares his willingness to join the club, providing Pixie can persuade Mercy to cook him vegetarian meals. Pixie decides the task is too formidable for her and delegates me. I decide I'm not brave enough to deal with Mercy either, and we all laugh. We always laugh a lot when Russ visits. He can inevitably be counted on to be good company.

Our change of diet isn't the only change though. There is a more disturbing change in Pixie that has to do with her work. I only find out about it when a cheque arrives from Cecily, with a covering letter explaining that she has managed to sell all of the paintings Pixie sent her. Pixie lets me read the letter. I have to smile; the large loopy handwriting clearly transmits Cecily's force of personality. The consonants and vowels seem to bounce along each line in a peremptory manner, marshalled at junctures by platoons of exclamation marks. The gist of the contents is that Pixie's new style has created quite a stir in the gallery, and Cecily sees this as Pixie's big chance to establish her reputation. She wants Pixie to 'work like the clappers' and produce enough paintings for an exhibition, to which will be invited 'all the press, and anybody who is anybody in the art world, sweetie'.

I fold the lavender scented pages and hand them back to Pixie. 'Congratulations. It's great news, isn't it?'

'The cheque is. It'll pay the bills for a while.'

Winter has arrived, and this particular evening is bitterly cold with a howling wind. We are sitting huddled over an electric bar heater in the living-room. I rub my hands and warm them on my mug of hot chocolate.

'If you have an exhibition, you could become rich and famous, my love.'

She smiles at my exuberance as she lights a cigarette. 'I can't have an exhibition.'

'Why ever not? All you've got to do is slave away in your studio as Cecily says in her letter. And bingo! . . . So what's the problem?'

'The problem is, I've decided I can't go on painting, and be like Nero fiddling while Rome burns. Even if I were able to paint masterpieces, which I'm not, they wouldn't do anything to alter the situation in this country.'

'I don't agree,' I exclaim fiercely. 'Anything you paint is a masterpiece.'

'You're very loyal, sweetheart.' Her hand touches my knee briefly. 'But you're missing the point. I feel it's time I did something more constructive with my life than paint pictures for well-off white people to buy and hang in their homes.'

'Why?' I ask, though I suspect, with a sinking sensation in the pit of my stomach, that I already know the answer.

She gives me a long hard look. 'You read the notebook,' she says tersely. 'You read newspapers. You aren't stupid or blind. You know what is being done to people in this country in the name of God, and democracy, and so-called white superiority.'

'Well . . .' I shrug. 'What can you personally do about it?'

'I don't know.' She blows smoke at the ceiling. 'Not much. I have no qualifications, apart from art. But I'd like to teach in a black school, or give art lessons to black kids in the townships.'

'You can't go into the townships,' I say in horror. 'It's far too dangerous.'

'Less dangerous than throwing bombs – which is another option, I suppose.' Her mouth has a little arch slant of a smile as she stubs out her cigarette. I presume she isn't being serious, but I'm not sure. 'So how did you get on at Wits today?' she asks.

I shrug. I'm feeling too upset to just leave it there, and change the subject. 'You know what I think the trouble is?' I tell her. 'I think you're simply going through a bad patch in your painting. You are an artist, and a damn fine one. It would be a terrible shame to give it all up.'

'A shame to whom?' she asks mildly.

'To me. To Cecily . . .' I almost add, to Bokkie, then

stop myself. I don't want to mention him if I can help it. ' . . . to the world.'

She laughs.

'You need a holiday. That's what you need,' I decide.

'You reckon?'

'Yes. Why don't we push off somewhere when varsity breaks up next week?'

'Push off where?'

'The coast? We could swim and—'

'Not me.' She shivers. 'The sea is too cold for me in July.'

'The mountains then. Or the North-Eastern Transvaal.'

'Maybe.' She shivers again. 'But it's freezing sitting here in this draught from the window. Let's go to bed, and have a cuddle, and get warm.'

Making love, I forget I'm upset. I forget everything in the voluptuousness of desire and mutual passion. Lying together afterwards, our limbs intertwined and our noses touching on the pillow, her sleepy eyes are soft with melting moonbeam light.

'Do you remember the butterfly, Sam?'

'What butterfly?'

'The one in Mrs Thornton's garden that afternoon we first met.'

'I didn't really see it. Why?'

'How long ago was that afternoon?'

'Five months, one week and two days.'

' . . . Two days . . . '

'Pixie? . . . ' I stroke her foot with my toe.

She sighs drowsily. 'It was a beautiful butterfly.'

She is smiling as she falls asleep. But a little later, she twitches in a dream and cries out, 'Don't hurt him!'

So it isn't over – the past. And now I can't sleep. Disturbing images from the story in her notebook start reeling through my mind. I clench my fists, hoping I will never meet her father because I feel, right now, I want to kill him. But I also feel jealous because she is dreaming of Bokkie, and not of me.

8

The day I bring home an armful of holiday brochures, Pixie brings home Jake. I'm waiting impatiently in the kitchen, with tempting photographs of mountain resorts spread out on the table, when she comes through the door. I switch off the radio.

'Where have you been?' I ask accusingly. 'You didn't mention this morning that you were going out. And you didn't leave a note.'

'Didn't I?' she says gaily, and gives me a kiss. Her face is pink and glowing with excitement. 'Well, I went to the Institute of Race Relations to try and find out about teaching art in Soweto. And guess who I bumped into? Jake.' She looks round. 'Where's he got to? Oh there you are. Come in Jake, and meet Sam.'

A big beefy black man looms up in the doorway behind her. I'm taken aback. I stare stiffly, as Pixie puts her arm through his and draws him into the kitchen. Smiling, he shakes my hand, while Pixie informs me exuberantly that it was just pure luck he happened to call into the Institute while she was there. She pulls out a chair for him, and busies herself filling the kettle and finding cups.

I become aware that I'm standing, bristling like a cat. I'm also aware that my wallet is lying open on the table within Jake's reach. I snatch it up and stuff it into my back pocket. His smile widens into a grin, but he doesn't say anything. He looks at the brochures.

'Planning a holiday?' He has a voice like an earth tremor; deep and rumbly, as if it comes from way down in his belly.

I continue eyeing him warily. 'Yes.'

'Soon?'

'Yes.'

He smacks his lips. 'Very nice. Then you won't be able to start straight away, Pixie?'

'What?' says Pixie. She's making a lot of noise rummaging in a cupboard.

'Start what?' I ask brusquely.

'I can't find the sugar. Can you see it anywhere?' Pixie asks me.

'It's here on the table,' Jake tells her.

'Oh good,' she says, and dumps a tray down without appearing to notice the brochures. 'So what were you saying, Jake?'

'If you're going on holiday, when will you be able to start?'

'Start what?' I say more loudly and forcefully this time.

'I'm not going on holiday.' Pixie frowns at me. 'Am I?'

'Yes. We talked about it the other day. Remember?'

'But I wasn't keen. Not in winter. It's too cold. I'd rather go in the summer. And now I've met Jake, and he's got this project, and he thinks—'

'It can wait,' Jake says hurriedly.

'No, it can't,' says Pixie.

I'm glowering at her. 'Do you mind telling me what all this is about?'

'Jake has started up a youth community centre in Soweto and he believes I might be able to help with it.'

'How?' I growl.

She shrugs. 'By giving art lessons maybe. I don't know. We haven't discussed it properly yet, have we, Jake?'

'No,' he says, smiling benignly from one to the other of us.

Pixie dunks a biscuit in her tea, and takes a bite out of it. With her mouth full, she says, 'Jake also thinks he might be able to get me a job in his school.'

'I'm a teacher,' Jake informs me. 'That's why I have so many grey hairs.'

'You haven't,' says Pixie.

He chuckles. 'My wife tells me I have.'

Pixie seems to become aware suddenly that I haven't touched my tea. 'Why don't you sit down, Sammie,' she says coaxingly.

'No! I've got work to do.'

Gritting my teeth, I sweep the brochures into a pile and dump them in the rubbish bin. So much for my hours spent in the travel agency! The route to the door is blocked by the great bulk of Jake in his chair. I try to squeeze past him. He gets up, knocking into me as he does so.

'I'm so sorry,' he says.

Ignoring him, I glare at Pixie. 'It isn't safe for you to go into Soweto on your own.'

'Well, you could come with me,' she suggests.

'You'd be very welcome, Sam,' says Jake, smiling.

'I'm too busy,' I tell him snappily.

'Sure. I understand.' Turning his back on Pixie, he looks me in the eye. 'Don't worry about your woman. She'll be safe in Soweto. We'll take good care of her, and see she comes to no harm. But here, *you'd* better take better care of this,' and he presses something into my hand – my wallet.

I gape at him. 'How did you—'

'It's a trick I learned from my nephew.'

'What trick?' Pixie asks behind him.

He chuckles. 'Nothing. Just a little private black man white man joke between Sam and me. Okay, Sam?'

I don't trust myself to speak. I walk out. In the passage, I check through my wallet; everything is still there: cash, driving licence, the photo of Jock as a puppy, and the photo of Pixie that she gave me. I go to my room and sit with a book open in front of me, fuming.

Jake stays a long time. After he has left, Pixie comes to look for me. She perches on the corner of my table, and prattles zealously about Jake's plans for her involvement in his youth centre – as if she's oblivious of my feelings on the matter. She isn't being obtuse though; I know she's simply choosing to ignore my mood, and that makes me all the more furious. I slam my book closed.

'Am I disturbing you? Are you studying? I'm sorry.' She slithers to her feet. 'I'll go,' she says. Instead, she pounces sideways and, locking her hands round my chest, starts nuzzling my ear. 'Such delectable ears you have, my Sam. Mhhmm . . .'

'Get off!' I mutter.

' . . . And eyebrows . . . mhhmm . . . and nose . . . and . . . mouth—'

I push her away. If I let her kiss me, I'll be a goner. Holding her at arm's length, I stare into her eyes. They are a seductive smoky blue. How can she be so desirable and sexy when I'm feeling so angry with her? Resentfully, I notice she is wearing a white silk blouse I haven't seen her in before.

'Is this new?' I ask, fingering the scalloped neckline.

'Yes. I bought it in a sale in town today. Do you like it?'

I remove my hands and my gaze. 'You'd better not wear it if you go into the township.'

'Why?' Her tone is amused.

'It's very revealing. Your bra is visible under it.'

'Only vaguely.' She laughs. 'I thought you'd like that.'

Aggressively, I repeat, '*If* you go into the township, you'd better not wear it.'

'I *am* going into the township,' she says, and she opens my book, places it in front of me, pats my head, and walks out bouncily.

'Pixie!'

She stops, smiling, in the doorway. 'What?'

'Have you gone crazy? Inviting a black guy you don't know into your home. You could have lost all your possessions and got both of us murdered. Didn't it even occur to you to think of the risk?'

'No,' she says mildly, 'but then I don't view every

black man as a potential thief, or rapist, or murderer. I knew I could trust Jake.'

'*Trust* him? You *knew* you could *trust* him?' I've lost control of myself. I'm shouting now. 'He *is* a bloody thief. He stole my bloody wallet.'

'So what's that sitting there on the table?' she asks, unruffled. 'Isn't that your wallet?'

'He *stole* it. He nicked it out of my pocket, then gave it back to me.'

'Oh . . .' Her face lights up. 'I see. It was the trick he mentioned. The little private joke. Well, he obviously had you sussed, didn't he?'

'Sussed?'

'You expected him to steal something, so he obliged. It's very funny. I'm going to make supper now. It will be ready in half an hour.' She disappears. A moment later, she is back. ' . . . And Sam,' she says, 'while on the subject of Jake, I expect you to be more civil to him next time he comes here.'

I snort. 'You do, do you?'

But she has gone again, without waiting for my reply.

* * * *

Pixie is very busy for the next few weeks, trying to raise money for Jake's youth centre. She is always on the phone, or rushing off somewhere in a purposeful manner, with a folder full of facts and figures and statistics. It is so unlike the Pixie I know; at least unlike the Pixie I've been used to, who had trouble getting up in the mornings, and who said she wanted to be a hermit in a cave with me and just paint all day. When she is at home now, Jake is often there. He goes out of his way to be friendly to me. I am stiffly polite in return. The two of them surround themselves with piles of documents at the kitchen table, and hold deep discussions. Sometimes I join them for a cup of coffee, but the conversation inevitably returns to politics or the situation in Soweto, and I start to feel tetchy and excuse myself and go.

Pixie has been into the township. Jake smuggled her

in without a permit, using back roads and alleyways to avoid patrolling police vans. She returned white-faced, and shocked, and angry, at some of the living conditions she had seen. Apparently, Jake had taken her into people's houses and introduced her to a lot of his friends. But she hadn't been able to see the youth centre. Jake decided it was too risky for her to turn up there in broad daylight because, he said, he had just learned the police were watching the place and looking for any excuse to close it down.

That information doesn't exactly make me feel less worried about Pixie's intended involvement in the centre. She isn't put off, however. Quite the contrary. It is after her visit to Soweto that she embarks on her fund-raising efforts, throwing herself into the task with sudden seemingly boundless energy and enthusiasm.

Now that I'm on holiday from university, I don't know what to do with my time while Pixie is so busy. My mother and Nick are away in Cape Town, where my mother is rehearsing for her next play – *Hamlet*. She is thrilled to be doing Shakespeare, but upset that she is too old to play Ophelia and has to settle for being Queen Gertrude. She rings up and invites me to come and stay with them in their hotel for a week, offering to send me the air fare. I tell her I've too much study-ing to do and can't afford the time. The truth is I don't want to go to Cape Town without Pixie, and my mother's invitation doesn't include her. Not that Pixie would agree to go, anyway, right now.

When Russ asks me to help him replace the clutch in his Morris, I'm glad of the chance to get out of the flat and spend a day in the fresh air, even if it does involve lying on my back under an oily engine, and having to cope with Mercy at lunch time. Russ warns me she is in a foul mood because her husband has been to see her and she can't stand him.

I stroke the head of the Alsatian who is sitting expect-antly next to my chair at the table on the verandah.

'Why does she stay married to him, if she hates his guts?'

Russ grins. 'You ask her, if you dare. Sshh! Here she comes.'

Mercy barges through the doorway, and dumps a dish of macaroni cheese down in front of Russ.

Pouting, she says, 'Don't finish it all up. It's for your supper too. I'm going to see the witchdoctor. Maybe I won't be back in time to cook.'

'The witchdoctor? What for, Mercy?' asks Russ. 'You aren't planning to cast a spell on your husband, I hope?'

'I want some medicine to keep him away from me.'

'Why?' I venture to ask.

She turns her scowl in my direction. 'Are you married?'

'No.' I resent the lack of respect in her tone, and the way she is looking at me.

'Men!' she exclaims, wrinkling up her nose in disgust. 'All they want from you is money, money, money, and to make babies – that's all. Tell Pixie, Mercy says she must never get married.'

Irritably, I snap, 'If you don't like your husband, divorce him.'

'Divorce? My husband?' Her eyes bulge at me. 'I can't do that.'

'Why not?' puts in Russ.

'Because he is my husband,' she says categorically, shaking her head as if we are small stupid children incapable of understanding simple facts.

Russ and I and the Alsatians watch her clump back into the house, her huge bottom wobbling behind her like an overloaded trailer on tow.

'You can't win an argument against Mercy,' Russ laughs. 'If you try to, you end up in a state of total confusion. Here, have some macaroni, and help yourself to salad.'

I think he's crazy to keep her on when she is so disagreeable, but I refrain from saying so. It is none of my business, and he wouldn't agree with me anyway;

and I have more important personal concerns on my mind.

After the meal, we carry on with the car repair. So far, neither of us has mentioned Pixie. Now he does. He asks me what she is doing today.

'Search me.' I'm having trouble trying to loosen a rusted nut. Testily, I hand him the spanner. 'You have a go.'

'Okay. But I'll need the wrench.'

'Where is it?'

'I might have left it next to the jack.'

'You didn't,' I say, looking. 'It must be in the tool-box.' Wriggling out from under the chassis, I find the wrench, pass it to him, and sit on the ground in the sun to smoke a cigarette. Frowning at his feet – the only visible part of him, I ask moodily, 'What do you think of Jake?'

'Jack? This jack, you mean? It's all right. It works as—'

'No, not jack. *Jake*. You met him the other day at the flat. The African teacher.'

'Oh, Jake. Yes... Damn! The blighter!... Aah! That's got it. Hang on, I'm coming out.'

He emerges, sliding on his back, and sits up, grinning. 'I liked him,' he says. 'He's a great guy. Great sense of humour. Why?'

I shrug. 'It doesn't worry you that he is putting Pixie into danger?'

'Danger? What danger? It isn't illegal for him to visit Pixie. She's allowed to entertain African gentlemen in her own home,' and he grimaces wryly, 'so long as she doesn't serve him liquor or have sex with him.'

He expects me to laugh. I don't. I glower at him through the smoke curling up from my cigarette.

'Oh come on, Sam,' he says. 'Surely you aren't jealous of Jake, because I really can't see there's any need to be.'

I shift uncomfortably. 'Of course not! But if the other

residents in the block find out how often he visits, all hell will be let loose.'

'True,' he admits. 'Let's hope they don't find out. At least he is being careful. Pixie told me he sneaks up the fire-escape in the side alley, and checks the coast is clear before approaching her front door. As the African cleaners use the fire-escape to get to their rooms on the roof, if a resident saw him they would probably assume he was visiting Solly or someone else up there.'

'I know all that!' Chucking my cigarette on the ground, I squash the glowing end aggressively with my heel. 'But he isn't being careful when he takes Pixie into Soweto without a permit. Did *you* know his youth centre is being watched by the police? – which means he is probably being watched as well.'

'It wouldn't surprise me,' he says mildly. 'You don't have to do anything subversive, or even be political, to be hounded by the authorities these days.'

'Yet it doesn't worry you?'

The accusation in my tone has no effect on him. He continues to regard me in an amiable manner, with his head resting back against the radiator grille of the Morris, and his lanky legs splayed out in front of him.

'I'm just glad Pixie is doing something she wants to do and that she feels is useful,' he says. 'I admire her for it.'

'Even if it lands her in jail? And me too?'

He laughs. 'The police aren't going to arrest you, Sam. You haven't done anything illegal. It's hardly likely they'll arrest Pixie either. They might put her under surveillance – for the hell of it, I expect. The sadistic swines enjoy playing a cat and mouse game with whites who don't share their racist—ouch!' He suddenly jumps, and starts shaking his foot violently.

A huge red ant drops out of his trouser leg and reels round in a drunken circle. Russ obliterates it under his thumb. Then he scrambles up hurriedly, rubbing his calf.

'The blighter bit me! Better watch out. There might be more.'

I stare blindly at the small indentation in the sand where the ant has been pulverized. A picture springs to my mind of a slim brown fawn of a boy lying naked on a rock in the sun. Ants are crawling over his back. His hand brushes them off carefully, so as not to injure their puny bodies.

'Get up, man,' advises Russ. 'Before you're nipped.'

I shake my head. 'They're only ants.'

'With jaws like sharks. I wouldn't stay there if I was you.'

I watch him lope over to the tool-box, and crouch down to consult the car manual. That day, lying naked on the rock next to Bokkie, Pixie had pretended her hand was an ant so she could touch him. That day was the day she felt the first stirring of adolescent desire. She and Bokkie kissed that day for the first time.

'Damn it!'

'What?' Russ looks round.

'Why can't Pixie let go? I know why she is doing what she's doing – it's because of how Bokkie died. She feels responsible in some sense, so now she's trying to work off her guilt by performing good deeds in Soweto. But why the hell won't she realize she can't bring Bokkie back to life? What's done is done. Why can't she forget the past and stop living with a bloody ghost?'

Russ gives me one of his discomforting laser-beam looks. Laconically, he says, 'If that's what's really bugging you, perhaps you need to ask yourself the same question.' Then he tosses the manual into my lap. 'Make sense of this, will you? It's double Dutch to me. I just hope the garage sold me the right parts. They don't appear to resemble the diagrams at all.'

We return to work. Neither of us are very mechanically minded, but we finally succeed in fitting the new clutch, and it seems to operate all right. We take the Morris for a test drive. Then Russ offers me a beer. I slurp it down in a hurry. There is a constraint between us because of what has been said. But I'm also feeling suddenly anxious to get back to the flat. I don't know where Pixie went today. I only know she was meeting Jake, and I have a nagging worry he might have whisked her off into the township again.

Russ walks with me to my car. As I'm about to drive away, he sticks his head in through the open passenger window. With a disarming grin, he says, 'Our Pixie is a free spirit. She also possesses a darn stubborn will of her own. So don't blow it, Sam. She has to follow her own conscience, and work out her own salvation – we all do. If you're too possessive or jealous, you'll screw things up.'

'Thanks for the encouragement,' I mutter.

He laughs. 'I know. I'm a pain in the butt. But I mean well.'

'Okay. Only what are you trying to tell me to do?'

'Nothing.' He flashes another grin at me. 'Just love her,' and he stands back.

By the time I've reversed and turned the Mini down the drive, he has disappeared into the house.

* * * *

I sense something is wrong as soon as I open the front door. Pixie's bag is standing next to the telephone in the hallway; but the flat is eerily silent, and gloomy with crepuscular shadows. Two empty coffee mugs and a scattering of biscuit crumbs on the kitchen table suggest Jake has been here.

Nervously, I call, 'Pixie!' and hear a mumble from the living-room.

I dive across the passage. In the twilight within the room, a dark lumpy shape is discernible on the sofa.

'Pixie?'

'Don't switch the light on,' she says.

'Why?'

'I'm thinking.'

'Can't you think in the light?'

'No,' she says. 'But I'd like a drink. I don't suppose we have any alcohol in the flat, do we?'

'As a matter of fact, we do,' I tell her.

When I had parked the Mini, I discovered a bottle of

wine under my overalls on the back seat, which Russ must have put there. I fetch it from the kitchen with two glasses and a candle. Pixie makes room for me on the sofa, and asks me how my day went.

'It went okay. We fixed the clutch. Russ sends his love.'

'Thanks.' As she lights a cigarette, I notice the elastoplast on her palm.

'What happened to your hand?'

'I cut it on some glass. I broke the lamp in here, and the bulb shattered.'

'Crikey! Let me look.'

'It's nothing,' she says, but she gives me her hand. Her fingers feel cold, as does the rest of her when I put my arm round her shoulders.

'What happened? Did you knock the lamp over?'

'No. I threw it on the floor. I was angry.'

I peer into her face. In the dark pools of her eyes, little fireflies of light flicker as miniature reflections of the candle flame. She smiles.

'It's all right. I'm not angry now,' she assures me.

'You're cold though.'

I get up to switch on the electric heater, and drag it closer. Then I cuddle her again. She doesn't respond. She lets herself be held like a rag doll, as if she has no volition of her own. I'm sure whatever has upset her concerns Jake, and so I'm afraid to ask. I wait for her to tell me. She does, finally, after a second glass of wine.

'The police have closed down the youth centre,' she says in a dull, matter-of-fact voice. 'They raided it last night and searched everyone there, and supposedly found some *dagga**. But Jake says the police brought the stuff with them and planted it as evidence.'

I can feel my heart beating faster. 'How did you find all this out?'

'Jake sent a friend of his to tell me this afternoon.

* dagga – cannabis

135

Jake didn't like to come here himself in case he was followed.'

'By whom?'

Her teeth flash white in a mirthless smile. 'The police – who else? They took Jake in for questioning last night. Then they let him go this morning with a warning. So now you know, I'll get us some supper.' As she tries to rise, I restrain her.

'Warning? What sort of warning, Pixie?'

'Ouch! You're pinching me.'

'Sorry.' I release her arm. 'But what did the police say to Jake?'

She swivels round to face me. It is too dark now to see her expression, or even her features clearly. The candle is behind her, and its wavering light forms a fluctuating ghostly radiance round her outline that adds to the creepy feeling of fear down my spine. When she speaks, it is in the same dead voice as before:

Jake is known to the authorities, not as a political activist – which he isn't, she claims; but as a teacher who, in his own meagre way, is trying to give his pupils a better education than is acceptable to the Bantu Education Department. The official strategy of the Department is to educate black children only up to the level at which they will have the basic skills necessary to be useful labourers in the white economy, while denying them access to the sort of learning that might encourage them to start thinking for themselves and begin to question the status quo.

Jake, explains Pixie, is a thorn in the flesh of the Department because, although he sticks to the syllabus as prescribed, he takes pains to point out its failings to his pupils, and provides them with free extra lessons out of school hours in which he uses textbooks and other teaching material not available at the school. His extra-mural teaching activities became known to the Special Branch through their efficient system of spies in the township; and that is why, according to Pixie, they are now embarked on a vindictive campaign against him.

'So why haven't they put him in prison?' I ask. 'Even if he isn't breaking the law, they could nail him on some trumped up charge, surely?'

'Why should they?' There is a sudden cutting edge to her tone. 'They're having more fun right now, trying to frighten and intimidate him. Anyway, it's possible, I suppose, knowing them, that they find it hard to believe he is acting off his own bat, and isn't part of some underground plot to overthrow the government. Maybe they're hoping to use him as bait to catch larger fish to fry.'

'Maybe he is a member of a banned political organization – maybe the police know more about him than you do,' I suggest, and sense her stiffen.

'I know him better than you or the police, Sam,' she snaps, and jumps up. 'You haven't even bothered to get to know him at all. If you had, you'd realize Jake is up front about everything.'

'Even something it might be dangerous to his own safety to mention?'

'He'd tell me because he knows he can trust me,' she says, marching out of the room.

I follow her to the kitchen. I have a question that can't wait. It is worrying me too much.

'Pixie, if the Special Branch are keeping tabs on Jake, do you think they're aware that he's been visiting your flat?'

'Quite possibly,' she says coldly, clearing a space on the table.

'Then they might come and interrogate you.'

'They might.'

'You don't seem too concerned.'

'I'm not going to let the bastards frighten me – if that's what you mean. Why should I give them that satisfaction? I'll just be glad to know they're wasting their resources and time.' She opens the fridge and fishes around in it. 'There's some left-over mushroom flan. That'll have to do. What do you want with it?'

'What's the choice?' I ask.

'Cold potatoes ... or ... cold potatoes.'

'You sounded just like Mercy when you said that,' and I laugh.

She smiles now; a tired smile, but at least a friendly one. 'How is Mercy?'

'In a bad temper because she has had a visit from her husband. She said to tell you that you must never get married.'

'Seems good advice to me.'

I study her while she is standing at the sink, slicing potatoes. The fair glossy thatch of her hair, overdue for a cut, is untidy at the back and tangled over the crown, looking as if a bird might have been investigating it for a possible nesting site. She is wearing old baggy slacks, and an even baggier jersey several sizes too large. The effect seems to diminish her somehow, making her appear smaller and younger and vulnerable. She no longer looks like the efficient energetic businesswoman of the past weeks. She looks now more like a little lost waif in hand-me-downs. But even in her Charlie Chaplin get-up, she is lovely, and desirable, and quixotically feminine.

I sneak up and slide my arms round her middle. She tenses, then relaxes, leaning back against me.

'I've missed you,' I mumble, squeezing her.

She turns, and hugs me tightly. 'Yes?'

I can feel her heart beating close to mine. I inhale deeply, savouring her closeness.

'You know what I think, Pixiebell? I think we need a second honeymoon.'

'Second? We didn't have a first.'

'Not officially, no. All the more reason, therefore, to have a second one.'

'What's this? A proposal?' she asks.

'Would you like to get married?'

She pretends to consider. 'No,' she decides. 'I couldn't cope with Mercy's wrath. I'll just take the offer of a honeymoon.'

'Where do you want to go?'

'Somewhere where there aren't too many people, and no cops! And we can sleep a lot. I feel worn out.'

She does look peaky. 'You've been working too hard,' I tell her.

'It isn't that. It's . . . I don't know. I always seem to end up powerless to help.'

'You don't!' I exclaim. 'You help me.' She shakes her head. It isn't what she means. I believe she is thinking of what happened to Bokkie, as well as about Jake and his youth centre. But I don't want her to think of them. I want her to think about us. A brilliant idea strikes me. 'How do you fancy a trip to a game reserve? There shouldn't be any policemen hiding behind trees in the Kruger National Park.'

She immediately perks up. Then: 'We'll never get a booking now though,' she says. 'It's the school holidays.'

'We *will*,' I promise. 'Leave it to me.' I feel prepared to bribe someone if necessary, or even hold a gun at their head. I feel capable of moving heaven and earth to make her happy. 'But first you must tell me you love me,' I demand.

She flicks my nose lightly with her fingernail. 'I'll tell you once you've made the reservations.'

'No! Tell me now!'

'There's no need,' she says. 'I'll always love you, Sam.'

'I don't believe you. How do you know? How can you be so sure?'

'Feminine instinct. I just *know* I will,' and she pushes me away, and gets on with preparing our supper.

* * * *

As it turns out, I don't have to move heaven and earth. I only have to lift a pen and write out a cheque in the travel agency, and I'm given a last minute cancellation in one of the smaller rest camps deep in the heart of the Kruger National Park. It sounds ideal. We pack and leave that same day in high spirits. From the moment we set off, I have a gut instinct that nothing will go

139

wrong. I know it is unwise to tempt fate. But I feel in this instance, fate is on my side. And perhaps it is.

For five blissful days, our home is a humble white-washed rondavel, under scraggy trees on the edge of the rest camp. There are other rondavels, inhabited by jabbering tribes of children and their parents who presumably, like us, have come to the game reserve to be refreshed by what is left of the real Africa. Beyond the wire fence enclosing the camp, stretch miles and miles of thorn trees, open grasslands, and thick bush, freely roamed by wild animals: ferocious lions, leopards, cheetahs; lumbering giant elephants; fleet-footed antelopes of all descriptions; plump, pyjama-striped zebras; and crane-necked giraffes.

Here, in this almost primeval wilderness, it is the animals who are free, and we humans who are locked up – albeit for our own safety – at night in our wired enclosure; and during the day in the mobile metal cages of our cars, staring out at all the beasts going about their natural business. But then, as Pixie drolly comments, 'Who are the real beasts in this environment? The animals or the humans?' Observing the beer-swilling behaviour in the camp, and the mess and litter that is cleared up each day by the black cleaners, I take her point.

She is happy here. She is a different Pixie. She is like a creature of the wild that has been released from captivity and returned to its natural habitat. She doesn't *walk* anywhere – she *skips*. She is carefree, and frolicsome, and full of fun. She chases me round our rondavel in the morning, threatening to throw a jug of cold water over me when I complain about getting up at the crack of dawn. She wants to see the sun rise, and smell the first fresh scents of the new day, and listen to the birdsong and the monkeys chattering in the nearby trees. After that, she entices me back to bed for an hour before breakfast. And still she is playful, doing the dance of the seven veils, while I lie back, grinning at her groggily and remembering that she was the one who said she was very tired and wanted to sleep a lot on holiday. But then she is full of surprises. *She. Woman.* My *Pixie-woman.*

I do believe we would be truly happy if we could live like this always, in a little rondavel in the middle of the bush. Except that we would probably get eaten by lions! I can't help wondering whether, if there had been lions on the farm in Natal, Bokkie would have been able to stop them eating Pixie. I'm tempted to ask Pixie, but I don't; I'm too afraid of Bokkie's ghost intruding on our present happiness.

After breakfast, we pack a picnic lunch, and drive off in different directions from the camp each day. We try to get away from the other cars; which isn't too difficult in a game park covering eight thousand square miles. Pixie has said she wants to see every animal there is to see. I promise her we will. But she is easy to please. She is as thrilled to observe ubiquitous graceful impala grazing under thorn trees, as she is to spot the funny-monster face of a hippo lying half-submerged in a muddy pool.

One afternoon, we almost literally bump into a bull elephant standing right in the middle of the road. He flaps his tent-sized ears at us, and I reverse away rapidly. Elephants have been known to charge vehicles in the reserve. Another afternoon, we come across a long line of stationary cars with eager faces glued to the windows watching two lionesses stalking some zebras. Pixie makes me turn the Mini round as fast as possible and drive off. She doesn't want to witness a kill. Neither do I; though everyone else does, it would seem.

The one question people always ask in the camp is: 'Did you see a kill today?' as if that is the highlight of all the sights the park has to offer. When the question is put to Pixie, she assumes her set sweet smile, and replies: 'No, but we saw something a lot more fascinating. We saw two baboons mating.'

The response is predictable. Faces stiffen, and parents immediately start talking loudly to their children about something else. The first time it happens, I'm embarrassed.

'Did you have to say that?' I scold her. 'They'll think we're weird.'

'Weird?' She snatches her hand out of mine as if my fingers have suddenly given her an electric shock. 'Who do *you* honestly think is weird? Me? Or mums and dads who believe their kids ought to see and enjoy life being destroyed, but not life being created?'

She looks so obdurate, pouting at me like a small kid herself. I have a fleeting image of her as a twelve year old girl, sitting at a dining-table in a farmhouse, stubbornly refusing to eat the mutton chop on her plate and braving the wrath of her tyrannical father. That must have needed a lot of guts.

She *is* gutsy. She *is* stubborn. She *is* self-willed. And she is right: making life should be considered more suitable family entertainment than taking life. Impetuously grabbing her, I swing her up in my arms off the ground. Her foot gets hooked between my knees. I lose my balance, and bring us both down on the sand in a heap. We laugh. We are making a spectacle of ourselves now. People are staring. Pixie leans her weight on me, pinioning me down.

'You haven't answered my question,' she says.

Her eyes are as burning blue as the sunlit sky behind her head. It isn't fair. Even after all these months, she only has to look at me like this and my pulses start racing.

'You're weird,' I gasp. 'But you're also beautiful. And I think you'd make a wonderful weird mum. And . . .'

She smiles. 'Go on.'

'So maybe we should make a wonderful weird little baby some day.'

I'm joking, though I also mean it. She knows. Suddenly solemn, she gazes back at me.

'Maybe we should. One day. If you can arrange for it to be a little boy.'

'What if I don't want a little boy?'

'Then we'd have to have two. A boy and a girl.'

'Two?' The whole idea strikes me as a bit awesome now. Even intimidating. I feel far from ready for fatherhood. Frowning, I watch her get up and dust herself off. 'I don't know that I could cope with two, Pixie.'

'It'd be worse for me. You'd only have to cope with two kids. I'd have to cope with three.'

'Thanks a lot!'

She backs off, laughing. 'Come on then, sonny boy, I'll buy you a beer.'

I catch her up, and take her arm. I'm glad to know she would like to have my kids. It makes me feel good. It makes me feel like swaggering a bit as I follow her into the restaurant bar.

On the morning of our departure, after packing the car, we decide to go for a final drive around in the park, before setting off home. It is Pixie's suggestion. My plan had been to spend the day enjoying a leisurely journey, choosing the most scenic route back, rather than the quickest. But Pixie said she would like a little more time in the reserve.

'Why?' I asked her. 'Is there still something you're keen to see?'

'I just feel I don't want to leave here yet. Do you mind?'

'No. Sure,' I said. 'I don't feel I want to leave either.'

Once we are away from the bustle of the camp, she becomes silent, sitting very upright beside me in the Mini, with her hands clasped round her knees, and her eyes alert, like a gundog's, to every shadow or movement in the thick grass and bush. Yet when we spot any animals, she only gives them a cursory glance, before asking me to drive on. Her behaviour this morning is so out of character, I suppose I should have guessed really; but I don't. It doesn't even occur to me that she is searching for one particular animal; until we come round a sharp bend in the road. And there it is, suddenly – a young duiker; standing motionless in the undergrowth, as if it is waiting for us.

'Stop!' Pixie yells.

The Mini skids and skews violently to a halt on the sandy road, raising a cloud of obliterating dust. Unbelievably, when the dust clears, the duiker is still there, crouched low on its spindly legs, staring straight at us out of deep olive-dark eyes. It emits a funny little snorting sound and, a moment later, it disappears, diving headfirst into the bush with a farewell flick of its wispish white tail.

There is silence now. A strange, almost palpable silence outside. Inside the car, we are silent too. Pixie's face is turned away from me. She is staring at the spot where the duiker stood. I realize I'm still holding my breath, and let out a sigh.

'You knew! Pixie! You were looking for it. How did you know you would see a duiker?'

She tilts her head round to face me. 'Because I dreamt I would last night.' Her eyes are brimming with tears, but she is smiling. 'Oh God, Sam, I'm so happy.' Throwing her arms round my neck, she kisses me. Then she sits back in her seat. 'We can go home now,' she says.

I gaze at her, dumb-struck. She laughs.

'Don't worry,' and she squeezes my fingers. 'Everything is fine.'

I'm nonplussed, but somehow I believe her. My hand automatically finds first gear, I take my foot off the brake, and we drive on.

9

Home. Back to the daily grind of lectures. And the prospect of the end of year exams looming. And the reappearance of Jake.

But my attitude towards Jake has changed. After

everything Pixie has told me about him, I look at him in a new light and decide that I like him. My nerves are still on edge though, when he visits. If the doorbell rings, I jump, fearful it might be the police; and I can't stop myself peering furtively through the bathroom window which overlooks the side alley to see if there are any suspicious-looking characters hanging around.

It doesn't reassure me that Pixie and Jake seem totally unconcerned about the possibility of the flat being put under surveillance. In fact, they joke about it. Their attitude might be bravado. I don't know. It isn't something Pixie and I can discuss. She has said quite adamantly that as she has nothing to hide, if the Special Branch want to waste their time trying to intimidate her, then good luck to them. She also reckons I shouldn't be afraid – 'because that's letting the bastards get to you' as she puts it. I can see what she means, but it doesn't diminish my fear.

I feel no incentive to cock a snook at Apartheid, and fall foul of the police. I just want to be left in peace to get on with my life. As Pixie doesn't share my attitude, there is nothing I can do, except hope Jake won't embroil her in any new scheme like the short-lived youth centre project.

Vain hope!

Simon *could* be described as a project. He turns up one day with Jake, and is introduced as Jake's nephew. Clearly, he doesn't take after his uncle in looks or temperament. He is on the short side and skinny, with a wiry frame and a narrow tense face that seems set in a permanent scowl. When he shakes my hand, he barely grasps my fingers before he snatches his hand back, and continues fidgeting with the string of beads round his wrist. He doesn't have much to say for himself either. Jake does the talking for him, explaining to me that Simon is sixteen and he has brought him to meet Pixie because he draws and paints all the time and would like to become an artist.

'He doesn't have to become an artist,' Pixie says, and

she smiles at Simon. 'You already are one, Simon. Jake has shown me some photos of your work.'

Without looking at her, or giving any sign of having heard her, Simon pulls out a small rusty tin containing tobacco and strips of paper, and starts rolling a cigarette. I'm fascinated to see how quickly and deftly his spidery fingers complete the fiddly operation.

'That's clever,' I comment, offering him a light.

Jake laughs. 'This scallywag does have clever fingers. Too clever,' and he gives Simon a cuff on the back of his head. 'They've got him into mischief. But no more. You hear, Simon?' he says sternly. 'Or I'll have you chopped up and given to Mama Sinzi to put in the beer she makes in her shebeen.'

For the first time, Simon reacts. He breaks into a grin. The effect is remarkable. His features are transformed. Suddenly he is engagingly attractive, showing sparkling even white teeth, and deep dimples in his hollow cheeks. He has sooty black eyes, but even they light up when he smiles. I notice Pixie gazing at him keenly, and I feel a sense of unease when Jake turns to her and says:

'We'll sort him out, hey, Pixie. But if he gives you any trouble at any time, you just let me know.'

'I will,' promises Pixie, and the covert look that passes between them, fills me with foreboding.

We have tea in the living-room. Then Jake and Simon leave. As soon as Pixie returns from seeing them off at the front door, I demand to know what is going on. She sinks into the chair furthest from me, drags her feet up like a drawbridge, and contemplates me defensively over the top of her knees.

'I'm going to give Simon art lessons,' she says.

'Where? Here in the flat?'

'There isn't anywhere else.'

I glare at her. 'You might have told me.'

'I'm telling you now. It was only confirmed just now as they were leaving. Jake wanted me to meet Simon first before agreeing to do it.'

'You should have mentioned it before,' I insist. 'You ought to have discussed it with me. Why didn't you?'

'I suppose,' she says, 'because I knew you would react like this.'

'Like what?' I retort.

A small resigned smile compresses the corners of her lips. I realize my hands are clenched, and make an effort to relax while she lights a cigarette.

But when she stays silent, I feel goaded into saying, 'I think you're crazy to do it. Wait till the neighbours find out. And the police. You're playing into their hands. Don't you care?'

'I care,' she says, after appearing to consider the question for a moment. 'I care that here is someone, young Simon, who has an amazing talent which he has never been given a chance to develop. He's more gifted than I am, but he doesn't even have money to buy paper and paints.'

'Because he is still at school?'

'Still at school? You're joking!' she says bitterly. 'He would be if he was white and didn't have to pay for his education. His mother, Jake's sister, is struggling to bring up five kids on her own. She can't afford school fees.'

'That's tough,' I admit. 'What happened to her husband?'

'He walked out on her. He was an alcoholic and used to beat her up, apparently – and the kids too. Jake does what he can to help. He paid for Simon's education up to Standard Four. But that's all he could manage; he has his own family to support. So Simon has been on the streets since the age of eleven or twelve. And it's a terrible, terrible waste of his abilities. That's what I care about,' she says, viciously knocking ash off her neglected cigarette on to a nearby saucer, 'not whether the ruddy neighbours—'

'Why is Simon still on the streets?' I interrupt her. 'Can't he get a job?'

She takes her time sucking in smoke and blowing it out slowly. 'No. Not easily,' she admits.

I've put her on the spot now. She looks uncomfortable. 'Why?' I press her.

'I suppose,' she says, 'it's only fair you should know. Simon has just come out of jail.'

'My God!' I jerk upright. 'What was he in for?'

'For relatively minor offences. Petty thieving – pinching handbags, money, that sort of thing.'

I explode then. 'I knew it! I knew there was something shifty about him. You could see it in his eyes and his manner. He's a criminal and you' – I jab my finger at her – 'want to let him into your home. Are you stark raving mad?'

She sits, staring me out in silence. The phone starts ringing. Neither of us moves. It rings on and on.

When it stops, she says mockingly, 'It's very easy, isn't it, to condemn someone for stealing when you've never gone hungry, or known poverty yourself.'

'It's not *him* I condemn. It's *you*! For being so incredibly stupid!' I leap out of my chair. 'I don't know why you bother to lock your front door.' I'm stamping about, gesturing wildly. 'You might as well throw it open, and yell to the whole world to come and clean you out of all your possessions.'

'Perhaps I should. They're only possessions, after all.'

I pull up in front of her. 'It's not bloody funny, Pixie! What about my things? I live here too.'

'Yes, you do,' she says almost regretfully.

Frowning, she stubs out her cigarette. I'm suddenly afraid she is going to tell me to pack my bags and find somewhere else to live. But I can't back down. I'm too incensed.

'So?' I say, trembling.

She breaks into a smile which doesn't reach her eyes. 'Simon won't steal anything. He's coming here to paint, that's all. I trust Jake's judgement. If he felt he couldn't rely on Simon not to abuse my hospitality, then he wouldn't bring him here. He is like a father to Simon. I know all about Simon's past. I know he has problems in himself. But Jake thinks I can help him. And that is what I intend trying to do. And if you don't like it, too bad!'

Getting up, she brushes past me and starts collecting the dirty tea things. I glower at her back resentfully. There doesn't seem to be anything more I can say. Turning on my heel, I march out.

'All the same, it might be sensible to keep temptation out of harm's way, and not leave money lying around while he is here,' she calls after me.

I glance round. She sounded as though she was teasing, but there isn't any sign of amusement on her face. I throw her a furious look, go and shut myself in my room, and switch the radio on very loudly.

*　*　*　*

Wednesday is the day Pixie has set aside for Simon's art lessons. He arrives quite early, sometimes before I've left for university. Pixie takes him straight into her studio, so I don't have to talk to him, or even see him. But it unnerves and irritates me just knowing he will be there in the flat all day. I'm always in a last-minute rush in the mornings, so I doubly resent the time it takes to check I haven't left anything lying around that he might steal. And he is often still there when I get home. Even if he isn't, the place smells of him; the cloying acrid odour of his hand-rolled tobacco assaults my nostrils as soon as I open the front door, and seems to permeate the atmosphere all evening. It doesn't bother Pixie.

She admits Simon isn't the easiest person to get through to, and she often looks drained by the end of the day. But she is pleased with his progress – to put it mildly. She sings his praises as an artist to Jake and Russ, and to Cecily over the phone. Her plan is to persuade Cecily to mount an exhibition of Simon's paintings in her art gallery in the New Year. Cecily, I gather, is open to the idea. She has offered to come up to Johannesburg at Christmas and view Simon's work and talk things over, providing Pixie also has some paintings of her own to show her by then.

'Which is pure bribery, and typical of Cecily,' says

149

Pixie. She *has* started painting again though. 'Dabbling,' she calls it, 'to keep Simon company.'

I ask her to let me see what she is doing. Reluctantly, she allows me a quick look at a couple of canvases. I don't know what to expect, but I'm intrigued. Both pictures are semi-abstract impressions of the sun-baked bushveld scenery in the game reserve. Lively brush-strokes do no more than suggest the multiplicity of natural forms and textures within the landscape, and the colouring is lurid – even somewhat surreal. Nevertheless, there is atmosphere and feeling and a strong sense of animation. Despite the absence of any sign of wild game, the landscape is so vibrant, it seems to be alive in itself, pulsating with energy and heat.

I still prefer realism in art, but I do find these two particular new paintings quite exciting and powerful. I want to study them for longer, only Pixie quickly covers them up again with a sheet, and starts talking enthusiastically about Simon's paintings which are displayed all around the studio.

I've already seen some of Simon's work. It gives me the creeps. I'm prepared to accept he does possess talent, as well as a fertile imagination. He is also prolific; he manages to finish one or two paintings every Wednesday. I can't look at any of them, however, without starting to feel uncomfortable and disturbed.

The world he portrays is so grim and menacing and dark – literally dark sometimes, as in his night scenes in Soweto, where frightened figures scurry through shadows, and monstrous human shapes lurk threateningly in pitch-black alleys with the glint of a knife or other weapon in their hands. Even the most innocent-seeming object is transmuted into a violent image by his brush. When he paints a still-life, the flowers in the vase reveal tiny prison cells at their centres, or mangled foetuses dripping blood into rose petals, giving them their colour.

Quite a lot of his pictures are totally weird. He depicts mountains mating like animals; trees growing upside-down, rooted in clouds and resting their crowns of leaves on the ground; people put together in bits like a jigsaw puzzle, with pieces missing.

'What's the purpose of it all?' I ask Pixie, flummoxed.

She frowns at me. 'Don't these pictures make you think?'

'Yes,' I snort. 'They make me think Simon must be mad.'

'Perhaps it's the world that's mad, not Simon.'

'Oh, sure!' I scoff, needled by her school-marmish tone. 'Trees actually do stand on their heads, do they?'

'The human eye perceives objects upside-down. It's our brain that makes us believe we're seeing them the opposite way round.'

'Then that proves my point,' and I laugh. 'There must be something wrong with Simon's brain.'

She gives me a withering look, picks up a paintbrush off the floor, and carries it over to the table. My gaze is drawn past her to the end of the room, where Bokkie's portrait is half concealed by two of Simon's paintings propped up against it. With only the right side of his face visible, Bokkie appears to be hiding, peering out soulfully from behind a corner. His one-eyed gaze is unnerving. Irritably, I kick at the pile of discarded paper next to my feet.

'This studio's a mess. How can you work in such chaos?'

'What *is* the matter with you, Sam?' Pixie asks, shoving things about on the table.

'Nothing.'

She peers at me sideways. Her one-eyed gaze is also unnerving. The effect suddenly strikes me as bizarre. I'm now being peered at by two eyes in the room: one blue and cold and censorious; the other brown and sympathetic and haunting. It is a weird experience – like looking at a painting of Simon's. For a zany moment, I almost believe the world *is* mad, or I am. Then she turns right round to face me.

'I know what it is,' she says. 'You're jealous. Of

Simon. You resent the time I give him, and you don't like me talking about him or his paintings. If his paintings were done by somebody else, you would feel differently about them.'

'Rubbish!'

'Well, you'll just have to get over it, because from now on, Simon is going to be around more often. I've told him he can come and paint here in my studio any day he likes during the week. It won't affect you as you'll be at university, and it's impossible for him to paint at home.'

I'm thunderstruck. I have to let her words sink in. Even then I can't believe what I've heard. 'Why?' I splutter.

'Simon's whole family – *six* people – live in a single roomed shack no bigger than this room so he can't—'

'No! Dammit! Why are *you* doing it?'

'Please don't shout at me, I'm not deaf,' she says evenly.

'Who's shouting?' I try to simmer down. 'You know how I feel about Simon coming here. You know *what* he is. You're giving up too much of your time to him already. What about your own work? Your own painting? And it's not as if he's even grateful for all—'

'I'm not doing it for gratitude.'

She has that stubborn look on her face. From past experience I've learned it means I'm wasting my breath. In exasperation, I cast my glance round the studio and contact Bokkie's eye again, staring at me steadfastly like a Cyclops. Suddenly, I feel I can't take it any more, any of it.

'It's *him*!' I point accusingly. 'Bokkie! That's why you are doing it. You're helping Simon because of what happened to Bokkie. Which is bloody ridiculous. Simon *isn't* Bokkie!'

'No, he isn't.' She lets out a brittle laugh. 'At least you're *right* about that! He isn't even a bit like Bokkie.'

'But he *is* black.'

'That is a very loaded statement!' There is a distinct

chill coming from her now. 'And I resent what you're insinuating. You are the one who is so colour-conscious, you can only think of people in terms of the shade of their skin.'

'Poppycock! But I don't see why I should have to like Simon just because he's black.'

'I think you'd better go,' she says.

My blood runs cold. 'Go?' I stare at her horrified. 'Are you kicking me out?'

'Out of my studio.' The brief curl of her lips only accentuates the tightness round her mouth. 'Trying to continue this conversation is obviously pointless.'

'You're too darn right it is!'

To calm down, I take myself off for a walk through Hillbrow. It is late Saturday afternoon, and there are lots of people about. Couples in evening dress, heading for somewhere to eat before going on to the theatre; shoppers lugging bloated plastic shopping bags; jean-clad hippie types swinging their long hair and beads as they saunter with conscious aimlessness; small children dancing round their mothers and fathers, and demanding ice cream although it isn't a very warm spring day.

The sky is a louring mask of papier-mâché clouds, obscuring the sun and casting an unusual grey gloom over the city. It matches my mood. I follow my nose and find myself in the main street of Hillbrow. It is snarled up with traffic as always. Outside a coffee bar playing loud music, the pavement is swarming with teenagers larking about and having fun – or trying to look as though they are. I elbow my way through them resentfully, and turn down a quieter side road to get away from the madding crowd.

At the entrance to an alleyway between buildings, I come across an elderly African man, smartly dressed, sitting slumped against the wall. He is very drunk and very happy, crooning quietly to himself, with his blood-shot eyes staring squiffily into space, and a big goofy grin reaming his tarry old face. I wonder briefly why he went to so much trouble to dress up in an immaculate suit and tie and shiny patent leather shoes, only to drink himself into a stupor and end up in a bedraggled wobbly heap in a filthy alley. Then I forget about him.

I walk all the way down to the bottom of the hill, and lean against a lamp post to smoke a cigarette. I'm no longer feeling angry. I'm just feeling sorry for myself because I don't want to go back to the flat, and there is nowhere else to go. Besides, I'm starting to feel cold. A dirty orange glow on the overcast horizon in the west marks the onset of dusk. The air already has a nip in it, and I'm only wearing a thin cotton pullover. Shivering, I reluctantly retrace my steps up the hill.

As I crest the brow, I discover a police van pulled up at the kerb some distance ahead. Two policemen are crouched on the pavement over a recumbent figure – the drunk African I passed earlier. I'm not near enough to hear what is being said, but it is obvious from the policemen's manner and gestures that they are demanding to see the old fellow's passbook. They start searching his pockets. Then they haul him roughly to his feet, and drag him towards their van. I catch a glimpse of the African's face. He isn't grinning any longer. He looks terrified. In a thin wailing voice, he begins crying, begging them to let him go. They drop him in the gutter to open the back of their van. He starts trying to crawl away. One of the policemen draws his gun; the other kicks the old man in the ribs, causing him to collapse like a rickety deck chair. The policemen grab him by the collar and the seat of his pants, throw – literally throw – him inside, and slam the doors. They stand for a moment, lighting cigarettes and laughing, before they jump in, gun the engine, and drive off at speed with tyres screeching.

It all happens so fast, I'm rooted to the spot. So are the only other visible witnesses; a middle-aged white couple further up the street. They stare after the van, glance at me, say something to each other, and walk on. The entrance door of the block of flats on my right opens slightly, and a face appears round it: a woman's face, heavily-made up, with hair rolled into tight curlers.

'What'd he do? D'you know?'

'Who?' I have to catch my breath. 'The old guy? Nothing. He was just drunk. They kicked him, and threw him in the van as if he was a bag of potatoes. Did you see? The bastards!'

'They're all bastards! Blerry kaffirs! I'm glad they caught him. He probably stole something.' Her face disappears. The door closes. I hear it being bolted on the inside.

My body has gone into a spasm of shaking. The empty street looks so normal, but it has taken on a sinister significance. The policemen's violence seems to hang in the air. I feel a reciprocal violence inside me; a sense of shocked outrage that makes me clench my fists and wish I could crunch them into the uniformed brutes' faces. Trembling, I lean against the wall. I have witnessed police brutality before, but not that recently; and one forgets.

Twenty feet away in the gutter, lies a pitiful memento of the old man – one of his patent leather shoes. I can't look at it. It is an accusation of my white complacency. I am guilty. I see Pixie's face in front of me. I see Bokkie's face. I see the policemen at Gerrit's farm, telling him to dispose of Bokkie's body and forget about it. And suddenly I'm afraid that when I get back to the flat, it will be too late. Too late to patch things up with Pixie. Too late to say I'm sorry for not being supportive about Simon. Too late to tell her I love her. I spring away from the wall, and break into a desperate run.

Pixie isn't alone. Russ is there. My heart sinks when I barge through the front door and discover him having coffee with her in the living-room. He informs me that he happened to be in the neighbourhood, and has just popped in for a cuppa. I hope he won't stay long as I'm bursting with the need to have Pixie to myself. But Pixie invites him to join us for supper, and opens the bottle of wine I have brought back. The other present I've bought her, I manage to hide.

I'm on tenterhooks all evening, mentally rehearsing what I want to say to Pixie. By the time Russ leaves, however, and we've got into bed, my prepared speech is beginning to sound hollow in my head. What had seemed so complicated and necessary before, now seems so straightforward and simple; a simple feeling. I don't want to talk. I just want to love her. From under my pillow, I fish out my concealed present.

'What's this?' she asks.

'It's my "sorry".'

'Chocolates. That's a very sweet sorry.' She kisses me.

'Am I forgiven?'

'Mhhm . . .' She puts her arms round me and kisses me again.

I'm forgiven. We make love wordlessly. It is beautiful. I go to sleep telling myself that all is well between us. But deep down, I'm not so sure.

10

Simon starts coming to the flat three or four times a week, and stays all day. To avoid bumping into him, I no longer return home as soon as my last lecture is over. Instead, I hang about on the university campus. My intention is to spend the time in the library, revising for my exams. But I'm all too easily distracted by whatever is going on around me, and I find I can only concentrate in short bursts. Sooner or later, I end up in the canteen, where I drink coffee and watch people and brood.

It is nearly a year that I have been at Wits, yet I haven't made any friends. I'm on nodding acquaintance with a few students in my lectures and tutorials, and there are one or two with whom I might pass the time of day; but that is about as far as it goes. I know I have only myself to blame. All these months, I have kept myself aloof, making no effort to form friendships, or to become involved in any social activities on the campus. It didn't really bother me before. I only wanted to be with Pixie. I couldn't wait to get back to the flat each day.

It is different now. I feel differently. I feel I'm missing out on student life, and I feel differently about going home too. After I have parked the Mini, I have to steel myself to cross the road and approach the front entrance to the block, keeping my eyes peeled for any signs of police surveillance. If I spot an unmarked stationary car with someone sitting in it – man or woman – my heart lurches. I retreat down the road, and wait until it drives away. Then, as I climb the stairs, my tension increases. I know, as soon as I enter the flat, whether Simon has been here because of the smell of his tobacco. That isn't all. He has taken to bringing Pixie flowers: handfuls of marigolds, or roses, or poppies, or sometimes sprigs of flowering shrubs. It is obvious to me that he has swiped them out of gardens or a park, and I complain about it to Pixie one evening. She laughs.

'No doubt he has,' she says. 'I only hope he doesn't get caught.'

She is in the bath. I'm brushing my teeth at the basin.

'Well . . .' I spit out the toothpaste. ' . . . Why don't you tell him not to do it?'

'I did tell him. I said it wasn't necessary to bring me anything. But he's very highly-strung and I don't want to hurt his feelings. He's actually an extremely sensitive and vulnerable kid underneath that tough macho front he shows to the world. Besides, I think it's rather sweet of him to give me flowers. It's his way of trying to show he's grateful.'

She puts an extra stress on the last word, as if she wants to make it clear to me that Simon is appreciative, despite my allegations to the contrary. I scowl at myself

157

in the mirror, then angle it so I can see her reflection without having to face her.

'Now you're getting as bad as he is,' I carp. 'Receiving stolen goods.'

'Oh, come on, Sam. It's not that serious. A few flowers will hardly be missed.'

'It's still thieving!'

'All right. Yes. You're right. I'll talk to him again about it.' Sighing, she slides down in the tub, disappearing from the mirror, so I'm forced to look round. She is submerged under the water with just her head and her toes sticking out. Teasingly, she says, 'Perhaps someone else will give me flowers.'

She doesn't need flowers. She *is* a flower – to me, anyway. A newly-opened flower: shapely and soft and pink and glowing. It bugs me that I can't prevent myself gazing at her hungrily. She knows it too. Stroking her fingers through the water in languid movements like an enticing sea anemone, she smiles up at me archly.

'Are you coming to join me, Sam-of-a-gun?'

I tear my eyes away and retreat to the door. 'I'm studying. I told you! I have to. I've got to read a whole damn book tonight, and also do some other revision.'

'Well, don't work too hard,' she says.

Work *too* hard? She doesn't realize – I'm not working hard *enough*. My exams start in just over three weeks' time, and I'm panic-stricken at the thought of how much revision I still have to get through before then. But I still can't will myself to concentrate.

I feel claustrophobic in my room; I feel claustrophobic in the flat. I've become very conscious of it being Pixie's flat – not *our* flat – and it is beginning to prey on my nerves. A lot of things are beginning to prey on my nerves; not least, the constant state of chaos in the kitchen. I've given up trying to persuade Pixie to put objects back in the cupboards. She says she can't find what she needs for cooking unless everything is kept right in front of her nose. But the mess and general disorder irritates me now every time I go in there.

It also irritates me that Pixie, these days, seems to live in old denim jeans and shapeless T-shirts or sweaters.

'Can't you wear any other clothes for a change?' I grouse.

She bridles. 'Why? What's wrong with what I've got on?'

'It's not very flattering.'

'Flattering to whom? To you, or to me?'

I put down my fork, and stare hard at her across the table. 'Aren't you concerned about how you look?'

'I'm concerned that I feel comfortable in what I'm wearing, especially when I'm painting.'

'But you aren't painting now, are you?'

'I might, this evening. Anyway, I don't see that it matters how I look. We aren't entertaining tonight. We aren't going out. And you are shut up in your room, swotting.'

'Is that a complaint?' I growl.

'No, it isn't. It's just a fact. You're so tense and pre-occupied with your exams, you don't seem to really notice me half the time.'

'Perhaps I would if you wore something a bit sexier,' I say churlishly.

She is suddenly cross; she wasn't before. 'Forget it! *This* is me. Like it, or lump it. If you want a dolly bird, there are plenty out there.'

'Yes! There are!' I get up and take my plate to the sink, and leave her to clear the rest of the table.

It is true. I've been amazed to realize recently how many attractive female students there are right in front of my nose at university. I must have been walking around with blinkers on for nine months. I sit at the window in the library and watch the passing parade of long-legged beauties in mini-skirts and tight blouses, and catch myself fantasizing about being single and free to ask one of them out, or play the field. But as soon as my fantasies develop into erotic daydreams, whichever female I happen to be visualizing making love to, takes on the features of Pixie. Immediately, I'm filled with remorse, and I have a sudden urge to rush home and grab Pixie and tell her how much I love her. But I don't go back to the flat as Simon is likely to be there. I go to the canteen instead, and drink coffee. By the time I do get home, I'm tired and nervy, and the sight of Simon's flowers (which keep arriving despite Pixie having said she would speak to him again about them) are enough to make me want to snap at Pixie, not kiss her.

I'm drinking gallons of coffee to keep myself going on very little sleep. Sitting up into the early hours, trying to cram facts into my thick head, I crawl into bed exhausted, only to toss and turn restlessly with my brain in overdrive. My mother, swanning in briefly on her way somewhere else as usual, strikes a pose of horror at my bleary-eyed, haggard appearance.

Hand on heart, she says, injecting a little quiver into her voice, 'Honbee! You look awful! You look as if you've just come out of a concentration camp. I knew it!'

'Knew what?' I ask.

'You're not getting enough nourishment from your new silly rabbity diet. It's got to stop. You must start eating normally again,' and she undiplomatically thrusts a twenty rand note into Pixie's hand and instructs her to buy me some red meat.

I intercede swiftly. 'Debs! There's nothing wrong with Pixie's and my diet. It's very healthy. Vegetarianism isn't to blame for my debilitated appearance.'

'Then what is?' she says, angling her face away from Pixie, and fluttering her eyelashes at me enquiringly as a cryptic code between the two of us.

'My exams. I'm in the process of having a nervous breakdown over them.' I laugh hoarsely. 'Don't look so worried, Debs. I'll survive. So! How are you?'

She sighs. 'I'm bound to confess I'm a little weary. The *Hamlet* was a great success, but I found touring very tiring this time, for some reason. I hope it doesn't mean I'm getting past it.'

'No, it probably just means you need a change of diet. You should try vegetarianism,' Pixie says, tongue-in-cheek.

My mother reacts by miming mock horror, then consults her watch. 'Twenty-to-eight! Oh dear, old Nicky-poo will be gnashing his teeth in the car. I mustn't keep him waiting any longer, as I had to bully him into taking me out tonight. He wanted me to stay at home.'

'Why?' I ask.

'Silly old quack's orders.'

She pirouettes precariously in her stilettoes, and reaches for the front door. I restrain her with my hand.

'Whoa! What are you talking about, Debs?'

'Nothing serious, honbee. Dr Cohen claims I'm slightly anaemic at the moment, so I'm supposed to be taking it easy and resting. Resting! . . .' She shudders. 'That ghastly word in the theatre.'

I inspect her. The light is dim in the doorway, but she looks her usual beautiful butterfly self. I walk her down the stairs, and kiss her goodbye in the vestibule.

'Aren't you coming out to say hallo to Nick?' she asks.

'No. You say hallo for me. I've got to get back to my studying. I sit my first paper on Monday.'

She is in a hurry, yet she seems oddly reluctant suddenly to leave. She fiddles with the strap on her bag. Then she starts straightening my collar. 'You are still happy, are you, honbee, living here?'

'Sure,' I say, not quite quickly enough. 'Why, what makes you ask?'

'No reason. Just checking. If you ever grow sick of Hillbrow, you can always come back home. Your room is there, waiting for you.'

I manage a grin. 'With room service?'

'Yes. I suppose I could always dress Nick up as a butler.'

'He'd love that. Better not keep him waiting, Debs.'

'No,' she says.

'Bye then.' I peck her on the cheek.

'Bye,' she says.

I watch her exit, as I have done so many times in the theatre. This time, though, there is something lacking in her performance. She isn't acting. She stumbles as she steps out on to the pavement, and she doesn't turn and wave. I suspect she is hurt I haven't confided in her. But I can't; it disturbs me that she has sensed an atmosphere between Pixie and me. My feelings are even more churned up now, than before.

Pixie waylays me in the passage. Holding out her arm, she drops the twenty rand note at my feet. 'If you want meat, buy it yourself,' she says.

'I don't want meat,' I mutter wearily.

'Your mother seems to think I'm your skivvy.' She bends and picks up the note and gives it to me with that quirky smile of hers, which means she might be joking, or she might not be. 'Like mother, like son,' she remarks, and disappears into her studio.

In my room, I thrust the money into the wardrobe with the intention of spending it on a meal out for the two of us after my final paper. I feel it will be something to look forward to. I persuade myself that Pixie and I will be able to patch things up once my exams are over.

* * * *

It has to happen, of course, on Monday, to coincide with my first exam paper, which is a stinker. I'm convinced I've failed. To add to my gloom, it is raining. I decide to go straight home because Simon isn't usually there on a Monday. Soaked and headachy and deeply depressed, I arrive back to discover the flat has been broken into while Pixie was out shopping for a couple of hours.

What is very creepy about it all is that nothing has been taken. The intruder, or intruders, have just had fun creating havoc in Pixie's studio, and destroying all of Simon's paintings and a few of Pixie's too – her most recent ones – including the two bushveld scenes I liked. It is obviously a deliberate act of vandalism. The ripped canvases have been left scattered about the floor in random piles, with upended pots of paint on them, suppurating greasy lava flows of colour over all that is left of weeks and weeks of creative hard work.

Pixie, I find huddled under the window in the room, staring at the destruction as if in a trance. Her face is chalky-white with shock. I can't get any sense out of her until I have made her drink a hot strong cup of sweet tea. Then she manages to tell me how she came home with a bag of groceries and found the lock on the front door had been forced, and the door was standing open.

Her teacup is rattling on its saucer. I take it from her, and grasp her hands to steady them. 'You didn't just walk straight in, did you?' I say, trying to control my own fear.

She nods.

'Pixie! That's crazy! You could have been murdered.'

She smiles weakly, as if she considers I'm being over-dramatic. 'I knew the swines had gone. If they were still in there, they wouldn't have left the front door open.'

'You couldn't be sure. It's insane to have just walked in. You should have gone and phoned the police, and waited outside for them to arrive.'

'Phoned the police?' She starts to laugh hysterically. 'That's very funny. Who do you think did this?'

My heart contracts. 'Who?'

'Our friendly Special Branch.'

'No!' I don't, can't believe her. She shows me the swastika daubed on the back of the door in red paint. I still don't believe her, but icy cold sweat is trickling down my armpits under my shirt. 'That d-doesn't prove anything,' I stutter.

'It does,' she says vehemently. 'Who else but the S.B. would choose a swastika as their calling-card? It's their sadistic idea of a joke, except that they mean it too as a deadly serious warning.'

'Of what?'

'Of their power.' She fumbles for her packet of cigarettes. 'Want one?'

'Y-yes.' I let her light it for me. Her hands are now steadier than mine.

We sit and smoke without speaking. Fear has frozen my mind; I can't think coherently. Then Pixie gives a sudden jerk.

'Bastards!' she says, and begins to cry. I sit and observe her dully. It is as if I'm anaesthetized, and unable to move, or feel anything. 'Have you got a tissue?' she gulps.

'What?'

'A tissue.'

My hand goes to my pocket and produces one. As she blows her nose, I look away, round the room. That's when it hits me. 'Oh my God! The portrait! Where's Bokkie? They didn't . . .?'

'Under the bed.' She sniffs, and almost manages a smile. 'It wasn't in the studio. I took it out of here last week because it was getting knocked about a bit, and stowed it under the bed.'

I experience an unexpected rush of relief. But Pixie has started crying again. I move closer and hold her.

Comfortingly, I say, 'At least they didn't destroy your old work. And I know, I'm so sorry, it *is* terrible about your new paintings – and Simon's. All the same, it could have been worse. I'm just so glad you weren't here, or they might have hurt *you*.'

'You don't understand, Sam.' She pulls away from me. Her eyes glitter through their wet shine. 'I don't *care* about me or my paintings. They *can't* hurt me. It's Simon. The bastards have done this to get at him. They're going to destroy him. But I won't let them.'

'You're right – I don't understand.' I think she is being paranoid. 'Why should the security police be so interested in persecuting Simon? He's only a petty thief.'

'He isn't.'

'He isn't?' I repeat stupidly.

'Only a thief,' she says.

Then she clams up, like someone suddenly realizing they've let the cat out of the bag. Lighting a fresh cigarette, she holds it in front of her as a smokescreen, and shakes her head when I ask her to elaborate.

'What else is he?' I insist. I can't see her face through the smoke. Pushing her hand to one side, I frown at her tensely. 'Tell me!'

'All right.'

She explains the whole thing in a garbled rush, as if she wants to get it over with as swiftly as possible. I'm too stunned to take in everything she says. But the gist of it is that when Simon was in prison, two members of the Special Branch paid him a visit. The officers made it clear that they knew everything about him; where he lived; the names of his mother and brothers and sisters; the school he had attended; and last, but not least, his relationship with his Uncle Jake. Then they told him they wanted him to spy on Jake and a few other people for them. If he agreed to do so, they said they would arrange for him to be freed from prison without having to serve the rest of his sentence. If, however, he refused to co-operate, he would be 'helped' to commit suicide. To demonstrate their meaning, the men tied one end of a sheet tightly round Simon's neck, looped the other end round the bars on his cell window, and hauled him up into the air until only his toes still touched the floor. Simon got the message. He agreed to co-operate. The officers were very nice to him then. They said they knew how short of money he was, so as soon as he had proved himself a trustworthy and reliable informant, they would start paying him for his services. They also gave him a packet of cigarettes when they left. Two weeks later, Simon was released from prison.

'And is that what he has been doing ever since?' I ask Pixie, appalled. 'Spying on Jake, and on you as well?'

'*Supposed* to have been doing,' she corrects me. 'But Jake has known about it all along.'

'Simon told him?'

'No, not Simon. Jake found out via the grapevine, from someone who knew someone who knew someone whose cousin's wife's sister's son – or such like – happened to be in the cell next to Simon's when the S. B. visited him. The information reached Jake even before Simon came out of jail.' She sucks on her bottom lip, frowning and half-smiling at the same time. 'Jake is a remarkable guy, you know. The police underestimate—'

I cut her off. 'How come *you* know all this? Did he tell you?'

'Jake? . . . Yes,' she says after a moment.

'When?'

She looks me in the eye. 'I've known about Simon being a spy from the beginning.'

'And it didn't stop you entertaining him in your flat?'

'Why should it? As I've explained to you before, I've got nothing to hide from the police. And it's not as if Simon chose to become a police informer. Poor kid. He had no option. It was either agree, or be killed.'

I shake my head violently! 'I can't believe that.'

'I guessed you wouldn't!' Her eyes blaze into mine. 'You also probably don't believe that the S. B. push political prisoners out of seventeenth storey windows and claim they committed suicide, or torture detainees to death and claim they just happened to fall over while being interrogated and fractured their skulls.'

I stare her out stonily. 'So you've known about Simon all this time. Yet you didn't tell me.'

'No,' she says. 'I didn't.'

'Why?'

'For obvious reasons.'

She tenses, waiting, as if she is expecting me to lose my temper. But I'm not angry. I'm beyond anger. A small inner voice says it is all over between us. This is the final straw. There is a hollowness inside me, a cold emptiness of emotion, which is almost a welcome relief after all the confused feelings of recent weeks. I cast a glance at the nearest pile of ripped, paint-splattered paintings. A torn-off section of a mutilated canvas shows the top half of a face with frightened eyes, staring, it seems, straight at the swastika on the door behind me. I recognize the face as that of a victim in one of Simon's violent township scenes. Something doesn't add up in all that she has told me, I realize.

'I still don't get it,' I say.

'What?' She is lighting yet another cigarette. ' . . . Get what?'

I point at the face. 'How can the Special Branch have done this? Why should they want to wreck Simon's paintings if he's working for them?'

'Last week . . .' she breaks off, and buries her head in her hands. ' . . . Oh hell, what does it matter if I tell you now.' But she doesn't take her hands away, and her voice is muffled when she continues. 'Simon broke down while he was here. He admitted everything to me. He was in a terrible state. He felt he had to get it all off his chest. And he's worried because he hasn't been playing ball with the police. He isn't supplying them with much information, and he keeps avoiding his appointments with the undercover contact. He's been going through the most terrible torment. I just . . .' She swallows.

'So you think this is their way of warning him to come into line?'

She glances up, fighting tears. 'Of course.'

'In which case, why did they destroy a few of your paintings too? Wasn't that intentional? Aren't they warning you as well?'

'Maybe . . . I don't know. But they haven't got anything on me. It's Simon I—'

'What are you going to do?' I ask coldly.

'I need to talk to Jake. I'm hoping he'll come this afternoon. I rang a number he gave me to use in emergencies. It's someone who will be able to get a message to him in the township.'

'Well, obviously you can't have Simon coming here any longer. It's too dangerous. Both for—'

'They'd really love that! The police. To know they had won with their Nazi tactics!'

'It can't be helped.'

'No way! I'm not prepared to give them that satisfac-

167

tion. Fascist bastards!' Crushing her cigarette packet, she hurls it at the swastika. It misses and hits the wall instead. 'I won't!' she says, seething. 'But it's not up to me. It's up to Simon. If he still wants to come and paint, we'll start again from scratch. We'll just have to work harder to get enough paintings done for Cecily to view at Christmas. And we'll have to find a safe place to store them.'

Observing her, I feel as if I'm watching a stranger, not the woman I love. I'm unaware of any emotion inside me other than an overriding sense of hopelessness, and a desperate longing to curl up somewhere peaceful and far away from all this, and go to sleep for a long, long time.

Almost mechanically, I ask, 'Do you really mean what you're saying?'

She doesn't answer. She doesn't have to; the defiant obduracy in her expression says it all. I stand up and dust myself off.

'Well, that's that then,' and I head for the door.

'Sam?'

I keep walking.

'Sam?' She is following me. 'Where are you going?'

I pause, heave a sigh, and turn. 'You seem to have forgotten that I'm in the middle of exams. I've got four folders of notes to revise before my next paper tomorrow morning. And I'm dog-tired as it is.'

'I'm sorry.' Contritely, she touches my arm. 'I should have asked you before, Sam. How did it go today?'

'It went.' And I walk on.

As I'm about to close my bedroom door, I stick my head out. She is still there, where I left her further up the passage.

'I'm so sorry,' she says hoarsely. 'It's a difficult time, I know. I hope you can study. I'll try not to disturb you.'

I shut the door.

* * * *

A difficult time? It is a nightmare, as far as I'm concerned. I try not to think about anything except my next exam paper, and get through each day as best I can. But my nerves are frayed to snapping point. I jump out of my skin at any unexpected sound in the flat, and if I hear a police siren I start quaking.

The nights are the worst. I lie awake with insomnia, despite being utterly exhausted. When I do finally drop off, I'm woken up by Pixie shouting in her sleep: 'Don't hurt him! Don't! . . . Run! Run! Please run!' The words are always the same. It is the old recurrent bad dream come back to haunt her, although in the morning she seems to remember nothing.

I'm all too conscious of Bokkie's portrait lying hidden under the bed. I fancy I can feel his omniscient gaze boring into my back through the mattress and bedlinen. I start to dream about him too:

He is buried in a coffin under the floorboards. But he is alive. I know he will suffocate if I don't get him out. I tear at the boards with my bare hands. They won't budge. He calls to me reassuringly. 'Don't worry,' he says. 'Open your eyes. Look! I'm not dead. Everything is fine.' Then a huge hole appears at my feet and the coffin plummets down through empty space. I fall with it at sickening speed, and wake up with a jerk. Lying bathed in sweat, I listen to Pixie gnashing her teeth and crying out urgently, 'Run! Quick! Run!', and I see a vivid picture of the scene she is re-living in her dream, and my blood runs cold.

After five nights, I can't stand it any longer. I decide to start sleeping in my own room. Pixie doesn't question my decision. We're living together now almost like strangers, avoiding all contentious subjects, and making polite conversation over the supper table. While I shut myself up in my room, she spends most of her time in her studio. She has embarked on a major spring-cleaning in there, clearing out a load of old stuff and rubbish. She doesn't know when Simon will turn up. Jake has told her he will talk to Simon, and send Simon to talk to her when the coast is clear.

The coast isn't clear. Nor is the future. Nothing is clear to me except the necessity to struggle through the rest of my exams. The day of the final paper arrives. This one is a godsend; for once I can answer all the questions.

From the examination room, I walk out into the brilliant sunshine of summer. There isn't a cloud in the sky. The leaves on the trees emulate the sparkle of emeralds. The campus lawns are a blinding blaze of green light. A flower-bed in front of me is a neon display of competing colours. And I am free to stand and drink it all in. I'm on holiday as from this moment.

Relief, and the dazzling radiance of the day, sweep away my depression. I feel like celebrating. Not on my own. With Pixie. The realization hits me like a punch in my midriff. *I want to be with Pixie*. Despite all the strain between us these past weeks, the force of my sudden certainty is irrepressible. I feel heady with fresh optimism. Anything and everything is possible on such a Utopian summer day. I'm convinced we can make a new start. I remember my mother's twenty rand note I stashed away in the wardrobe. I remember I had intended to use it to take Pixie out to dinner. Impulsively, I decide to surprise her and stop off in Hillbrow, and book a table in a restaurant and buy her flowers.

For once, I can't wait to get home. I bound up the stairs without bothering to check for signs of police surveillance in the street outside. As I tear along the corridor, Pixie emerges from the flat. I wave the flowers at her.

'Hi . . . Guess what?'

'You passed?'

'Who knows? Who cares? But it's all over for another year – thank God! . . . And these are for you.'

She looks flustered. Then she smiles, and sniffs the bouquet without taking it from me. 'Heavenly! I adore the scent of roses. Thank you, Sam.'

I was hoping she would kiss me, but she has stepped back. She seems in a bit of a flurry.

'They're beautiful. Thank you,' she repeats.

'Well, take them then,' I grin, pushing them at her. She moves away. 'I will. When I get back – I've just got to go to the corner shop. Uh . . .' she pauses '. . . Simon is here, by the way. He's in my studio. I was making him some coffee and found we're out of sugar. I'll be as quick as I can.'

I stand, staring after her, with my stupid grin frozen on my face. *Simon! Bloody Simon!* He would have to turn up today! In a fit of pique, I hurl the bouquet on the floor, and collapse against the wall, cursing. So much for my optimism! So much for the beautiful day!

The sun is in my eyes. I press my hands over them, and rest my head back. I'm dead-beat. The sensible thing to do would be to collapse on my bed for the afternoon. But I don't want to go inside while Simon is there. I decide to stay where I am until Pixie returns. Impatiently, I frown at my watch. The corner shop isn't far. She should only be a few minutes. I wait several minutes. Only then it suddenly occurs to me that Simon might use the opportunity of being left alone in the flat to try and steal something. For my own peace of mind, I realize I have to go in and check up on him.

Retrieving the flowers, I insert my key in the lock, and open, and close the door softly behind me. Then I listen. When Simon is in Pixie's studio, her radio is always on. Loudly! Pixie has told me Simon needs the background noise because he can't stand silence – it makes him nervous. But I can't hear any radio playing now; I can't hear any sound at all; and I'm immediately suspicious.

Very gently, I lay the bouquet down on the hall telephone table, and tiptoe to the doorway into the passage. From there, I listen again. It is abnormally quiet; so quiet a tap dripping in the bathroom is audible. Then a floorboard creaks somewhere. The hair on the back of my neck starts to rise. Another creak. This time it doesn't sound like a floorboard, it sounds like a bedspring in Pixie's bedroom. And there is another noise now as well – a low moaning. With my heart hammering, I creep down the passage. The bedroom door is ajar. I'm trembling so much, I have to grasp the handle for support before I peer through the aperture into the room.

Simon is sitting on the end of the bed. The moans are coming from him. He is crouched forward, clutching himself round the middle. My first impression is that he's in terrible pain. Then he starts rocking back and forth, and I see that he is hugging Pixie's nightie, pressing it tightly against his body, and rubbing the silky material in rhythmical movements with his hands.

'Hey! . . .' Shock, and a violent sense of outrage propel me into the room ' . . . What the hell do you think you're doing?'

He bounds up in fright, dropping the nightie, and makes a run for the door, trying to dodge past me. But I manage to grab his arm, and haul him round with such force that he loses his balance, reels sideways, and falls flat on his face on the floor. As he picks himself up, he glares at me, his eyes constricted to coal-black chinks of animosity.

'You filthy black bastard!' I'm out of control, shaking from fear as much as from fury, expecting him to retaliate. Searching wildly about for a weapon, my eye lights on Pixie's school hockey stick standing in the corner. I snatch it and point it threateningly at him. 'Stand still! If you move, I'll—'

'No! Sam! Don't. Don't hurt him!'

I whip round. Pixie is standing in the doorway. Her face is as white as a ghost.

'Run!' she says to Simon. 'Run!'

Instantly, he is out of the room, and sprinting down the passage. The front door slams. In the following hush, Pixie's words reverberate through my head with a jolting familiarity. My mind is disorientated; for a few seconds I almost believe I'm re-living a dream, a recurrent nightmare, or experiencing *déjà vu*.

Then Pixie advances on me. Wordlessly, she snatches

the hockey stick from my hand, strides away and starts smashing it against the wall. After the third or fourth blow, the stick snaps in two. She hurls both bits through the open window. Then she turns and confronts me with a look of contemptuous fury.

'Okay,' she snarls through clenched teeth. 'Now tell me what happened.'

Shakily, I start to explain. She lets me get as far as describing what Simon was doing with her nightie on the bed before she interrupts me.

'Christ!' she says. 'Is that all? You were going to hit him just for that? I thought at least he must have stolen all your damned money, or threatened you.'

'What he was doing was far worse.'

'It was harmless. He was only fondling my nightie, for pity's—'

'And turning himself on. It's disgusting!'

'Of course!' she says with virulent sarcasm. 'You've never done anything like that, have you? You're so pure and holy, just like Gerrit!'

I look at her in horror. 'I am not like Gerrit.'

'No. And I suppose you'll also deny you called Simon a filthy black bastard! But I heard you.'

Feeling sick and wobbly inside, I lower myself on to the edge of the bed and clasp my head in my hands. From behind me, she starts shouting. I realize she is telling me to get off her bed, and get out of her room, and get out of her flat, and to take my things with me. She is chucking me out. It means it is finally over between us, but I don't care. If anything, it is a relief. I stand up, and walk numbly to my room, and begin packing.

11

Everything looks the same – as if time has stood still in Saxonwold while my world away from it has fallen apart. The garden is as neat and verdant and colourful as ever, with all the old familiar summer flowers festooning the edges of the carefully curved paths, and the lawn its usual lush green, like a newly-laid thick-pile carpet that not even moles would dare to disturb. The gnomes round the fishpond are the same as well. And the live black gnome, Benjamin, is there with them, scooping up leaves from the surface with a long-handled net, and pausing every now and then to relax and scratch his grizzled old man's beard. Like the rest of the scene, he doesn't seem to have changed at all.

Squinting past him, I can see that the arbour is empty. But I know my mother and Nick are at home because Nick's Mercedes is standing in the garage. They must be indoors. Benjamin notices me and doffs his hat and beckons enthusiastically, grinning from ear to ear. I pretend not to notice. I can't face his cheerfulness this afternoon. I don't feel up to facing my mother and Nick either. Steeling myself, I drag my feet back round the side of the house and through the kitchen door.

They are in the lounge, which looks exactly the same, crowded with dark Victorian mahogany furniture and teak display cabinets, all smelling of perfumed polish. They are sitting primly on the settee as usual, like Tweedledum and Tweedledee, with cups of tea balanced on their knees. Tea, of course! It is four o'clock. Tea-time in Saxonwold.

I force a smile. 'Hi.'

I'm expecting a scowl from Nick, and a show of

delighted surprise from my mother. Instead, they both appear startled, and my mother spills some of her tea. Nick immediately removes her cup and saucer and mops at her skirt with the clean monogrammed hankie he always carries in his breast pocket, while my mother fishes in her bag, produces a tissue, and dabs at her cheeks and nose almost furtively. Neither of them answer me.

'Sorry,' I say, advancing into the room. 'Did I give you a fright? Did you think I was a burglar?'

'No, it's not that.' My mother blows her nose, something she normally never does in front of anyone. 'It's ... it's ... well, uncanny you should happen to walk in now, honbee, because we were just talking about you, and we were hoping to get hold of you as soon as we'd finished our tea.'

'Why?' For a split-second I feel a flicker of wild crazy hope that Pixie has had a change of heart, and has rung while I was on my way here. But I can't believe it, and I'm not even sure I really want to talk to her. 'What's happened?' I ask.

My mother looks at Nick, as if she expects him to answer. He lays his hand over hers.

'Deborah has to go into hospital tomorrow for an operation,' he informs me gruffly.

'Operation?' My heart falters. 'What for? What's wrong with you, Debs?'

'Oh, honbee. Don't look so worried.' She tries to smile, but she can't sustain it; her lips waver. 'It's just a spot of gynae trouble.'

'She has to have a hysterectomy.'

'Nick!' She turns on him. 'You make it sound so melodramatic.'

He jumps up, mumbles something about a fresh pot of tea, and barges past me out of the room. My mother gathers herself together, rearranges her skirt, and adopts her best stage manner.

'Well, honbee, it's so lovely to see you. Come and sit down, and tell me how your exams—'

175

'Not now.' Hollow legged, I sink on to the settee beside her. 'I want to know about your operation. Why wasn't I told before?'

'We didn't know before today. I had an appointment with a gynaecologist this morning, and he decided I had to have all my bits and pieces out immediately.'

'Why, Debs?'

'It happens, honbee, it happens. It's the cross we women have to bear.'

'Yes. But why does the operation need to be done in such a rush? Did he tell you?'

She pulls a face. 'Let's not go into the gory details, darling. It's embarrassing. I've been having some female problems, a bit of bleeding – you know. And this will sort it out.'

'Is that the reason you've been feeling tired?' I ask her.

'Probably.' She tucks her chin in, peering coyly at me through her lashes. 'Do I look tired to you?'

Her mascara is smudged on her lower eyelids, and there is a faint dried tearmark down one cheek. The reassurance I want to give her won't come out; my throat has closed up. I shake my head helplessly, wishing I had inherited her acting ability.

'I'm so glad you're here,' she says, pressing my hand between both of hers. 'Can you stay and have supper with us?'

I nod, but I can't look at her any longer. I get up, and walk away. Staring out of the window, I croak, 'Actually, I've come to stay. I've brought all my things with me. Is that okay?'

'Of course.' She sounds delighted. 'Do you mean you're moving back in? For how long?'

'I don't know.'

'Will you stay until I'm better?'

'Yes.'

I turn. She doesn't ask me why I've left Pixie's flat. We just smile at each other stiffly, like two lost souls on opposite banks of a fordless river.

'Would you like a biscuit?' She lifts the plate.

'No, thanks. I'd better unpack the Mini first,' I say listlessly.

As I'm pulling things out of the boot, Nick appears. He casts his eye over all of my belongings, then walks right round the car, as if he's inspecting it, and starts kicking at the front tyre.

'It's serious, you know,' he says.

'What is? Damn! . . .' I stop tugging at the plastic bag full of shoes that has become hooked on the boot catch, and go to investigate. 'I haven't got a puncture, have I?'

'The operation. Did she tell you?'

'No.'

He moves off to the other side of the Mini. Leaning his arms on the roof, he says, frowning past me at the garden. 'They've found tumours.'

My heart stops for a second. The birdsong behind me sounds terribly shrill in my ears. My own voice sounds even shriller:

'She has cancer? Is that what you're saying?'

His face is a tormented mask. He lifts his hands up in a gesture of helplessness. 'She might . . . be okay. Please God! . . . If they've caught it in time.'

I stare down at my feet. When I look up, he is already on his way back into the house. Above the roof, the sky is still a clear ink blue, but late afternoon shadows are sketching elongated charcoal cartoon shapes of trees and shrubs across the lawn. I was wrong. The garden does not look the same. Nothing can be counted on to remain the same – not even in Saxonwold. Right now, I desperately wish I could see Bokkie's golden light in everything. I wish I could see God inside myself. I wish I could believe in something to help me through the next few weeks.

* * * *

The surgeon cuts my mother open, looks inside, and sews her up again without removing anything. In private afterwards, he explains to Nick and myself that there wasn't any point in putting her body through the trauma of a hysterectomy, as the cancer had spread into her bowel and her liver and her lymphatic system. In medical terminology, her condition is described as inoperable terminal cancer. The surgeon can't tell us how long she will live; it might be a matter of months, or only a matter of weeks – it all depends on her own strength of will to survive, and how slowly or quickly her constitution succumbs to the cannibalistic onslaught of the disease.

On a day of dramatic thunder and hailstorms, Nick and I wrap my mother up in a travelling rug on the back seat of the Mercedes, and drive her home from hospital. Her bedroom is garlanded with voluptuous arrangements of flowers and humorous or sentimental cards from dozens of well-wishers.

She knows she has inoperable cancer. The surgeon took the responsibility on himself of at least intimating to her the seriousness of her illness the morning after her operation. But she pretends, or chooses to believe, that it has all been a false alarm and she is going to get better. It is her final acting role, and she performs it with brave aplomb. Myself, and Nick, and the servants, and all her visitors, have no option but to join in her theatre of make-believe.

From the first day she is back home, there is a marked and, frighteningly sudden, rapid decline in her health. Her body literally seems to start wasting away. Yet she keeps insisting she is feeling stronger and will be back on her feet soon. She is an old trooper. She is a star. Her bedroom is her stage. People flock in to see her; old friends she has known all her life, as well as all the theatre mob: actors, actresses, directors, producers, impresarios, stage managers, lighting technicians, set designers, stage hands. She puts on a marvellous show for them all, which leaves her so weak and drained at the end of the day, she can barely open her eyes and sit up to be spoonfed a sparrow's portion of light supper. But she won't let any visitors be turned away. She becomes angry at the very suggestion. She might be dying, but the show must go on. And she loves all the fuss and attention, even though it is killing her faster.

She loves too, having her 'boys' as she calls Nick and me, dancing attendance on her. Nick never leaves her bedside, except to wash and shave and change his clothes. He looks terrible. He looks as if he is wasting away with my mother, and he seems genuinely incapable of making any practical decisions. I've had to take over the running of the household; planning the meals, doing the shopping, answering the door and the constantly ringing telephone, and organizing endless cups of tea for the perpetual flow of visitors. At times I resent being landed with the whole load of it. At other times I feel good about having proved myself so capable, and thankful I'm kept so busy I have no time to dwell on my own thoughts.

The only opportunity I have to be alone is when I go out shopping. I both long for and dread these brief escapes. It is a relief to get out of the heavy atmosphere of impending death in the house, and breathe fresh air, and walk in the sunshine. It is somehow reassuring to know that life is continuing much as usual in the outside world. But sooner or later, I start thinking. That's when all the suppressed pain surfaces, and I'm afraid I'm going to crack up. Not only over what's happening to my mother. I start thinking about Pixie too. I can't avoid it; her image pops up no matter where I go to do the shopping.

As I drive past Zoo Lake, I see her sitting in a rowing boat, wearing a big floppy hat and a wicked grin as she scoops a sheet of mucky lake water over me with her oar. As I'm choosing apples in the greengrocer's, I see her sneaking up behind me and pinching my bum. Stopped at a red traffic light in Louis Botha Avenue, I see her looking at me from the passenger seat and smiling, or gazing out of the window and commenting on something that has caught her eye. Every time I see her image, a sharp pain like a razor cut rips through my midriff; and I don't understand why, if it's over between us, it should still hurt so much to think of her.

One afternoon, the pain is unbearable. I have to drive to Hillbrow. I stop the Mini outside Pixie's block of flats, and stare at the entrance with my heart thumping and my stomach tied up in knots. I don't get out. I start crying. If Pixie did suddenly appear, I would try to hide. I wouldn't want her to see me in this state. I'm not even sure if I'm crying because of her, or my mother, or simply because I'm feeling so lonely and sorry for myself. Then I remember the groceries on the back seat, and my promise to my mother that I wouldn't be away long. I pull myself together and hare back to Saxonwold at breakneck speed.

Nick is sitting on the front steps, waiting for me. 'It's about bloody time!' he snaps. 'Why were you so long?'

'Does it matter?' I snap back. 'Oh God!' I drop the bags I'm carrying. 'Is she . . .?'

He shakes his head, squinting up at me against the sunlight. 'She's begun coughing up blood,' he says hoarsely.

'Then why the hell aren't you with her,' and I charge past him, but he grabs me by the shirt.

'Don't go in there now. You'll disturb her. She's sleeping. The doctor came and gave her a strong sedative.'

I collapse on the step beside him. 'How much blood?'

He mutters something under his breath.

'What?'

'I can't . . .' His shoulders heave, and I realize he is crying. 'I can't stand seeing her . . . suffering like this.'

I gaze blindly at a crack in the bottom step.

'I just don't know . . . how I can . . . live without her.'

What about me? I want to say. *She's my mother.*

'She has been everything to me . . . Everything!'

I lay my hand on his shoulder. But he tenses at my touch, so I get up and retrieve the groceries.

'I'll make you a cup of tea,' I mumble, and head along the path outside to the kitchen.

Benjamin hails me from the rose garden. 'Master Sam! . . . Master Sam!'

I avert my face, and quicken my steps to avoid him. 'Master Sam!'

There's no escape now. He's hurrying after me, and will catch up before I reach the door. I stop.

With an edge of desperation in my voice, I ask, 'What is it, Benjamin? If it's to do with the garden, I can't—'

'The madam. How is she today?'

'Not very well.'

'Shame!' He sucks in his lower lip, contracting his cheeks into a mesh of wrinkles. 'Shame! And you, Master Sam?'

'Me?'

He takes off his hat. 'Since you are this small' – with his gnarled hand, he pats the air about two feet off the ground – 'I watch you grow. Now I see you are a big chief.'

'What do you mean?'

'Now the madam she is ill, the other master here he's no good. I see' – he jabs two fingers at his rheumy eyes – 'I know. I see Master Sam must do everything. Look after everything very very nice. Now I see you are a big man.' Straightening his bony little back, he puffs his chest out to demonstrate, and grins. 'The old master who died, your daddy, he be too much proud.'

His dried-up prune face starts swimming in front of my eyes. I blink furiously. 'Thanks, Benjamin.'

He bobs his head in acknowledgement. His own eyes are brimming. Donning his hat, he shambles back to pick up the fork he dropped on the path in his hurry to catch me.

I wipe my sleeve across my face and continue on my way with a lighter step.

* * * *

My mother has become very fragile. We have to lift and move her in bed extremely gently, so as not to bruise her paper-thin flesh. She is on morphine for the pain, and can no longer cope with a roomful of visitors. Some days she isn't well enough to see anyone. But she never complains. She sleeps a lot of the time and often wakes up vague or confused.

Nevertheless, she still manages to be concerned about her appearance, as if she is about to go on stage. She will suddenly ask if she looks all right. I can truthfully tell her she looks beautiful, because in an awesomely mysterious way, she does. As her butterfly beauty fades and shrivels, I see her body taking on the appearance of a chrysalis. And sitting by her bedside, watching her through half-closed eyes, I fancy I can glimpse within the pale shrunken husk of her former self, a more resplendent ethereal butterfly shining through. I'm aware of it especially when she first opens her eyes after she has been dozing. Her gaze doesn't seem to focus on anything, yet she smiles and there is such peace in her face, as if she is seeing something beautiful inside herself. Then, when I speak to her, the spell is broken. She frowns, as though she is trying to remember where she is. All the tension and pain come back into her expression; and I sense her disappointment as she recognizes her surroundings.

I keep remembering the scenes in Pixie's notebook where she described Bokkie sitting or lying very still, and appearing to go somewhere far away inside himself. He looked very peaceful to Pixie at such times. Like my mother. It's odd, I feel very close to Bokkie at the moment. I imagine him gazing at me from the shadows in my mother's darkened bedroom. I imagine him saying, as he said to Pixie, 'We don't die. Not really die.' I wish he could tell me what he meant.

The doctor has told us to be prepared for my mother to die any day now. He said she might lapse into a coma first. But she doesn't. On Christmas Eve, we hang a few decorations in her room. She barely notices them, and sleeps through most of Christmas Day. In the evening, alone with her while Nick is having a bath, I take her hand.

'Debs?'

Her eyelids flutter and open. She winces.

'Are you in pain?'

She blinks at me. 'What are you doing here? I was just talking to you a moment ago in your garden.'

'My garden?'

'You were showing me all your flowers.' She tries weakly to raise her head. 'Your hair! What have you done to your hair, Keith? It's different.' Keith was my father's name.

'I'm not Keith. I'm Sam, Debs,' I remind her gently.

'Oh.' A faint smile quivers on her lips. 'So you are.'

I stroke her hair. 'You know I love you, don't you, Debs?'

'You do? I'm glad.' Her fingers squeeze mine slightly. 'That's very sweet of you. I'm tired now. I must rest before the performance tonight. Will you be there?'

'Of course.'

I let her down. I'm not there. No one is. It takes place in the middle of the night, while I'm crashed out in my own bed, and Nick is in the kitchen boiling water. But perhaps it doesn't matter. Perhaps my father and others were waiting to greet her backstage, when she made her final exit quietly in her sleep. I like to think so.

* * * *

We postpone the funeral until the New Year because it is difficult to organize everything, and make all the necessary arrangements over the holiday period. It is a ridiculously hectic time. Death shouldn't have to be so complicated. By the time it is all over, I feel on the point of collapse, emotionally and physically. But there is still the will to be dealt with, and the whole estate to be sorted out.

The will, fortunately, proves to be fairly straight-forward. I inherit the house and some money, and my mother's personal possessions are divided between Nick and me. Every item is individually listed, so there aren't any problems over that. However, it will take months for the estate to be wound up; and in the meantime, it is clear that Nick and I can't stay together under the same roof for very much longer. We didn't manage to get on while my mother was alive. Now she has gone, we are failing to find anything in common at all.

He's hitting the bottle. I'm worried about him. But I'm worried about myself too. I feel as if I've lost my bearings, and any sense of direction in my life. I've had my exam results, and I've passed. That's one bit of good news; only I'm unable to work up any enthusiasm at the prospect of returning to university in a month's time.

I just can't keep Pixie out of my mind. Images of her plague me even more now than before. Images of Simon do too. I find myself imagining what it must be like to be in his shoes: poverty-stricken, and being toyed with – like a cat plays with a mouse – by the police. Sometimes, lying awake at night, I conjure up erotic pictures of Pixie and appease my sexual longings. Afterwards, I feel sick with shame, remembering my hypocritical furious disgust at discovering Simon doing the same thing. I cringe, remembering Pixie's despising sarcasm: '*Of course, you're so pure and holy – just like Gerrit.*'

I'm afraid she was right about me. When I read her notebook, I hated Gerrit for what he did to Bokkie. But I experienced an uncontrollable violence towards Simon that afternoon in Pixie's bedroom. I break out in a sweat thinking about it. I suppose that is why every time I go to the phone to dial Pixie's number, I chicken out at the last moment. If she was prepared to talk to me, she would have rung me by now, as she must have known of my mother's illness and death – it was in all the newspapers.

One morning, about a week after the funeral, Nick tells me we ought to start answering the hundreds of condolence cards. I've just got out of bed, and shambled into the kitchen, where he is making breakfast for himself.

'I've sorted the cards into two piles,' he says. 'I'll answer the ones from people I know better than you. I've put your pile on the hall table.'

I open the fridge and poke around in it. 'Where's the orange juice?'

'I finished it.'

'The whole carton?'

He grunts, like a bear with a sore head. He always has a hangover in the morning these days. 'Did you hear what I said about the cards?'

'I heard!' I snap. I'm feeling like a grizzly myself, having slept badly.

The maid, Janet, appears at the back door, and looks at me with a long face and a load of dirty washing in her arms. 'There's no more mealie-meal for porridge for Benjamin and me,' she complains. 'And the vegetables are finished yesterday, the jam too, and now the washing powder. Can you go to the shops today?'

'Don't ask me.' I jerk my thumb over my shoulder. 'Ask him. I'm tired of doing all the shopping always,' and I slam the fridge door. When I turn round, Nick is disappearing down the passage, carrying a tray.

I have a long soak in the bath. Back in my room, I discover a pile of cards on the table which Nick must have put there. I sift through them, glancing at the names below the messages of sympathy. Near the bottom of the pile, the handwriting on one card looks familiar, and the name jumps out at me: Pixie.

She has only written a few lines. I read them over and over again:

Dear Sam, I'm so sorry to hear about your mom. I hope you're okay. Thinking of you. Love, Pixie.

I'm not imagining it; she has actually used the word: *Love*. Of course, it might not mean anything. But it might. There isn't a date, so I have no idea when the card arrived. Nick must have opened it, probably in a hurry without checking the envelope, and then just added it to all the others, leaving it up to me to go through them. But he should have told me.

I career around the house in my towel, looking for him. He is in the shower. I decide I can't be bothered to wait for him to come out. Throwing on some clothes, I grab an apple from the kitchen for my breakfast, jump in the Mini, and screech down the driveway, startling the neighbour's cat digging a loo in one of the flowerbeds.

I don't rehearse what I'm going to say to Pixie. I march up to her front door and ring the bell before I can change my mind. Seconds tick by. I start to have a sinking feeling that she isn't at home. Then I hear footsteps, heavy footsteps, and wheezing as the key is turned and the door opens a crack. Cecily's face scowls at me through the aperture.

'Sam?'

'Yes.'

The door opens wider, wide enough for me to see what she has on: striped men's pyjamas and a silk smoking jacket. Her expression is formidable. She doesn't smile. Neither do I.

'Is Pixie expecting you?' she asks.

'No. But is she here? I'd like to—'

'She's in bed. Is it important? Could you—'

'What's wrong?' I feel panic. 'She isn't ill, is she?'

'No, not ill. She's tired. She needs the rest.' Cecily juts her double chin round the edge of the door. 'Look, Sam, this isn't a good time. Pixie really isn't up to visitors this morning. I'm keeping her in bed. Perhaps you could come back another day.'

I stare at her, undecided as to what to do.

'I'm sorry I can't let you in,' she says. 'But I could give Pixie a message.'

'Are you sure she isn't ill?'

She nods, allowing her face to relax briefly in a token smile. 'I'll tell her you were asking after her, shall I?'

I stare at her again. She stares back.

'Well, I'll tell her you called. Goodbye, Sam,' and she withdraws her head.

'Give her my love,' I growl, before the door closes.

I get in the car and drive, not back to Saxonwold, but out of town, away from the traffic and people. I want to go somewhere Pixie and I have never been, somewhere quiet in the country, so I can be on my own and think.

When I pass the turn-off to Wendywood, the road in front of me blurs into a carpet in the living-room of Robert Thornton's house. I see a jean-clad figure sitting cross-legged, balancing a sketch pad on her lap. We are introduced. She looks up, and my solar plexus is electrified. It is only a memory, yet the physical reaction in my midriff makes me catch my breath. I grip the steering wheel, and put my foot down, and focus on my driving.

A signpost informs me I've reached Buccleuch. I leave the highway, and let the Mini coast down a curving hill, past properties with paddocks and orchards and smart painted gateposts. The road eventually ends at some sort of country club, built in the shape of a ship. But I don't go that far. There is a narrow bridge crossing a shallow stream at the bottom of the hill. I pull on to the verge, and sit on the bridge, and watch the water gurgling past underneath. It has a soothing effect as I replay the scene at Pixie's flat over and over in my mind.

Each time I reach the same conclusion. It seems so obvious now. I must have been dense not to have realized immediately. Ten o'clock in the morning. Pixie still in bed. Cecily coming to the door in her pyjamas. It all adds up. '*I'm keeping her in bed*,' Cecily said. She was practically spelling it out to me. God! She must have enjoyed shutting the door in my face. I imagine her gloating to herself. I imagine all sorts of nasty things about her. It makes me feel better, though it doesn't stop it still hurting like hell.

I sit there a long time, watching rainbow-winged dragonflies hovering like helicopters among the reeds, and ants building a nest in the bank, and a lizard sunning itself on a rock. I remember on field trips with my father how the two of us used to sit happily for hours, observing all the little creatures going about their business in our campsite. If he were here with me now, I know what he would say: 'It's all water under the bridge, son.' I smile at that.

Then it occurs to me that Bokkie spent most of his time like this; solitary, communing with nature. I don't want to forget Bokkie, even though I want to forget Pixie. I decide I must write out his story while it is still vividly imprinted on my mind. I also decide I have to get on with my life. I haul myself up, and climb into the stifling hot Mini, and head back to town.

* * * *

Nick is sprawled on a sun-lounger in the middle of the lawn, reading the newspaper. He only looks up when my shadow falls across the page. I take a deep breath.

'Nick, we need to talk.'

'What about?'

'Things. The present situation.'

Frowning, he removes his Hollywood-style sunglasses. 'What about it?'

'Well . . . I mean, it doesn't really work, does it – the two of us living here together?'

'It might, if you were to inform me when you decide to suddenly disappear and don't come back for hours,' he grumbles. 'Where were you today?'

I grit my teeth. I've been priming myself not to react to his sniping this time. 'There was someone I had to see – a friend. Then I went for a drive. Then, on the way home, I did a big shop. We'd run out of a lot of provisions. I bought you a slab of mint chocolate. That's what you like, isn't it?'

'Yes . . . Thanks,' he mumbles. ' . . . And thanks for the shopping.'

'That's okay. I—'

'But how can I be responsible for you if I never know where you are half the time?'

I raise my eyebrows. 'Who says you have to be responsible for me?'

'Your mother would have wanted me to be.'

'No, she wouldn't,' I retort. 'She knows – knew I can look after myself.'

He is about to say something, but changes his mind and takes a swig from his glass instead. It might just be water with a slice of lemon in it, but I suspect it is actually vodka and tonic. The amount he is drinking really worries me.

'You're the one who needs looking after, I reckon,' and I laugh tersely. 'You used to drink tea at four. Not alcohol.'

'I used to do a lot of things, I don't do any more.' A note of self-pity has crept into his voice. He smiles at me sourly. 'So, anyway, what's this all about? You want me to move out? Is that what you're trying to tell me?'

'No. You've got the wrong end of the stick,' I say hurriedly. 'I'm—'

'I do realize, you know, that it's your house now.'

'It's your home too.'

'Home? Home is where the heart is,' he cracks feebly.

'This is your home for as long as you like,' I reiterate. 'But I'm moving out. That's what I've come to tell you.'

He muses, sipping his drink. 'Are you going because of me?'

'No. Not really. It would be more convenient for me to be nearer university, for one thing. But also, I just don't want to live here.'

'Nor do I.'

'How come?' I'm surprised.

'Too many memories,' he says. 'So you might as well sell the house once the estate is sorted out. I can stay until then. It shouldn't be left empty.'

'That's fine by me. And when it's been sold, Benjamin must be pensioned off with enough money to live on comfortably. And I'd like Janet to get some money too. I know she has only worked here for two years, but that's longer than any of the other maids managed to last. She deserves a bonus for that.' I grin at him.

He shrugs. 'It's your house, your money, your decision,' and he picks up his newspaper.

'One other thing, Nick.' I'm embarrassed now. 'I

haven't got any cash in the meantime, to pay my university fees, and accommodation, and living expenses.'

'Of course,' he says instantly. 'I'm sorry, I ought to have thought of that before.'

'It's understandable. There's been so much else to think about.'

'When you've worked out how much you'll need, I'll write you out a cheque. And you can always ask me for more.'

'Thanks. I appreciate that. I'll pay you back,' I assure him.

'With interest.'

'Sure.'

'I'm joking,' he says.

'I'm not.'

He puts on his sunglasses and starts reading. I walk round the lawn and come back.

'Nick, do you know yet what you'll do after the house is sold?'

'Does it matter?' he mutters.

'It does to me.'

'I might go to America. I have a friend in New York who's offered me a partnership in his theatrical agency.'

'Sounds a good idea.'

He grunts.

'You'll be okay though, won't you?'

'I'll survive.' After a moment, he asks, 'What about you?'

'Me?'

'Will you be okay?'

'I'll survive.'

We look at each other. There seems nothing more to say. I go away and leave him to his newspaper.

12

I find suitable accommodation surprisingly quickly from an advertisement on a noticeboard at Wits, and move in immediately. I'm now the occupier of a small square room in a small square tumbledown cottage, built on the crest of a rocky outcrop in Melville, only a few minutes drive from the university campus. The other inhabitants of the cottage are two guys a few years older than me. Mike is a post-graduate science student. Phillip is doing a B.A. Honours in linguistics. They are both easy to get on with and gregarious.

Within the first week of living with them, I meet a lot of people, mainly students. The new term hasn't yet started at Wits, so everybody is making the most of what is left of the holidays. I'm invited to play tennis and squash, and to go swimming, and to parties in the evenings. I keep telling myself I'm having a ball, but I'm still suffering restless nights. I wake at four, and can't get back to sleep. I finally give up trying to; I struggle out of bed and switch on the bedside lamp, and begin writing down the story of Bokkie. It is a good time to work. The house is quiet, there are no distractions; as soon as I put pen to paper, it all comes back to me. I can recall practically every word of every sentence of every page of Pixie's handwritten notebook; yet I only read it once, months ago now. But it has been like a tape playing over and over in my mind ever since.

I write very quickly for a while. Then I stop and picture in my imagination, the scenes and events I'm recording. The whole exercise is a form of catharsis, as I realize it must have been for Pixie as well. But it is more than that for me. It is a form of quest. If Bokkie

191

really was able to perceive a mystical union and oneness in all life, then I want to discover how I can perceive it too. I've never been very religious in an orthodox sense. Recently, though, I've started feeling desperately that there has to be a hidden spiritual purpose behind the suffering in existence, otherwise I can't see any point in being alive.

When the birds begin twittering sleepily outside, I open the curtains and watch the dawn spill colour into the sky. The rock-strewn ridge at the top of the sloping back yard becomes gradually visible. In my mind's eye, I see a small, lonely boy crouched up there. I see him peering over the edge, watching a small girl riding her pony in the valley below, desolately searching for him.

I see the same small girl turn into a woman with a mop of unmanageable bright hair, telling me, after her pony has died, that we should celebrate, not mourn death, as it is the end of suffering. I see her dancing determinedly to prove it. I see her smiling at me seductively. That's when I yank the curtains closed, and climb back into my cold bed, and pull the pillow over my head to try and shut out further images of her.

Then, at a Saturday luncheon party in someone's garden in Parktown, I meet Penny. She isn't a student. She is a laboratory technician at Modderfontein Dynamite Factory, and lives near there. We hit it off. She is vivacious, and forthright, and funny too. She makes me laugh. I offer her a lift home, and feel flattered when she accepts.

At her house, she informs me her parents are away on holiday, and her brother won't be back until later. 'Nobody is inside,' she says. 'I'm frightened to enter on my own in case there are burglars. Will you come in with me?' She says it in a sort of jokey manner, making her eyes look big and fearful.

'I'll be right behind you,' I assure her.

'No. You go first. You have to protect me,' and she pushes me to get out of the car.

We have coffee sitting on the chaise longue in the

living-room. It is quite a posh house. Penny is flirtatious and snuggles up close. I take her hand. Pixie's fingers used to fit mine like a warm velvety glove. Penny's long painted nails feel awkward and grasping, as if I'm clutching a claw. I realize being here isn't what I want. I'm only going through the motions. I don't want Penny, nor anyone else, except Pixie – even if I can't have her.

I make my excuses, and leave. Penny accompanies me out to the car.

'Will I see you again?' she asks.

'Sure,' I lie.

'When?' she says bluntly.

I rub my chin, dithering.

'Well, spit it out,' she demands. 'I can bear it. You don't find me attractive.'

'Not true. You're very attractive.' I look at her objectively. She is pretty. She has lovely long sleek dark hair, vivid blue eyes, and a sand-glass figure. I must be mad. 'The truth is . . . to be honest, I'm still trying to get over someone.'

'Aren't we all! You're a fool. I hope she was worth it?' And she flounces up the drive.

I think about her question while I'm driving. I can't answer it. You can't put a value on the feeling of missing someone. But the feeling makes me take the turn-off to Linbro Park.

I haven't seen Russ since Pixie and I split up. He sent me a condolence card after my mother died. I sent him a brief thank-you note back. As it is a Saturday, I'm half expecting him to be out gallivanting. However, he appears from the verandah to meet me, and shakes my hand warmly.

'It's nice to see you, Sam.'

'I was just on my way back from somewhere, and popped in to find out how you are,' I say lamely, stroking the Alsatians who are snuffling round my feet with their Geiger counter noses.

'Great. Come and have a drink, and meet Bonnie.'

'Bonnie? Who's Bonnie?'

'My assistant. I've been receiving a lot more orders for my pottery recently, and I needed help. She's proved a Godsend.'

Bonnie could be mistaken for Russ's sister. Tall and leggy, she has a pleasant freckled face like him, except that her cropped ginger hair is very curly. Her manner is also friendly and easy-going. I like her. But my opinion doesn't count. For her sake, I just hope she has managed to pass muster with Mercy.

Over a drink, we discuss Russ's expanding business. Then Russ leans across and clasps my shoulder.

'I was so sorry to hear about your mother,' he says. 'It's been a really tough time for you.'

'It hasn't been easy,' I admit.

'And now? How are you now? Are you still living at home?'

'No,' and I explain about my digs in Melville.

'Are you coping okay? Do you need anything? Money?'

Before I can answer, Bonnie jumps up.

'I gather you two haven't seen each other for a while,' she says. 'You must have a lot of catching up to do. So I'll vamoose.'

'You don't have to,' Russ tells her.

'I might as well go and start unloading the kiln.'

As she passes Russ, he grins up at her fondly.

'She's nice,' I comment when she is out of earshot.

'She sure is,' he agrees.

'Does Mercy approve of her?'

He laughs. 'She does now she's established Bonnie can't cook. Mercy is very territorial about her kitchen. She doesn't mind Emma, Bonnie's six year old daughter, in there. It's us grown-ups who have to keep out. I'm sorry you can't meet Emma today,' he says ruefully. 'She's a clown. But she's spending this weekend with her father.'

'Bonnie's married?'

'Divorced. Emma and Bonnie are living here – did I tell you?'

'No, you didn't.' I'm trying to adjust to this surprising and unpredictable change in his life-style.

'It's fun. Emma's company really livens the place up. Bonnie's too. Makes a dramatic change from Mercy and I rattling around on our own in the house.'

'I bet.'

'More punch?' He fills our glasses.

We drink in silence. I'm aware of his scrutiny, and realize I probably look very glum. I put on a smile.

'You are okay?' he asks. 'I mean really okay?'

'I'm surviving,' I tell him.

'And you're all right financially?'

'I've got enough to live on for the time being. Once the estate is wound up, I'll have plenty. So cash is not a problem.'

'Well, that's something, at least.'

One of the Alsatians lying at his feet, begins scratching. Russ bends down and rakes his fingers through its fur, searching for fleas. This seems a suitable moment to ask what I've come here to ask. I take a gulp from my glass, then put it down in case my hands start shaking.

'How is Pixie?' I say, trying to sound as if I've only now thought of her. 'Have you seen her recently?'

'Not very recently. I've been too busy to see anyone. But I've spoken to her on the phone.' He rolls the dog over on to its back, and inspects its tummy. 'She seems a lot better now.'

'Better? She hasn't been ill, has she?'

He looks up. 'When did you last see her?'

'I haven't since we – since I moved out of her flat in November. I went round there a few weeks ago, and Cecily answered the door and said Pixie was in bed. She didn't tell me Pixie was sick. She claimed she was just very tired and not to be disturbed.'

He plays with the Alsatian's tail, deliberating. ' . . . Is that all Cecily told you?'

'Yes.' I can feel my heart pounding. 'Why?'

'I presumed you knew, but obviously you don't.'

Straightening up, he directs his full attention on me. 'Simon died,' he says a bit hoarsely.

The shock stupefies me. I listen in horror as he explains that Simon's body was found lying next to the main road to Soweto, in the early hours of the morning on the third of January – the day of my mother's funeral. It was thought that Simon had been killed by a hit-and-run driver. But Jake discovered electric burn marks on the toes and fingers and chest of his nephew's corpse when he brought it home from the morgue for burial. He was convinced the Special Branch had tortured Simon, and then flung him – possibly still alive – from a speeding police car, so that his death could be passed off as a traffic accident.

'It's possible,' concludes Russ. 'The police have done this sort of thing before.'

He reaches for his glass, and takes a gulp from it. I'm gripping the arms of the chair so hard, my knuckles have turned white.

'When did . . . Pixie find out?' I stammer.

'I can't remember exactly, though it must have been about the time you called round at the flat, if Cecily was there. Pixie was in such a bad state over the news, Cecily flew up from Durban to look after her for a few days.'

I'm galvanized suddenly out of my shock. 'Cecily isn't *still* there? I thought she and Pixie had got tog—' I break off, and spring up. 'I have to go. Thanks for the drink. Bye, Russ.'

He starts to speak, but I don't wait, and whatever he says is drowned by the Alsatians' barking as they leap after me down the steps, and pursue me across the grass to my car.

* * * *

She opens the door. 'Oh, it's you,' she says, which is exactly what she said a year ago, when I arrived at her flat with all my luggage, and my heart in my mouth. She smiled that first time and put me at my ease. This time she doesn't smile. She looks at me and continues to look at me, with a small frown of uncertainty on her face while she waits for me to speak.

My heart is hammering against my ribs, my knees are trembling, and the words I had rehearsed all the way from Linbro Park have disappeared in a tumult of feelings I don't know how to express. I hold out the flowers I've bought her. She takes them wordlessly. The longing to touch her is almost unbearable.

'I'm so sorry, about Simon, I've just heard,' I choke out.

Her eyes fill up. 'I'm sorry about your mother.'

'Pixie, I . . .'

She makes a little move towards me. It is enough. I grab her and press her against me. She squeezes me tightly.

'Oh God, it's so good to see – you feel so good!' I'm on the verge of crying with relief.

'I've missed you too; terribly!' she admits, and shuffles backwards, drawing me into the hall.

I kick the door shut behind us, then we pull apart and gaze at each other.

'You've got thinner,' I admonish her.

'You're not meant to say that.' She smiles. 'You're supposed to say I look beautiful.'

'You *are* beautiful.' There is a lot more I want to say to her. But it can wait.

She slips her arms round my neck. 'Hold me again, Sam. Just hold me.'

We stand there for several minutes, with our foreheads pressed together and our noses touching. Then I kiss her.

'Mmm,' she says.

'Mmmmm!' I agree. And I scoop her up and carry her, laughing, along the passage to the bedroom.

13

Pixie says I have grown more hairs on my chin, and more muscle on my shoulders. My body does seem to have filled out a bit, but I don't know about the hairs – I shave every day, and you can't count stubble. She doesn't mean it literally, anyway. It's her way of saying I have become more mature.

'I agree with you,' I tell her. 'But why did the growing pains have to hurt like hell?'

'Because,' she says, 'we have to go through hell to be able to appreciate heaven.'

I grin at her smugly. 'Well, I'm glad I've got to heaven.'

'You haven't!' she snorts. 'I reckon you've got a lot more hell to go through first. And I'm here to see you suffer. So keep stirring that sauce. And when it's ready, you can slice this onion and have a good cry.'

I've moved back into her flat. But it is on a different basis this time. I've moved in, not as her lodger, but as her lover. Her bedroom is now our bedroom. We've rearranged the furniture, and reorganized the cupboards to make space for my clothes and personal possessions. The room is more cramped, but it's cosy. And we have two pictures on the wall. Pixie's painting of our kloof, and the portrait of Bokkie. It was my decision to drag the portrait out from under the bed and rehang it. I wanted it to be where I could look at it. The eyes no longer disturb me. Since writing out Bokkie's story, I feel a strange affinity with him. I feel, now, when I look at the portrait, that his gaze is trying to tell me something; something I want and need to know: that death is not the end.

The spare room has officially become my study. I have to spend some time in there, unfortunately. Lectures have started again, and I'm trying to discipline myself to keep up with the workload this year. I'm also making an effort to participate more in campus life. I know quite a few people through Mike and Phillip; I chat to them in the canteen, and join in student activities between and after lectures.

But university is still not my main concern. The best part of the day is coming home to the flat and Pixie. That, and waking in the morning and feeling her lying snuggled up next to me in bed – especially at the weekends when we don't have to get up early!

During the week, she is as busy as I am, painting portraits again to help pay the rent. Cecily has taken back to Durban the few paintings Simon managed to do after the rest were destroyed, and also a selection of Pixie's. A few of Pixie's have sold; but none yet of Simon's, which upsets Pixie. She thinks it is because the affluent white visitors to Cecily's art gallery aren't interested in hanging paintings by a black artist in their homes. Cecily doesn't altogether agree with her. Just as likely a reason she feels, is that Simon's pictures aren't comfortable to live with.

'But that's just my point,' Pixie protests angrily. 'Simon portrayed the reality of life in a black township, and white people don't want to be faced with it, especially while they're relaxing in their lounges, sipping gin and tonic, and checking on the state of their investments in the financial pages.'

Pixie and I don't talk much about Simon. I did tell her that I felt terribly guilty about him, and sometimes wondered if I wasn't partly to blame for his death.

'We're all to blame,' she retorted. 'And anyway I'm more guilty than you are for what happened to him.'

'That's preposterous!' I said. 'You of all people! Why?'

I didn't receive an answer. For some reason, she

looked uncomfortable and shrugged, and changed the subject.

It is unfortunate that her inspiration for her own paintings seems to have dried up again, though it doesn't appear to bother her. She is spending all her spare time reading her way through a lot of banned political literature, lent to her by someone she met at the Institute of Race Relations. I've given up worrying about the possibility that the police might still be keeping a surveillance on the flat. It seems less likely now Simon is dead. But I do get a bit anxious at the effect Pixie's reading has on her. She becomes very worked up over a collection of Nelson Mandela's speeches, writings, and court statements at his trial in 1964.

'This man should be the prime minister of South Africa,' she vehemently claims, 'not incarcerated in prison on a life-sentence.'

'But he's a terrorist,' I say unwittingly.

Clenching her teeth, she looks daggers at me. 'Oh God, Sam! *When* will you wake up? The terrorists in this country are the people in power. For pity's sake, read this speech of Mandela's,' and she chucks a dog-eared typescript at me in bed.

I read it. I'm impressed. 'But how do you know he's being honest, and genuinely means what he says?' I ask.

She snatches the document back, lies down, rolls over away from me, and switches off her bedside lamp. 'I give up on you, Sam,' she says coldly. 'Goodnight.'

However, she doesn't give up on me. She is never angry for very long. In the morning, when I rouse her with a cup of coffee, she smiles at me sweetly. I know I'm forgiven, and I climb back into bed, and we have a cuddle. She is so sleepy and soft and appealing at this time of the day, like a tousled dormouse. I remember Russ warning me last year not to be jealous and possessive, or I would screw things up. '*Just love her*,' he had said simply.

Love is simple at moments like this. I look at her, and

I'm happy because I know I love her. And I can believe I've overcome any jealous, possessive streak.

I have no way of knowing my complacency is about to be put to the test.

* * * *

Pixie makes the announcement as we are washing the dishes after supper.

'I went to the doctor today,' she says, handing me a plate to dry. I almost drop it.

'You didn't tell me.' I peer at her anxiously. I can't see anything visibly wrong with her. 'You just said you were going to town this morning.'

She smiles, almost apologetically. 'I didn't want to worry you.'

'Well, I am worried.' I put down the plate, and take hold of her shoulders, turning her to face me. 'Nothing's the matter with you, is it?'

She shakes her head. But she isn't looking me in the eye, and her smile seems stuck on, as if she is trying to hide herself behind it.

'Then why did you go to the doctor? Was it just a routine check up?'

'Yes. I thought I ought to have one, as I've been missing my periods.'

'But you haven't been. You had one last week. And last month.'

'I lied to you. I had a spot or two of blood – hardly really even that.'

I grip her harder. 'How long has this been going on?'

'I've missed two...' She shrugs. 'Three, I guess. The first month I wasn't too bothered as I'm often very irregular, especially if I'm feeling below par, which I was in January.' She wipes a wet soapy hand across her brow, leaving a smear of tiny foam bubbles on her skin. 'But then, after the second month I—'

'Pixie!' I shake her. 'Why didn't you tell me? Why did you lie to me?'

'Because I didn't want to concern you unnecessarily. I know your mom had cancer of the uterus, and I thought if I said anything, you might start to worry that . . .' She swallows. ' . . . Well, I was getting a bit worried, myself. That's why I made the appointment today.'

I feel as if my legs are going to give way under me. 'And . . .?'

'The doctor says I'm okay.'

'Thank God for that!' I move to hug her, but she steps back.

'I'm pregnant, Sam.'

I do a double take.

'I know,' she says abjectly, 'it was a bit of a surprise to me too.'

'But . . .' I flounder, flabbergasted. 'You're on the pill. I thought it was supposed to be safe. Are you sure you're pregnant?'

'The doctor says I am.'

'Crikey!' I have to think about it for a moment. Then I grin, and grab her.

'Don't! . . . Please,' she says, as I try to cuddle her, and she backs off. 'It's not your baby, Sam. I'm so sorry. It's Simon's.'

The stuffing is knocked out of me suddenly. I have to sit down. There is a chair behind me. I collapse on to it, staring at her with a glazed expression.

'I'm so very truly sorry, Sam,' she says.

I shake my head, uncomprehending. 'I don't understand.'

'No, I know.' She bites on her lip. 'I don't either – I mean, understand why it had to happen,' She comes and flops down at the table, opposite me. 'But if you're prepared to listen, I'll try to explain.'

I narrow my eyes at her in hostility. 'Were you having an affair with Simon while I was living here?'

'Of course not!'

'So it was after I left?'

'No! I never wanted to have an affair with Simon. He was just a boy, for pity's sake. I felt motherly towards him, that's all.'

'Oh come off it,' I sneer. 'You aren't going to suggest you became pregnant putting on your nightie after he had been rubbing . . . unless . . .' I sit up suddenly, clenching my hands. In a hollow voice, I ask, 'Pixie, he didn't rape you, did he?'

She half-shakes her head. 'I need to explain the whole thing from the beginning if you—'

'Beginning? Beginning of what? You having it off with him?'

'Sam! . . . Sam, please!' Her eyes are pleading, her face white and forlorn. She looks on the point of tears. 'This is very painful and difficult. It is for both of us, but I can't talk about it if you keep jumping down my throat.'

I swear, bound up, and storm across the kitchen. At the window, I stand, glaring out. Her confession feels like a knife in my guts. For a few moments, I hold my breath, gnashing my teeth. Then I breathe out heavily, walk back, sit down again, and fold my hands in my lap.

'Okay,' I say. 'Explain.'

She sniffs, and smiles at me apologetically. 'Have you got a tissue?'

I pass her my hankie. She blows her nose. Then she shifts in her seat, and begins her explanation in a monotone, as if she's trying to detach herself from feeling what she is telling me.

'After that day you confronted Simon in the bedroom,' she says, 'I didn't see him for weeks. He just disappeared. Even Jake didn't know where he was, until Simon suddenly turned up at his house on Christmas Eve. He told Jake he was living in a shed in someone's back yard in Soweto, hiding from the police who, he claimed, were going to kill him for refusing to co-operate with them. Jake said he was in a terrible state; filthy and frightened, and unable to talk without stammering. He stayed the night, stole some money out of Jake's wallet, and took off again in the early morning while the rest of the household were still asleep. It was the first time he had stolen anything from Jake. Jake tried to discover where he was living, without success. Then . . .' She breaks off. 'Have you got a cigarette?' she asks me. 'I've smoked all mine.'

I pull out my packet, give her one and light it. She sucks on the filter as if she's gasping for oxygen, not nicotine. It occurs to me that she shouldn't be smoking if she is pregnant, but I don't say anything. I light up, myself, and scowl at her.

'Well, go on,' I mutter. I want to get it over with. 'When did you see him again?'

'Not until New Year's Eve – night – whatever.' She tips ash clumsily into the ashtray, and sits back, away from me. 'He unexpectedly arrived on my doorstep at about two o'clock in the morning, looking as if he hadn't slept for days. He was shaking uncontrollably, and talking gibberish; I couldn't get any sense out of him. But I managed to calm him down a little. I wrapped him up in blankets and gave him a hot drink laced with whisky. That seemed to knock him out. So I put him to bed in the spare room, and when I was certain he was asleep, I went back to bed myself.' She pauses to puff on her cigarette. Her hands have started trembling.

Frowning, I ask, 'Are you all right?'

She jerks her head. 'It's just . . . I'll never forget the terrible mewling noises he was making, like an injured kitten. They woke me up. And I found him, naked, down on his hands and knees on the floor, trying to climb under his bed. He didn't seem to recognize me, or know where he was. But when I spoke to him, he started pleading with me to hide him because they were after him. I made him sit on the bed and tried to comfort him. . . . Oh God!' She covers her face with her hands. 'I don't think I can go on with this.'

'You must,' I encourage her gruffly, though I'm dreading hearing the next bit. 'You've managed to get this far. Just let it come out. Did something happen then?'

She takes her hands away, and looks at me. Clearing her throat, she says, 'I could see he had an erection, but he wasn't . . . he was just so frightened. I know fear can do that sometimes.' Her face has reddened. Her gaze, though, doesn't waver from mine. 'His body was shaking so much, his teeth were chattering. I tried to get up to pull the blanket off the mattress to wrap round him. But he must have believed I was leaving him, because he grabbed me and clung on desperately, gibbering in terror. I lost my balance, and we fell back on the bed with him on top of me. I could have pushed him off,' she says with a tortured expression, 'but I didn't. And it happened so fast. It wasn't even sexual. He was still shaking, and I was holding him and I could feel the awful convulsions of terror wracking him, and it was like an' – she catches her breath – 'automatic release. I mean, he wasn't even really inside... That's why it seems so incredible that I could be pregnant – even though I had stopped taking the pill after you left.'

I grasp my lighter and press it tightly between my palms. 'So what happened next?'

'Can I have another cigarette?' she rasps.

I light her one, and hand it across the table. She slumps back in her chair, smoking for a while without answering. I watch her eyes fill up with tears.

'He cried,' she says suddenly. 'Like a baby. He just cried and cried and cried. I couldn't get him to stop. Finally, he cried himself to sleep. I went and had a bath. When I returned, he was gone. He'd left the flat. Two days later his body was found. So you see...' She lifts her hands up in a helpless gesture. ' ... If I hadn't had a bath, I could have stopped him leaving, and the police might not have caught him. He might still be alive.'

'That's nonsense,' I say hoarsely. 'It isn't your fault. You can't blame yourself for his death.'

She rubs her eyes fiercely. 'Do you want a cup of coffee?'

She gets up and makes it. I doodle with my finger on the table, drawing invisible circles and squares and triangles.

'We haven't finished the washing-up,' she says.

I don't look round. 'It can wait . . . Will you have an abortion?'

'No,' she says. 'Did you want coffee? Or tea?'

'Coffee . . . You won't even consider it?'

'An abortion? No,' she says, and I somehow knew that would be her answer. 'I can't. I didn't wish this to happen. But it has. And this little guy inside me is obviously determined to exist. So who am I to stand in his way?'

I draw a large question mark on the wood with my nail. 'How do you know it's a boy?'

'Or girl.' She lays her hand on my shoulder from behind. 'I'm truly, terribly sorry, Sam. I really am. I know this changes everything. But you don't have to stick around. It's my responsibility. You're free to push off whenever you like.'

I feel the touch of her lips on the top of my head. Then she puts down my cup and walks round to sit on the other side of the table. We drink our coffee in sombre silence. We both have a lot to think about. I look up at some point and catch her gazing at me in the way she does after we've made love. The same tender soulfulness is in her face now. As our eyes meet, she smiles sorrowfully. I reach out and take her hand.

'Okay,' I say, thick-voiced. 'So what will we call it?'

She strokes my fingers with her thumb, studying my face. 'Are you sure you want to stay?'

I shrug. 'I have no choice. I love you.'

'But can you love the baby?'

I hesitate. I'm not certain but I want to be, and I feel determined enough. 'Yes,' I decide. 'So what will we call him or her?'

She laughs nervously. 'I think that's going to be the least of the problems.'

'You'll have to give up smoking.'

'Yes,' she agrees. 'Can I have a last one now?'

'No.' I kiss her hand.

'All right,' she says.

We go to bed. But neither of us sleep very well.

14

Autumn. The foliage of Liquidambar and other decidu-
ous trees become firework displays of sulphur, gold, and
scarlet sparks on the brightest days. The fallen leaves
weave themselves into brown quilts round the base of
the stems, suggesting the trees are tucking up their feet
to keep their toes warm in the coming winter. As the
sun sets further north each day, it departs in a mellow
gold illumination.

I see gold everywhere; in the sky, in the trees, in the
shafts of sunlight slanting over buildings and the ground.
I tell myself humorously that perhaps I am seeing Bokkie's golden light in everything at last. But I am more
inclined to believe the glow is reflected from my Pixie-
woman.

It is amazing. Pregnancy has transformed her. She
seems to emit a radiance that is almost awesome. I don't
know whether this is a common feature of pregnancy,
or whether it is just that Pixie has unexpectedly found
a deep source of fulfilment in her pending motherhood,
deeper than any other experience in her life so far. At
times I feel jealous that it is the baby growing inside her
who has caused her such contentment, and not me. I
grumble about it in a sort of jokey manner.

'Oh dear, is your little nose out of joint?' she teases,
and gives me a hug. 'Don't be silly. It's a circle, don't
you see?'

'What is?'

'Happiness.' She traces a circle in the air. 'One line,
see? Not two or three. Just one line making a circle;
you, me, the baby, all joined up together. If you weren't
here, the line would be too short to complete the circle.'

'It could complete a smaller circle though,' I point out logically.

She snorts disparagingly. 'Men! You're so irrationally rational. I'm not talking about a geometric circle. I'm talking about a happiness circle. It's different.'

'Oh.' And I smile at her indulgently, and take her arm to help her up the flights of stairs to the flat.

Not that she needs a helping hand. She is fit and strong, with seemingly boundless energy. She says she has never felt so well. She eats like a horse – but then she does have two mouths to feed. We've both given up smoking. I miss it. Pixie doesn't, even though she was more addicted than me. The smell of cigarettes makes her feel nauseous now. So does the smell of raw flesh and blood when we pass a butcher's shop. Despite that, her doctor keeps crossly insisting she ought to eat meat while she is pregnant.

'I'd only bring it up again,' she tells him.

He draws his eyebrows together and squints down his short-barrelled nose at her, as if he is lining her up in his sights. He is a hunting, shooting, and fishing man. 'You could try, at least,' he complains.

'Dr Smart.' Pixie lets go of my hand and leans forward in her chair, plonking her elbows down on his desk. 'I'm healthy, aren't I?'

'Yes,' he admits almost reluctantly.

'I'm not anaemic, or short of minerals, or vitamins, or protein?'

He glances through the notes in her file, as though he is hoping to find some evidence to the contrary. Usually he ignores me during the consultations – possibly because he disapproves of us not being married. But he turns to me now.

'You have to think of the development of the baby,' he says.

'I am,' retorts Pixie before I can answer, and she fixes her deadly sweet smile on him. 'The fear and pain of a slaughtered animal must be registered in its flesh. I don't want to pass that on to my baby. I want my baby to be happy and healthy and placid. After all, we are what we eat, are we not?'

'That is a very interesting opinion, Miss de Jager.' And he heaves himself to his feet to indicate our time is up.

Back out in the street, I tell Pixie I wish she would change her doctor. I've said it to her before. 'I don't care if he's a good doctor, there are others,' I insist.

'I know. But his consulting rooms are the closest to the flat, which is handy. Besides, Dr Smart is a challenge. Sometimes seeds do sprout, even on the stoniest ground. I'm not ready to give up on him yet.'

He doesn't annoy her, like he does me. Nothing aggravates her these days. Or worries, or disturbs her. She seems content to take each day as it comes, and leave the future to look after itself. That is what worries and disturbs *me*. We *need* to start making some crucial decisions, but she keeps avoiding doing so.

It is obvious we have to leave the country before the baby is born. If we stay, I can imagine the possible headlines: *White Woman Gives Birth to Coloured Baby in White Hospital*, and: *Son of Famous Actress Claims Fatherhood*. My mother would turn in her grave.

But that would be just the start. The baby would immediately be classified non-white, making it illegal for it to live in a white area. We would then be evicted from our flat, and have nowhere else to go. When I point this out to Pixie, a little glint comes into her eye.

'In that case,' she says, 'you and I would have to get ourselves re-classified as coloured, and move into a coloured township.'

'Forget it!' I protest in horror. 'No way. Not me.'

'All right then. You stay white, and just come and visit baby and me.' She grins. 'But we wouldn't be able to indulge in any hanky-panky because that would be against the law.'

I am not amused. 'This is no time to joke. Be serious! We have to—'

'I am being serious.' She arranges a cushion at the end

209

of the sofa, and flops down on her back, resting her feet on my lap. 'So we'd better make the most of the hanky-panky while we still can,' she says, and starts tickling me with her toes, rolling her eyes suggestively.

I push her feet away, get up, and switch off the record player. Then I turn and confront her from this safe distance. 'Pixie, just please listen to me for a minute. In a few weeks time, the money I've inherited from my mom will be in my bank account. And soon, with any luck, the house will be sold. Nick's put it on the market, and he's already received an offer.'

'Yes. You told me,' she says. 'What will Nick do when it's sold?'

'He's moving into a friend's flat in Killarney for a while.' I haven't seen Nick, but I've spoken to him on the phone a few times. He seemed in better spirits, not the liquid kind, and sounded almost friendly. 'But, anyway, the point is, Pixie, we have cash now. And we've *got* to get out of here before the baby is born. You *know* that. We can't stay in South Africa. It's insane to even contemplate it.'

'This country is my home,' she says mildly.

'We can make another home somewhere else.'

'Where?' she asks.

I shrug. 'England? America? Canada? Australia? New Zealand? With the funds we have' – I gesture grandly – 'the world can be our oyster, m'dear.'

'And you don't think we'll come up against racism in any of those places?'

'Pixie! Dammit! What are you asking for? Heaven? Isn't it enough just to escape from hell?'

She smiles at my theatricality, and sits up. Her eyes search my face. 'Do *you* really want to leave South Africa, Sam? I mean, never mind about what's best for me. What's best for you? What about your degree?'

'To hell with my degree. To hell with everything. Let's just get away from the laws of this country before it's too late,' I plead desperately.

She holds out her arms. 'Come here,' she says huskily.

I give in. I can't resist that look in her eyes. I go to her.

'I love you, Sam,' and she takes my fingers and presses them to her cheek.

'Good. Then listen to me for—'

'Sshh!' She lays my hand on her abdomen. 'Can you feel?'

'What?' There is a sudden slight flutter under my hand. 'Oh, my gosh!' I look up at her in wonder. 'Is that the baby?'

'He's kicking like a kangaroo,' she exaggerates.

'He or she.'

'No. He. I'm sure it's a boy.'

'You can't be sure,' I say with male logic.

She just smiles her little mysterious woman's secret smile. The baby kicks again.

'I know what he's saying,' I tell her. 'He's saying "Let's go to Australia, you guys." '

She laughs and lies back, turning on her side to make room for me to lie down with her on the sofa. It is a tight fit, but very snug.

I kiss her. 'Shall we?' I say. 'Go to Australia?'

'Maybe,' she murmurs. 'Let's talk about it tomorrow. Not now. Now's too precious ... Uh-huh, he's at it again. Did you feel that?'

'Yes.' It is awe-inspiring – the miracle of the new little life moving inside her. I wrap my arms round them both, and relax, and forget about the need to make a decision.

'I see what you mean,' I say.

'About what?'

'The happiness circle.'

She just smiles.

* * * *

Winter. The mornings are now crisp, and frosty sometimes, the nights cold. When the wind blows, it has a freezing abrasive edge, scouring skin dry and raking dust from the pavements into the air. People's faces look chapped and colourless, like the faded flowers in neglected gardens.

But Pixie blossoms. While the rest of Mother Nature contracts and shrivels, she expands and blooms. The changing shape of her body is a source both of amusement and amazement to the two of us. Her waistline has disappeared, her breasts are swelling, and her stomach is now the first part of her to enter a room. I delight in watching her undress and climb into bed. She might have become more ungainly, but there is a sensual womanly beauty in her ballooning flesh – like the beauty of a ripening peach.

If only she wasn't so darn stubborn! Time is running out, and she still keeps postponing making any plans to leave the country. She seems unable to consider the future. She is totally bound up in the present, taking each new day as it comes. My own increasing panic doesn't appear to get through to her. She acts as if she believes motherhood will give her the unassailable might to keep the whole apartheid system at bay from her child; like an invincible lioness protecting her cub. I think there is a part of her that feels leaving the country would be cowardly, and that she should stay and fight the enemy, not run away in defeat.

But if she feels that, nobody else does. The three friends who are in the know about the baby; Russ, Cecily, and Jake; all feel as I do. Cecily came and spent a weekend, and told Pixie in no uncertain terms that she had to pack her bags and clear off; for her own sake, as well as the baby's – and for Sam's sake too, she even added. It was the first time I found myself on the same side as Cecily. We had a few chats together alone, and she started to grow on me.

Russ advised Pixie along the same lines – only he didn't put it quite so bluntly as Cecily. And then Jake turned up late one night and had a long talk with Pixie. After he arrived, I couldn't prevent myself peering out furtively through the window, as I used to do. He noticed and laughed.

'It's okay, Sam,' he said. 'The Special Branch dogs seem to be leaving me alone at the moment. I guess they're sniffing up some other poor guy's trouser leg.'

'They aren't dogs,' Pixie put in. 'Dogs are nice. The S.B. are Nazi psychopaths.'

I excused myself and went and made coffee. When I returned, Pixie was explaining that she didn't think she could survive away from Africa. 'I draw my nourishment from the African landscape,' she said. 'The light, the colours, the textures of the rocks and the veld, the smell of the earth.'

'Me too,' Jake told her. 'Africa *is* the marrow of my bones. But you don't have to leave Africa. You don't even have to leave southern Africa. Go to Swaziland, Lesotho, Botswana. I have relatives in Lesotho, and contacts in Swaziland and Botswana who could help you settle in.'

Pixie looked at me questioningly.

'Sounds a good idea,' I said. 'It means we wouldn't be too far away, and friends could visit us.'

Jake smacked his thigh. 'Well, that's settled then.'

'Perhaps.' Pixie smiled at him. 'But I'm not sure. I need to think about it.'

I cursed under my breath. Jake shook his head at me.

'What are we going to do with this woman of yours, Sam?'

'Ask her, not me,' I grouched. 'I give up. She won't even agree to marry me. She wants us to wait until the baby is born and see how we both feel then.'

'I didn't say I didn't want to marry you.' Pixie stood up and stretched, rubbing her stomach. Then she walked over to me, and planted a kiss on the back of my neck. 'There's plenty of time yet,' she claimed placidly, and took herself off to the loo.

'Keep trying,' I urged Jake. 'If you don't get through to her, nobody will.'

He tried, and failed, and went home when Pixie said she had to go to bed because she was falling asleep in her chair.

To stop myself worrying about it all, I carry on with my university work. But it has become a drudgery. I can't see myself completing my degree at the present time. And I'm no longer even sure I want to be a journalist. I've been feeling there must be something more useful I could do with my life, though I don't know what.

Just recently, while I'm shut up in the spare room, Pixie has taken to painting again. She paints me, flowers, chairs, babies, landscapes, buildings, and lots of animals – especially duikers. She says she is just having fun, and her pictures reflect her mood. Her portraits of me look happy; her inanimate objects look happy; her babies smile; and so do her duikers as they spring about, or stand, or hide in foliage. She paints more duikers than anything else. I feel I know the reason: she is thinking of Bokkie. It doesn't surprise me. I imagine she is hoping her baby, being coloured, will turn out to be a bit like Bokkie. I catch myself hoping the same thing.

I'm knocked sideways, therefore, when she announces one evening that she has settled on a name for the baby. 'I've decided I'd like to call him Sam,' she says.

'Sam?' I gape at her over the book I'm reading. 'My name? How come?'

'Why do you look so surprised?' Her face is amused. 'Don't you fancy him being called after you?'

'Yes . . . but – yes, of course. Only won't it be a little confusing having two Sams?'

'We can give Sam Junior a nickname. Roo, or Poo, or something.'

'And if it's a girl?'

'We can still name her Sam, short for Samantha.'

'But Sam isn't very original,' I protest self-consciously.

'He is,' and she gives me a loving smile.

A little later, I go out to buy her some marshmallows. She has started developing these sudden unpredictable cravings. As I step out of the building, a cold blast of air hits me. I pause to zip up my wind-cheater. Overhead, the evening sky is showing a trillion specks of light, uncurtained by clouds. Judging from the temperature, there will be a frost later. With a big grin on my face, I stamp my feet to warm them.

I'm on a high. It isn't the naming of the baby that is significant to me. It is the sentiment behind Pixie's decision. She is intimating that she considers me, Sam, to be the father of her child.

Shoving my hands in my pockets, I swagger along the pavement, whistling.

* * * *

Pixie is six and a half months pregnant. I'm on holiday from university. She wakes me up one morning with a smacker of a kiss, and a beaming smile.

'Let's get married,' she says. 'And let's go and live in Lesotho. And let's make love.'

I wipe the sleep from my eyes. 'In that order?'

'No. In the reverse order.'

'We can't.' I struggle to sit up. 'We can't make love.'

'Why not? We have up until now. What's so different about today?'

'You weren't prepared to marry me before. Now that you are, I think we should do the proper thing, and wait until we've tied the knot, or we're at least officially engaged.'

'In that case,' she says, 'get your tail out of bed, and go and buy me a ring, pronto.'

'All right.'

I push the bedclothes back, and lift my feet on to the floor. She snatches at my arm.

'Sam. Come back. I'm only joking.'

My heart drops. 'You're only joking? About going to Lesotho, and getting married?'

'No, I'm serious about that.'

I peer into her face doubtfully. 'What's caused you to decide so suddenly?'

'I don't know,' she says. 'But it feels right.'

'You won't change your mind?'

'I promise.' She crosses her heart.

'Okay. Then stay here. Don't move.'

I pad down the passage to the spare room and return, hiding something in my fist. She looks at me with big eyes as I kneel on the bed, take her left hand, and slide a ring on to her finger.

'It fits,' I say, with satisfaction.

She ogles the sparkling diamond. I kiss her.

'Well, do you like it?' I demand.

'Sam!' . . . She flings her arms round my neck, and squeezes the breath out of me. 'How long have you had this?'

'I bought it the day after you told me you were pregnant. I've been waiting for you to come to your senses.'

'Yes!' she says instantly.

'What?'

'I agree to marry you.'

'About time too.' I plump up her pillows. 'Now lie down.'

'Lie down?'

'Both of you.' I grin. 'I'm going to love you to death.'

In the evening, we invite Russ to join us for a meal out to celebrate. We would have invited Bonnie too, but she and Emma are away for the weekend, visiting Bonnie's mother in Benoni. Pixie chooses a Chinese restaurant. Her latest craving is for noodles, of all things. We're in good form, the three of us. We stuff ourselves, and laugh a lot, and Pixie and I play footsie-footsie under the table – like two adolescents out on their first date.

It is quite late when we pay the bill and leave. Halfway back to the car, Russ discovers he doesn't have his reading glasses, and returns to the restaurant to look for them. It is too cold to stand about waiting for him. Pixie and I walk on to where I've left the Mini in a narrow cul-de-sac, which is deserted now at this time of night. Earlier it had been full of parked cars. I'd had to let Pixie and Russ out before I squeezed the Mini into the only free space, alongside a skip of builders' rubble on the pavement.

I jump into the car to move it away from the skip, so that I can open the passenger door wide enough for Pixie to get in. The engine is cold. I have to rev it loudly to keep it going. And that is probably why I don't hear them come out of the alleyway behind the skip. It is only once I have set the car in motion that I'm suddenly aware of voices raised in argument very close by; two African voices – a man's and a woman's. I jerk my head round in consternation to check on Pixie. She is still standing where she was on the pavement. But now she has been joined by two scuffling figures.

Yanking on the handbrake, I fumble for the door catch in blind panic, wasting precious seconds, before the door flies open and I practically fall out into the road. It's only a short distance I have to cover, and I've never run so fast in all my life. But I don't get there in time. That is the nightmare that haunts me afterwards. I see it happen, and it is over in a trice, but it seems to take place in slow motion because I can't get there in time!

I see the man raise his hand and I catch the glint of a knife. The woman screams, and ducks behind Pixie as she steps in between them, shouting at the man. I see the man lunge forward, and jump back. A split-second later, I canon into him. The force of the collision sends us both sprawling. By the time I pick myself up, he is scrambling to his feet yards away, with blood pouring from his nose. I'm aware of him breaking into a limping run and fleeing, as I turn towards Pixie. I'm aware of the terrible high-pitched wailing in my ears coming from the woman who is now supporting Pixie in her arms.

Pixie's hands are clasped across her breast, and her face is very pale, but she manages to smile at me as I gently lift her fingers and discover the small tear in the bodice of her maternity dress. There is only a little blood oozing from it, which I find reassuring. I grab the woman's shawl and lay it on the ground with my jacket. Then I lower Pixie down on to her back, press my clean hankie against her wound, and tell the woman to fetch a cushion from the Mini for her head.

I'm shaking like a leaf, and from now on, everything that happens, seems to happen in a blur. Russ appears and instantly disappears again to call an ambulance. I take off my jersey and wrap it round Pixie's shoulders. She keeps saying she is all right, but she feels very cold. I strip off my shirt and vest and cover her feet and legs with them.

The woman kneels beside her, rocking back and forth, and crying, 'I'm so sorry, Madam, I'm so sorry, Madam, I'm so sorry, Madam.' She isn't altogether sober. I can smell the alcohol on her breath.

I tell her to shut up. But she doesn't. She starts whimpering and pleading.

'Please, Master. I haven't got a pass, Master. If the police catch me, I'll be in big trouble. I'm so sorry, Master, but can I go now?'

Pixie nods at her weakly. 'Yes . . . go,' she whispers, and closes her eyes.

The woman starts to rise.

'You stay!' I shake a trembling finger at her. 'We need you for a witness. You know the man. You can identify him.'

She begins crying again, more quietly this time, thank goodness.

Russ returns. Pixie is very white and cold. She opens her eyes only briefly when we add Russ's jacket and jersey and shirt to the inadequate coverings over her. It feels like an eternity before we hear sirens in the distance. Pixie's eyes flicker, and focus on the woman.

'Run!' she whispers urgently. 'Run!'

The woman crawls away on all fours. Then she struggles stiffly to her feet, and makes off in a shambling gait. Pixie raises her head to watch her. After the woman has disappeared into the alleyway, Pixie looks relieved and shuts her eyes again. Moments later, a police car and an ambulance draw up.

I can't handle any questions about what happened. Now that I know Pixie is in expert hands, I've fallen into a state of blank shock. I follow her stretcher into the ambulance, leaving Russ to deal with the police and drive the Mini to the hospital.

On the way there, Pixie dies. I'm holding her hand, and I feel the life leave her fingers. It is a very peaceful passing. She dies with a faint smile on her lips.

The ambulance man attending her is taken by surprise. He tries to revive her, but it is useless. Her wound hadn't appeared to be that serious. But according to the coroner's report at the inquest later, the point of the knife just nicked Pixie's heart, causing it to leak into the pericardium and fill it up; with the result that her heart literally drowned in its own blood.

'She's gone, hasn't she?' I say dully. I feel as if I'm dead too and nothing is real now.

He nods gravely. 'I'm sorry.'

'What about the baby? Can you save it?'

'How many months old?'

'Seven . . . seven and a half . . .' I can't remember. 'No – six and a half.' Someone else seems to be talking for me; it is strange to recognize the voice as my own.

He purses his lips, looking doubtful.

In the casualty department, they whisk Pixie away somewhere. I sit on a hard chair and wait. I'm shivering and my teeth are chattering. A nurse wraps a blanket round me, and gives me a hot drink. Russ turns up. We wait together. Eventually a doctor comes and tells us they couldn't do anything for either Pixie or the baby inside her. Both were dead on arrival at the hospital.

It is well after midnight when we walk out into the black cold night. Russ puts his arm round my shoulders.

'You're coming home with me. Okay?'

My head nods automatically. It doesn't feel like it's my head. It doesn't feel like it's my body. It all feels like a dream – a horrendous nightmare. I cling to the hope

I will wake up soon, and find myself in bed with Pixie asleep beside me. I get into the Mini.

In silence, Russ drives to Linbro Park, and pours each of us a stiff whisky as soon as we arrive. Mercy suddenly appears at the doorway of the living-room.

'What's wrong, Russ?' she says. 'Something's wrong. I saw you come home. But where's your car?' She glances in my direction. 'And where's Pixie?'

'I'll explain, Mercy.' Russ crosses the room and takes her wrist. 'Let's go to the kitchen.'

As he leads her away, she stares back at me over her shoulder with a frightened expression. I hear the kitchen door close, and the muffled sound of Russ's voice, followed by an awful blood-curdling shriek from Mercy and loud sobs. I feel the shriek inside me as a tearing open, and an awareness of an excruciating anguish that my mind can't face. I blank it out, gulp down what's left of my drink, and shakily pour another tot from the bottle.

Russ returns. Numbly, I contemplate his drawn, haggard face.

'Sorry about that,' he says, 'but she knew something was wrong. She's psychic. I'm just going to take her a whisky. Help yourself to another one. I'll be back in a minute.'

For a while after this, he and I sit, nursing our drinks, listening to the grandfather clock ticking in the corner. Then Mercy joins us. Her face has assumed its usual censorious appearance. Wordlessly, she holds out her empty glass for Russ to refill.

'More,' she demands, and grasps the bottle and pours from it herself. Taking a huge swallow, she wipes her lips, grimacing, and puts down her glass. Then she waddles over to my chair and, bending forward, unexpectedly envelops me in her ample arms. My face is smothered in her huge bosom. I can't breathe until she lets me go, and turns, and waddles back to pick up her drink. I suddenly want to cry, but I won't let myself; if I start, I'm afraid I'll never stop.

'You go to sleep now,' she orders us both from the doorway. 'It's late.'

'We will,' Russ assures her. 'And you must go to bed as well, Mercy.'

She scowls at him. 'Me? I can't sleep tonight. I will sit in the kitchen and pray.'

I don't believe I will be able to sleep tonight either. Swallowing the sleeping tablet Russ has given me, I burrow under the blanket, and hug the pillow for comfort. The nightmare ends abruptly in a blessed blackout of consciousness.

* * * *

The birds wake me at dawn. I surface from a semi-conscious sense of well-being into the shock of full awareness and memory; and the pain is all-encompassing. I can't go on lying there and bearing it. I have to get up and get dressed.

The kitchen light is on. Mercy is sitting slumped over the table, her head cushioned in her arms, snoring. I manage to slip past her, and open and shut the outside door without her stirring. I push the Mini all the way down the drive and into the road, before I jump in and start it. I don't want Mercy or Russ rushing out to stop me.

There is very little traffic on the road at this hour of the morning. I reach Hillbrow in record time. But it is harder than I had anticipated, stepping through the front door into the emptiness and silence. I imagine I can smell Pixie's perfume, and it is torture. Yet that was the reason I came here; to feel her presence; to have something to hold on to. I thought it would be a solace. It isn't. It's like sticking a needle in a fresh wound.

I wander into each room, and stand, and look around. And the only way I can contain the pain is by refusing to let myself think. I look, and I walk out again. It is a silly thing that tips the balance. In the bathroom, Pixie's hairbrush is on the basin. I pick it up. Strands of her hair are caught in the bristles. I drop it. I feel I will explode if I stay there a moment longer.

I run, out of the flat, and out of the building, and don't stop until I reach the car. The Mini's tank is almost empty. I fill up at the nearest garage. Then I drive to Buccleuch, and sit on the bridge where I sat before, and watch the burbling flow of water under my feet. It doesn't soothe me this time. The solitariness of the scene simply reinforces the anguish of the finality of this separation from Pixie.

I don't know where to go from here. I just drive, following the main road to Pretoria until, without pausing to think about it, I turn off on to a smaller road. I can no longer see clearly. I'm crying, uncontrollably; I can't stop; it feels like a dam bursting within, a deep black bottomless pit of grief.

I'm driving down a steep gradient. There's a right hand bend at the bottom. Straight ahead there's a large blue gum tree. I should slow down to navigate the bend. I don't bother. I stop steering and take my foot off the accelerator, and let the Mini drive itself towards the tree. But at the last moment, I panic. I hit the brakes and wrench violently at the steering wheel. The landscape kaleidoscopes, into a rushing darkness, into oblivion.

* * * *

The dreams are vivid:

I see Bokkie lying dead in some long grass. He sits up and smiles. 'Fooled you,' he says. And I laugh. He beckons me to follow him, and takes me to a tree. A blue gum tree. It has a huge gash in its trunk which is seeping blood. He strokes the bark. 'You shouldn't have hurt it,' he says.

Then he disappears, and so does the tree, and I become aware of throbbing pain, until I drift off again.

I meet Pixie. She isn't dead. She's alive. She smiles at me. But I can't get to her because there's a deep canyon between us, or she passes me in a lift going up, while I'm in one going down and I can't make it stop. She has the baby with her. She holds it up. 'Look, it's a boy,' she calls. Only I can see it's a girl. But that happens only once or twice. Usually the baby is a boy. Sometimes he looks like Pixie, sometimes Bokkie, sometimes Simon, sometimes me. They're always happy when I see them, and they get cross if I tell them they're dead. Except Bokkie, who just gazes at me compassionately before he disappears. I wake up feeling reassured.

There's no pain in the dreams. The pain is in my body when I come back. It is a few days before I am able to comprehend the full extent of my injuries. The list is quite long: a hairline fracture of the skull with severe concussion and contusion, a broken arm, broken ribs, broken ankle, torn muscles in my back, and cuts and bruises all over.

'I goofed,' I say apologetically to Russ, on his second or third visit to the hospital. I'm feeling sufficiently compos mentis, and strong enough now, to admit it.

'You did,' he agrees. 'Can you remember what happened?'

I nod carefully. My head still hurts; so does everything else.

'The police believe you must have suffered a temporary brake failure. Did you?'

'That's what I told them when they came to interview me yesterday,' I say expressionlessly.

'And then your brakes suddenly recovered miraculously at the last minute – judging from the tyre marks.'

'Something like that.'

It's obvious he knows the truth. He studies my face, and I sense his reprobation that he's trying not to show.

'But who told you about the tyre marks?' I ask guiltily.

'I went to collect the Mini. It had to be towed away. It was a write-off.'

'What about the tree?' I try to raise my head. 'Was the tree damaged?'

He raises his eyebrows at me comically. 'You're all smashed up. Your car's smashed up. And you want to know if the tree's all right?'

'Did I hit it?' I persist.

'No. Which is just as well, or you'd probably be dead now.'

I relax back. 'I'm sorry I've been such a bother. I've put you to a lot of trouble.'

'You have. You've given Mercy indigestion from worrying about you so much. And when she has stomach gripes, she takes it out on me. She says I must bring you home – she doesn't trust hospitals. She wants to look after you. She reckons she'll have you back on your feet in no time.'

'I bet she would. Tell her not to worry. I'm okay. And give her my love.'

'I will,' he says.

He shifts his chair to look around the ward. It is a large ward, and there is a lot going on in it. But his gaze doesn't settle anywhere, and his hands are restless in his lap – which is unusual for him. I sense he is thinking how to broach the subject that is uppermost in my mind too. We have to discuss it sooner or later.

To make it easier for him, I say, 'The funeral, Russ; what are we going to do about it?'

'Yes.' He looks relieved. 'The funeral. We need to— but firstly, what do *you* want to do? Would you like it postponed until you're well enough to attend?'

'No, let's get it over with,' I tell him.

'I agree.' He lays his hand on my plastered arm. 'You needn't worry yourself over anything. I'll take care of it all. We have to decide a few things though.' He uncrosses his legs, and leans nearer. 'You sure now?'

I nod; it hurts. A shooting pain flashes through my temple, setting off a throbbing ache round my skull. I wait for the pain to subside. 'She'd like to be cremated, I know that. She said so once, when I was talking about my mom's funeral.'

'All right. And do you happen to know if there's a will?'

'There isn't. We meant to do something about it, both of us, because of the baby, and we hadn't got round to

it. Oh damn!' – I've suddenly realized the implications
– 'that means Gerrit...'

'It's okay. He won't be a problem,' Russ assures me.
'Cecily has had a word, or rather words with him.'

'With Gerrit?'

'He had to be informed, Sam. He is Pixie's next of
kin. He told Cecily he didn't want anything of Pixie's
except a painting, any painting of hers, to hang on his
wall. He isn't even coming up for the funeral. He
claimed he wasn't well enough to travel.'

I feel a tremendous surge of relief. I couldn't bear
the thought of him poking around in Pixie's personal
possessions, and removing all her things.

'What's wrong with him?' I ask.

'Cecily thinks he's probably riddled with gout. She
suspected he had already had a few drinks when she
rang him at ten in the morning.'

I grin feebly. 'I could do with a stiff whisky myself
right now.'

'From the look of you, you could do with a painkiller
and a kip,' he says. 'I'd better go.'

'I'm fine.' I eye him shamefacedly as he gets up. 'I'm
sorry to saddle you with it all, Russ. I'm really sorry.'

He regards me for a moment, as if he is considering
what to say. 'You're forgetting something, Sam.' His
voice is quite harsh. 'I loved her too, you know.'

I watch him walk the length of the ward and disappear
through the door without looking back. I can't get
comfortable. My pillows have slipped, and every part of
my body seems to be aching. But I feel it serves me
right. I realize I've let myself down very badly. And
Pixie. I owe it to her to prove my mettle, and make
something of my own life.

15

It isn't easy to find. I get lost several times, and have to keep stopping to ask anyone I come across if they can direct me to Gerrit de Jager's farm. Eventually, an elderly African man, mounted on a scraggy pony, informs me that he used to work for Gerrit, and knows the farm well. He offers to lead me to it.

As I follow him in my hired car at a snail's pace, it makes me think of the day, eleven years ago, when the local sergeant and constable in their police van had followed Pixie on her pony, Ifu, back to the farm to investigate her claim of a murder. I try to push the thought out of my mind. I don't want to meet Gerrit feeling angry. I haven't come to open up old wounds. I have come on a quest, and a mission of peace.

The old man leaves me at the start of an overgrown rutted track, after assuring me it leads to 'the house of the oubaas Gerrit'. Navigating round all the potholes requires my total attention and driving skills, especially with my stiff left arm and ankle. But when I have to jam on my brakes suddenly as a huge green mamba slithers across the track in front of me, I sit for a moment and look about. The land on either side must have once been cultivated; I spot the rusted remains of a tractor upended in a donga. Now the ground has been reclaimed by rampant wild grass and the indomitable creeping bush of the Natal coastline, and the colouring is vivid green following the first spring rains. I feel as if I'm right out in the wilds. Apart from the tractor, there is no sign of human habitation to be seen. But the farm-house must be somewhere ahead, hidden behind one of the contours of the soft rolling hills that stretch away to the horizon.

A small forlorn group of buildings reveal themselves, finally, standing at the end of the last straight stretch of the track. I steer through the broken gateway, and pull up in the dusty yard. The single-storey farmhouse looks almost as dilapidated as the empty cattle barn and various sheds opposite it. Its corrugated-iron roof is badly rusted, and paint is peeling and flaking off the outside walls. But the back door is open, and I can see a face – a black female face, peering at me curiously through a window.

I switch off the engine, feeling sick suddenly with nervousness. What if Gerrit refuses to see me? What if he isn't even here? A young African woman emerges from the house, and stands, looking anxious and uncertain. Judging from the desolate air of the place, I shouldn't think unexpected visitors turn up very often.

Picking up the parcel I've brought, I get out. My ankle is puffy and aching after the long drive. I've been on the road since four a.m. and it's now nearly noon. I flex my foot a few times, then limp over to her.

'I've come to see Mr de Jager,' I tell her. 'Is he at home?'

'The baas is here,' she says. 'He's inside,' and she turns to lead the way.

'Wait! What's your name?'

'Mary,' she says.

'Mary?' I'm disappointed, even though I realize that by now Florence would be quite a bit older than Mary looks. 'Where's Florence?' I ask. 'Is Florence still here?'

She looks bemused.

'You don't know Florence? She used to be the kitchen maid.'

'There's only me and the baas,' she says. 'Nobody else. I take you to him.'

I follow her through a scruffy bare kitchen, and along a dark passage to a doorway.

'Baas, there's a man to see you,' Mary announces, and

leaves me standing where I am, and goes back to the kitchen.

'Who's it?' a voice growls from behind the open door.

I've been anticipating this moment in trepidation for days. I take a deep breath, and step into the room. Slouched in an armchair in the corner is a man with a gnarled red face, slovenly dressed in a dirty vest and badly creased old khaki trousers. He has one leg propped up on a stool, and is holding a glass of what looks like brandy. For a moment, we stare at each other. I swallow nervously, and put on a smile.

'Mr de Jager? I'm Sam. I—'

'What do you want?' he snarls in a strong Afrikaans accent. 'I can't buy anything.' He points at the parcel under my arm. 'I've got no money.'

'I'm not a salesman,' I assure him. 'This is a present I'm delivering. It's a painting done by your daughter, Pixie. You said you wanted—'

'Priscilla?' Something happens in his face. He's obviously startled, but his expression also becomes suddenly more animated, and he sits up a little. 'You've got a picture of Priscilla's?'

'Yes. I'll show you.' I untie the string, and start pulling the wrapping off carefully. 'I hope you like it,' I say.

He grunts. I'm aware, though, of his eyes watching keenly as I remove the cardboard padding from the glass.

'I've had it framed so it's ready to hang on the wall. It's a picture of a duiker that—'

'Hold it up, man,' he says impatiently.

He looks at the duiker. He looks at the whole painting. He studies it for a long time. And he doesn't say anything, but his eyes grow moist, and his lower lip starts trembling. He sucks in his mouth, and sits back, and nods at me.

'It'll look nice on the wall.' He gulps some brandy. He has to hold the glass in both hands to keep it steady. 'So you know Priscilla? I mean my daughter – you *knew*

228

her?' he corrects himself. 'I forget, man – what's your name again?'

'Sam.'

'You a friend of my daughter?'

'Her boyfri – fiancé. We were engaged,' I say thickly. I still can't think about our last morning together without becoming emotional. I turn my back and put the painting down, leaning it against the wall.

'They told me Priscilla was pregnant.' Gerrit coughs. ' . . . Was it your child?'

I hold my breath. Then I nod. 'Yes,' I lie. I wait a few moments longer, before I turn round and face him. He is looking at me kindly for the first time.

'You better sit down,' he says. 'Have a drink. What you want? Brandy? Tea? Coffee?'

'Tea,' I mumble. 'Thanks.'

'Pull up a chair, man.' Then he yells, 'Mary, bring the baas some tea. And some biscuits.'

Mary appears in the doorway. 'We haven't got biscuits,' she informs Gerrit.

'Then bring some bread, and some butter and jam. And for me too,' he snaps at her irritably.

My tea arrives in a cracked mug. And the bread is stale. But I swallow it down because I'm hungry. I didn't stop to eat on the journey. Gerrit refills his glass from the bottle hidden under his chair, and lights his pipe. To make polite conversation, I ask him about the farm. That really sets him going. I've obviously touched a raw nerve. In a long bitter tirade, I'm told the whole story of how he had to sell all his stock and his machinery as he wasn't making any money. I'm told how much he had to suffer, and how it has ruined his health. Then he mentions there are people who want to buy his farm, but he won't let them.

'Why not?' I ask

'They want to grow sugar cane. They want to tear up all the grass and the bush, and plant sugar cane.' He is suddenly beside himself with fury and almost shouting at me, as if I'm a representative of 'them' whoever they are. 'Sugar cane! That isn't blerry farming!' With a shaking hand, he slurps some more of his brandy. A malevolent gleam comes into his bleary blue eyes. 'But I won't let them have my farm. I don't care how much money they offer me. I've told them they can stuff their money up their blerry backsides.'

'Good,' I say.

He squints at me suspiciously. 'You agree with me?'

'Yes, I think it would be a shame to tear up all the bush.'

'So' – he grins unexpectedly – 'you and me are on the same side, hey?'

I'm not sure we're on the same side for the same reason. But I grin back at him.

He peers into my empty mug. 'You want some more tea?'

'No thanks... Actually, if you don't mind,' I say, 'there's something I'd like to do before I leave. I'd like to go for a walk; stretch my legs; because it's a long drive back to Johannesburg.'

He immediately looks grumpy again. 'I can't walk. Not much now. I can't come with you. You'll have to go on your own.'

Trying to appear disappointed, I stand up.

Stretching, I ask casually, 'In case I get very hot on my walk, is there a river, or a stream, or a creek or something I could have a swim in?'

He frowns at me. I'm afraid I might have alerted his suspicions. He must wonder, after all, how much Pixie has told me about her childhood.

'You can swim in the reservoir. It's behind the barn.'

'But I'm not hot now. Is that the only water supply on the farm?'

Again he looks at me, and his eyes seem suddenly as sharp as an eagle's. 'There are a couple of springs and a pool that way.' He points the direction with his finger. 'But you won't find them. They're hidden in thick bush.'

'How far away are they?'

'About half an hour walking, if you're fit.'

I shrug. 'Well, if I find them, I find them. It'll be nice just to wander about anyway. I'll pop in to say goodbye when I get back.'

He grunts, and pulls out his tobacco pouch, and busies himself filling his pipe, as if he has already lost interest in me.

I fetch the small urn from the car. Aware he could be watching me from somewhere inside the house, I hide it under my shirt, before I set off in the direction he indicated.

My ankle slows me down. I have to stop and rest it every so often. But I find the creek. Perhaps through pure chance; perhaps not. Crazy as it may seem, I felt I was being guided to it intuitively. Crouching down on the edge of the enclosing bush, I can hear the water trickling into the pool. I hunt for a way in, and discover several tunnels made by small animals. I choose the largest, and crawl and slither along it. My knees and elbows are grazed, and I'm covered in scratches, by the time I emerge into the leafy seclusion of the glade.

There is the flat-topped rock, and the chaliced pool below it, and the spotted sunlight under the trees. I stand and take it all in, attuning my senses to the stillness and tranquillity. My mind starts conjuring up images of Pixie and Bokkie lying on the rock, splashing in the crystal water, eating sandwiches and consulting books on the grass. The pictures provoke other more painful memories. I realize I'm torturing myself, which isn't why I came to the creek. I make my mind go blank. There is no pain here now, only peace. And that is what I have come to find in myself.

Undressing, I step into the pool and sink into the deepest part. The clear spring water eddies round my body, dissolving the blood from my scraped and scratched skin. I feel cleansed and purified of the suffering of my flesh. But the temperature is too cold to stay in for long.

Climbing up the rock, I stretch out on my back. The sun relaxes the tension and fatigue in my muscles, spreading a glowing warmth through me. I start to doze. After a little, the fiery pink radiance of sunlight on my closed eyelids fades. My body feels cool suddenly. I look up at the sky. The sun has disappeared behind a cloud.

Bokkie had said we never *really* die, like the sun never *really* sets.

I don't know. I can't prove Pixie is still alive. But I believe she is, somewhere.

I lie quietly, and wait for the sun to come out again. It doesn't. But deep inside I'm aware of a glow, a warmth of well-being. Pixie has left me, but not my love. I feel peculiarly at peace. Sitting up, I look around in stillness, with a sense of wonder. Every leaf and every branch of every tree, every stone, every blade of grass is as it should be. The bird calling out suddenly to its mate, is as it should be. Even the dead branches and the dead leaves on the ground are as they should be. Even the green leaves fallen prematurely are as they should be. I can see an interconnectedness in it all, a unity, a wholeness, a oneness. But the oneness isn't visible. It is a feeling. The feeling of love.

The sun re-emerges from behind the cloud. I lie back and close my eyes. It seems to me that only we human beings aren't as we should be because we don't feel the oneness in our love. And so we go on killing each other, over a difference in skin colour, or religion, or political belief. And while we're busy killing each other, we're killing all the other forms of life too – out of greed, not need. We're wantonly destroying our home, our Earth. In fifty years time, how many of Bokkie's friends, the wild animals, will be left? But we don't care. By the time we do care, it might be too late. Well, not if I can help it, I decide, for I know now what I want to do with my life.

I get dressed. Then I take the urn of ashes, and scatter them around the glade. It's not important. It is only dust to dust, and ashes to ashes. I'm aware it isn't Pixie, merely her body. I imagine her smiling at my sentimentality, and telling me I should dance, not grieve. But I can't stop myself crying.

I wash my face in the pool, before I crawl back through the tunnel. Halfway along, my shirt snags on a thorn. And that's when I see it, hiding in the dark thicket. A young duiker. I stare at it. It stares back. Then it lifts its nose to sniff my scent, and I swear its lips form a smile. I disentangle myself. When I next look, it is no longer there.

The farmhouse is cast in lengthening shadows by the time I arrive back. Mary meets me at the kitchen door. 'The baas is waiting for you,' she says.

Gerrit is still in the same chair. But he has moved it round to face the wall. He doesn't appear to notice me when I enter the room. His head is down, his chin sunk into his chest, and his empty glass is leaning at an angle in the loose grasp of his knobbly fingers. He could be asleep, except that his eyes are open. His gaze is fixed on the painting propped against the skirting board. He looks as if he has been crying. I retreat to the door, and knock loudly.

'It's Sam. Can I come in?'

He grunts, which I take to mean yes.

But he doesn't stir, or even glance at me, or speak, as I sit down to take the weight off my throbbing ankle. He continues staring at the painting. I look at it too. It is one of the last paintings Pixie did. The young duiker is crouched in dense bush, its head turned sharply towards the viewer, so that its face is the focal point. The ears are pricked forward, half concealing the sharp little horns, and the nostrils are flared. Yet the tiny antelope doesn't appear to be frightened, only shyly curious. As I focus on it, it seems to gaze at me with an intense soulful expression.

I was feeling nervous about putting my proposition to Gerrit. But I'm not now, suddenly. I just come straight out with it. I tell him that I want to buy some of his land – as much of it as I can afford, and turn it into a nature reserve – a sanctuary for wild animals and plants. I explain about my inheritance from my mother, and tell him I would like to invest it all in the project.

I can't be sure he is listening to me. He doesn't bat an eyelid, or move a muscle, even once I have finished talking. He seems sunk in his own self-pity, or sorrow, or regret. I'm beginning to think I have been wasting my breath, when he gives a long wheezy sigh, and mutters something.

'Sorry' – I lean forward – 'I didn't catch that. What did you say?'

He swivels his glaucous eyes up at me. 'I said, take it. Take the lot. You can have the whole blerry farm. It's no good to me any more. Make your nature reserve. Just leave me the house. You can have that too after I'm gone. Then at least I can stop worrying about them coming and planting sugar cane here when I'm in my grave.'

'Do you mean that?' I'm thunderstruck, but I'm also only too aware that he has had quite a bit to drink, and possibly doesn't even know what he is saying.

'Man!' He scowls. 'Why would I say it if I didn't mean it. Fetch the deeds. They're there' – he points at an old stinkwood table under the window – 'in the drawer.'

I find them and bring them to him. He pushes the folder back at me irascibly.

'You take them. You get a lawyer. You sort it all out. I'll just sign.'

In the same irritable manner, he dispenses with my offer to write him out a cheque as a deposit.

'Keep it,' he growls. 'Cheques are no good to me. I don't use banks. And I don't want a lot of money in the house. You can send me some cash every month, enough to keep me going.'

I realize then that he is practically giving away all his land to me, albeit in ill-humour. But I can't comprehend it – his sudden generosity. It doesn't make sense. I'm afraid he will change his mind as soon as I've gone.

'Wouldn't you like a bit of time to think it over?' I ask him.

'Do you want your blerry animal reserve, or don't you?' he snaps.

'Yes. I do. Very much.'

'Then get on with it,' and he waves his fingers at me in dismissal.

I stand still, watching him shakily pour more brandy into his glass, and drink. His eyes contact mine over the rim. He sits up a little.

'You said you were going to marry my daughter. Not so?'

'I was going to, yes. I lov—'

'Okay,' he cuts me off. 'So the farm would have been hers. So now it's yours.'

I look at him, not knowing what to say. A skew smile flickers faintly across his mouth.

'And you brought me the picture,' he says.

Then he sinks down in his chair, and withdraws back into himself. It's as if I no longer exist for him. His brandy-befuddled gaze is concentrated on the painting. He merely grunts when I try to thank him, and say goodbye. From the doorway, I glance back at the duiker's pointed brown face. Like the portrait of Bokkie on the wall at home, its eyes seem to have followed me across the room. No doubt it is a trick of the light, but its lips appear to be smiling.

Mary is in the kitchen. I pull out my wallet and hand her a fifty rand note. I know it doesn't change anything. For the time being, I feel it is all I can do for her.

I am relieved to get in my car and drive out of the yard. As soon as I'm beyond sight of the house, I stop, and just sit and soak up the scenery. I would like to sit there for longer. I can't. I have a long drive ahead of me. Steering slowly over the bumpy track, I decide that if I ever have a son, I will call him Bokkie.

There is a golden light in the west. The sun is setting.

But, of course, the sun never *really* sets!

Epilogue

Sunrise at Pixie Creek is the best time of the day. I like to sit on the flat-topped rock and meditate as the grey light of pre-dawn alchemizes into gold, melting the mist, and the night silence of birdsleep into a resonance of song. I empty my mind of thoughts, and go down very deep within myself, into the feeling of well-being at centre. It is as if the birds are singing inside me in a wonderful inner space of stillness, and I am totally at peace. At such times, I feel very close to Sam.

Pixie Creek is my favourite place in the reserve, although there are dozens of other pools and streams and watering places for the animals. Sam's dream came true. The land that was Gerrit's farm is now only a tiny area of the entire park, which stretches over many thousands of square miles. Sam was a very gentle and kind and wise man. He was my father, and I loved him dearly.

I don't look like him. I take after my Indian mother, Sita. I have inherited her features, and her cocoa-coloured eyes. Sam often used to tease Sita that he only married her because she had the dark soulful gaze of a duiker. When I was born in 1994, he said the happiness circle was now complete, and he built a circular rondavel with a thatched roof near the creek for the three of us to live in. He also said the timing of my entrance into the world couldn't have been more propitious. In 1994, the long nightmare of Apartheid finally ended in South Africa, and Nelson Mandela became the president of the new multi-racial government. There were huge celebrations in the country. Sam told me he thought of Pixie at the time, and imagined she must be celebrating too. It was then that he decided to rename the nature reserve Khulula Park – a Zulu word meaning to untie or free. Sam intended the meaning to apply to both humans and animals. For him, animal rights were as important as human rights. He believed that all sentient beings have the right to be treated with loving kindness. And so do I.

However, even 1994 is quite a long time ago now. A lot has happened and changed in the world since then. There is more compassion and understanding. There is still cruelty and greed and wanton killing. But, at least, conservation has become a major world issue.

Sam and Sita lived to a ripe old age. They are both dead now. Sam left Khulula Park in my charge; and the story of his relationship with Pixie, which he wrote before he met my mother and kept in a box file in the bottom drawer of his desk. He also left me the portrait of Bokkie. It now hangs in pride of place on the wall of my rondavel. I look at it often. I feel a strong affinity with the small strange boy whom I believe was an Enlightened Being. He didn't die in vain. People come to Khulula Park from all over the world, to see animals that have become extinct elsewhere.

Whenever I'm lonely at any time, I go to Pixie Creek. I have a friend there. A young duiker. He eats out of my hand, and sometimes we romp together on the grass. Then I lie on the flat-topped rock, and become very still in myself, and feel the interconnectedness of everything. And I know it is all as it should be. As Sam said, with a ruminative smile, shortly before he died: Love simply is!

P.S. I forgot to mention – Sam didn't have a son. I am his daughter. Bokkie.